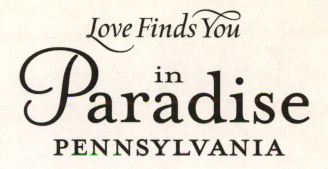

Love Finds You

in

Paradise

PENNSYLVANIA

Love Finds You

in Paradise

PENNSYLVANIA

BY LOREE LOUGH

summerside
PRESS

Cover and Interior Design by Müllerhaus Publishing Group
www.mullerhaus.net

Published by Summerside Press, Inc., 11024 Quebec Circle,
Bloomington, Minnesota 55438 | **www.summersidepress.com**

Fall in love with Summerside.

Printed in the USA.

Dedication

....

For Larry, light of my life and stirrer of my soul, for whom I'm happy to obey 1 CORINTHIANS 7:10: "Let not the wife depart from her husband."

Special mention to Rachel and Connie, the best editors ever; to Jason and Carlton, who welcomed this humble author with open arms; to my once-abused and now-spoiled dog, who put aside his Frisbee addiction long enough for me to write this story; and last but certainly not least, to Sandie Bricker, the first to say, "Send something to Summerside!"

WHEN FRENCH HUGUENOT SETTLERS ARRIVED in southeastern Pennsylvania in 1712, they must have suspected that their beautiful new homeland might one day be called Paradise. The name was chosen by one of the town's founders, David Witmer, who was a friend to George Washington and supervisor of a section of the Philadelphia and Lancaster Turnpike. Today, that road is Lincoln Highway, where historic inns and restaurants like Revere Tavern have stood since the 1700s. Steeped in rich history, the town's friendly people and peaceful vistas inspired the 1994 film *Trapped in Paradise*, which stars Nicholas Cage. Home to the National Christmas Center and the National Toy Train Museum, Paradise boasts dozens of gift and craft shops, antiques stores, delightful eateries, quaint B and Bs, and a thriving Amish community. Visitors to Paradise can view acres of rolling green countryside while steaming along the tracks of the Strasburg Rail Road and wave to Amish farmers who travel in traditional horse-drawn buggies. Few leave this township without tipping their hats to David Witmer, for he truly understood the meaning of Paradise.

Prologue

....

A warm wind whiffled through the open car window, mussing Julia's hair. Turning onto Lincoln Highway, she drove past shops and businesses still bustling with activity, though the workday had nearly ended. Cars and minivans bearing license plates from all over the country still sat in the Basketville parking lot, and even the Amish Trader still seemed to be doing a brisk business. Julia couldn't help but smile.

Before returning to her birthplace, she'd gone out of her way to avoid crowds. When she'd first come back "home," she'd taken long roundabout routes to get to and from her job in Lancaster *just* to avoid the noise and traffic that went hand in hand with the flutter of tourists who flocked to Paradise every day of the year. And now? Julia laughed to herself, because she'd gotten almost as caught up in the happy beehive of activity as the sightseers themselves!

After steering onto Pine Hill Road, she turned up the volume to the song playing on WJTL…the only radio station her old beat-up sedan could pull in. Why not sing along? Just because her attitude toward church and God had changed over the years didn't mean she couldn't enjoy her favorite hymn.

Should she credit "Amazing Grace" for the calm that settled over her? Or was it the knowledge that just over the next lush green hill, her house would come into view? The questions broadened her grin. If anyone had told her six months ago that she'd move back to Paradise, Julia would've pooh-poohed the idea. And if they'd suggested she'd be happy here? *I'd have laughed out loud!*

No matter how hectic her day had been, pulling into the driveway of her very own place felt good—so good that Julia almost felt guilty. What had she done in her twenty-eight years to earn three rambling acres and a two-story house, complete with a white picket fence? *Nothing, that's what,* she told herself.

And just that fast, an all-too-familiar sadness pricked at her consciousness. "Shake it off, Julia. Put it out of your mind, right now!" Her take-it-on-the-chin attitude about the hard knocks she'd survived resurfaced as she took another breath of clean country air. So what if she didn't have a single living family member? And so what if her dreams of a husband and children could never come true? She'd met some wonderful people, and she had a good job and her four-legged friends at the Wolf Sanctuary. Lots of people would count themselves lucky to have her life. "Some aspects of it, anyway...."

Chapter One

....

"Why would anybody *do* such a thing?"

Simon had no idea how to answer the five-year-old boy, so he shrugged helplessly. He'd stopped by to visit Levi—the closest thing to a son he'd likely ever have—and came to a halt when he realized what had commanded the Gundens' full attention.

Levi's father ran a hand over the bullet holes that had pierced his white-painted barn. *ottes wille,"* he said, nodding.

Simon stared slack-jawed at William Gunden. Having known the Gundens more than a decade, he considered this man a friend; but while he had a lot in common with the family, the differences between them and him never seemed more obvious than at times like this. Far be it from him to tell William how to raise his children, but his conscience hammered at him to say something, anything, that might erase the look of shock and fear from Levi's face. "The world can be a strange place," he said, "and not everybody is kind and loving." Simon got onto one knee and plopped a palm onto each of the boy's shoulders. "Sometimes people make bad choices, choices that hurt others."

Levi's blond brows drew together. "Shooting at our barn wasn't a bad choice," he snapped. "It was mean."

While Simon couldn't have agreed more, he didn't say so. Already he'd overstepped his bounds, as evidenced by the stern expression on William's face.

"It is hard, I know," William said, "to understand such things. But God does not call us to understand. He calls us only to obey."

Crossing both arms over his chest, Levi shook his head. If the look on Levi's face was any indicator, the boy would've given anything to state the opposite. Loudly.

"It is by God's grace," William continued, "that they were such poor shots." Winking at Simon, he added, "Missed the cows, there, and the horses, too." Then he pointed at his youngest son. "Levi, go to the house and see if your mama needs help collecting the eggs. And tell her I will be up soon for lunch."

The boy gave the bullet holes one last glance and did as he was told. Only when he was out of earshot did Simon say, "I worry about you, William."

The farmer stroked his dark beard. "And why is that?"

"You're way out here in the middle of nowhere, for starters. Sitting ducks for the wackos and weirdos who do things like"—he gestured toward the damage in the barn wall—"like *that*. At least let me call the cops and report it, so they can drive by once in a while and keep an eye on—"

William held up a hand. "No, Simon. You must not involve the police. It will only make things worse. Remember what happened when the Beachys talked to them."

If only Simon *could* forget.

Adjusting his straw hat, William smiled. "Do not worry for us." Then he gave Simon's hand a hearty shake. "But now I am keeping you from your work, and from my own as well," he said. "Remember as you go that we are safe in God's hands."

Simon thought about that during the half-hour drive to the Wolf Sanctuary. About a year ago, a carload of rowdy teenage boys had decided to target the Beachy farm. Night after night they had assaulted the family, first paintballing the house and then tossing cinder blocks onto the mailbox. Throughout the summer the attacks continued, until a neighbor dialed 911 to report that a little Amish girl, on her way to the schoolhouse, had been knocked unconscious by a full soda can tossed from a passing car. The boys—identified by the concerned citizen—served a year in jail for their crimes, and not long after their release, the Beachys' buggy was forced from the road, killing their horse and eldest son.

As occasional vet to the Beachys, Simon had attended the funeral and watched as they quietly and uncomplainingly buried their boy. Then, as now, he couldn't help but think that, somewhere, one of those vengeful teens smirked at the knowledge that the peace-loving Amish refused to report even deadly attacks.

He breathed deeply as the sanctuary's sign came into view. Few things satisfied him more than time spent here. The strong, magnificent beasts behaved as though they knew he'd come to help them, and for the most part, they cooperated with his exams. Chuckling under his breath as he slipped through the sturdy chain-link gate, Simon glanced at proof not quite healed on his forearm that not every member of the pack agreed with the need for periodic veterinary checkups.

"Attaboy, Casper," he said. Crouching slowly, he extended a hand. The wolf approached slowly, head down and tail tucked as he sniffed Simon's palm then happily accepted a doggy treat. Casper was one of the sanctuary's few outcasts, and Simon made a point of paying special attention to him. He pitied any creature—two-legged or four—that didn't enjoy a sense of belonging. But here, as in the wild, wolves had rules, and only they understood what Casper had done to earn his shunning.

Without warning, Casper's ears perked and he stared at something beyond Simon's right shoulder. Simon turned, too. Neither he nor the wolf could afford to let their guard down for an instant, for if a member of one of the sanctuary's four packs decided that Casper shouldn't communicate with Simon or enjoy a treat, things could turn ugly in an eyeblink.

He breathed a sigh of relief when he spotted the source of the wolf's curiosity—a young woman crooning softly to Fawn, another outcast. Clad in denim coveralls and tiny white sneakers, she was oblivious to him, though he crouched no more than twenty yards from her. "She's mighty easy on the eyes, isn't she, buddy," he whispered.

Casper sat on his haunches and gave Simon a big doggy grin then licked his lips, hinting that he'd like another of the biscuits hidden in his pal's shirt pocket. Simon carefully placed two more near the animal's forepaws and slowly rose to his nearly-six-foot height. "Enjoy, buddy. I'll be back later to say g'bye. Right now, I've got things—and people—to check out."

Casper's demeanor changed the instant he realized that Simon would leave. Eyes wide and ears flat, he mouthed the treats and hurried toward the thick underbrush to hide from those who might steal his snack and inflict severe punishment for delighting in creature comforts. Simon shook his head and wished life could be gentler for the big white wolf. Things were better here than in the wild, where Casper would surely have starved. Still…

A husky female voice floated to him on the warm spring breeze, interrupting his thoughts. "Such a pretty girl," she sang. "You like gettin' your belly scratched, don't you?"

Amazingly, she'd coaxed the wolf onto her back. More amazingly, Fawn wallowed and whimpered with gratitude, paws digging happily at the air…until she spotted Simon. In one swift move, she stood on all fours, head tilted slightly to the side, assessing the situation. Recognizing his scent, she relaxed some, but he didn't fail to note the way she'd scoped out a potential escape route, should she need one. Nor did he fail to notice the way the young woman's bright smile dimmed. "Sorry," he said. "Didn't mean to startle you girls."

She shrugged one white-sleeved shoulder and nodded toward the treeline. "No biggie. Better you than one of those bullies over there."

Simon followed her gaze. Sure enough, five wolves stood along the pines, watching with suspicious interest. "Murphy's the biggest one," he said. "Alpha male of Pack One. He's a pretty gentle sort—"

"—usually," she finished.

True enough, he thought. But how would she know that unless she spent a lot of time around here, too? He would have asked if those big, long-lashed eyes hadn't distracted him. Simon had never seen eyes that color before. At least not on a person. Once while in vet school, he'd assisted in a delicate operation on a lion. Just before the anesthetic took effect, he'd looked right into her big, golden eyes and—

"They're all pretty gentle, most of the time."

He watched her tuck both hands into the back pockets of her coveralls, but not before he caught sight of pale-pink fingernails. "You're, ah, sorta new here, right?"

Another shrug, this time from the other tiny, white-sleeved shoulder. "Guess that depends on how you define 'new.' "

When she tilted her head, a length of shiny brown hair cascaded over that same shoulder. *Like a cinnamony waterfall,* he thought. Blinking, Simon removed his Orioles baseball cap and ran a hand through his hair, wondering where on earth *that* thought had come from. He decided to try a different tack. "Name's Thomas," he said. "Simon Thomas."

Her eyes widened, and a glimmer of the smile she'd given Fawn brightened her face. "So you're the vet who volunteers his services here. I've heard good things about you. Julia Spencer," she said, drawing quotes in the air, " 'ordinary volunteer.' "

Nothing "ordinary" about you! he wanted to say. "How long have you been coming here?" he said instead.

Fawn chose that moment to remind them that they had an audience near the pines—and that it had decided to move forward. She darted for the safety of the scrubby pines that ringed the main enclosure.

"I love them all," Julia said, narrowing her eyes at the advancing pack members, "but sometimes I'd like to give those guys a piece of my mind for being such terrorists." Satisfied that Casper and Fawn had returned to their small assigned thicket, the others backed off.

He knew how Julia felt. "It's instinct in its purest form, and we'll never fully understand what makes them force one of their own to live alone."

Her sigh rode another breeze, caressing his ears and his heart in the same breath. Simon didn't for the life of him know what was going on. He hadn't felt this addled about a woman since before meeting Georgia! *Get a grip, dude, before you say something you'll regret.*

"I know. It's just tough watching those two live their lives from the periphery. Family life is so close they could touch it, if they tried. But they know if they do, they're doomed."

"Sounds like you've seen an encounter or two."

"Just one. But it was one too many," she said, standing. "Those bullies over there nearly killed Fawn."

Simon remembered it all too well, along with the frantic call from Matt asking him to come and shoot the she-wolf full of antibiotics and stitch up her wounds. The memory of it was written all over her pretty face, a sadness that simmered in her soul and glittered in her big eyes. If he didn't think it would spook the pack, he'd have wrapped her petite little body in a comforting "there-there" hug. "So how often do you come out here?"

Now both shoulders lifted. "Not nearly as often as I'd like, but I try to put in a few hours every weekend." A slanted grin put a dimple in her right cheek when she added, "Never know what you might miss, not being here."

A picture of her, wrapped in his arms and looking up into his face, flashed through his mind. Simon blinked. And swallowed. He'd blame the sun or the unrelenting cold for his goofy behavior, except that the temperature, last he checked on this springlike Saturday, had been fifty degrees, and a massive oak sheltered them from the sun. For all he knew, she had a husband and kids waiting for her at home....

Home.

Not his favorite place since Georgia died, and Simon did everything humanly possible to put off going there. He hated every room in the big Victorian she'd fallen in love with. Hated sleeping in that enormous bed all alone. Hated the oppressing silence. Simon cleared his throat. "So, are you finished for the day?"

"I promised to ready-up a few things in the gift shop, and then I have to pay a visit to the Gunden farm."

"Oh?" Grateful for the change of subject, Simon headed for the gate. Maybe, if he was lucky, she'd agree to let him buy her a cup of coffee so they could continue getting acquainted. Surely her husband and kids wouldn't mind sharing her for a few minutes.

"They bought a parcel of land," she explained, falling into step beside him, "and I've agreed to handle filing the deed and stuff."

"So you're a lawyer, then…." He slowed his pace so she wouldn't have to half run on those short legs of hers to keep up with him.

Julia nodded. "I enjoy working with the Amish." She giggled. "They're quick to pay and always insist on adding a homemade pie or jar of jelly to the fee."

"The shelves in my pantry are lined with stuff like that," he told her, grinning. "I've never figured out a polite way to tell those gracious ladies that a man living alone can only eat so much in a year."

"So you're a bachelor, eh?"

Her *"eh"* echoed in his ears. Odd that he'd never run into her before; from the sound of things, she'd grown up in the area. "Not a bachelor, exactly." He hated telling people that his wife had died. Not only did it remind him of those horrible last days with Georgia, it never failed to paint an "aw, poor baby" expression on the face of the listener.

"Divorced or widowed?"

"My wife died three years ago." He braced himself for the barrage of questions that would surely follow.

"Sorry to hear it."

They walked the remaining distance between the eight-foot-tall chain-link gate and the gift shop, the crunch of gravel under their shoes the only sound. He hadn't noticed a wedding band when he spotted the perky pink polish on her nails, but that didn't mean a thing these days. Maybe she knew how to bite her tongue. Or maybe she just didn't give a hoot about the details of his past.

He didn't like that idea, and it surprised him more than he cared to admit. Why should it concern him one way or the other *what* she thought of him? He'd only met her moments ago, and while they had the sanctuary and helping their Amish neighbors in common, they—

"So do you live nearby?"

Simon opened the gift-shop door, wincing when it squealed in protest. "Wonder where Matt might have stored a can of oil…."

In place of an answer, Julia's eyes narrowed and her lips thinned, proof, he believed, that she thought he'd deliberately sidestepped her question. "I live just outside of Paradise."

"I admire your dedication. What is that—a thirty-minute drive each way to get here?"

"Some days. Depends on weather, traffic…. What about you?"

"My grandparents left me a house in Paradise."

The soft, dulcet tones of her voice vanished and the sweet expression on her face hardened like a protective mask. Obviously she regretted having provided the information, telling Simon that "sharing" wasn't something Julia did often. Again, he fought the urge to wrap her in a comforting embrace. "Big enough for your husband and kids, I take it?"

"No husband. No kids."

He was on the verge of breathing a sigh of relief when she added, "Thankfully…"

No way he intended to touch *that* one. All he needed was another "Let's wait till we're older and rich and see some of the world before we have kids" woman in his life.

And so much for the invite to join him for a cup of coffee. Yeah, he'd been big-time lonely and, sure, he'd like to remedy that with a gorgeous little gal like Julia. But he was a veterinarian, for the love of Pete, not a shrink, totally ill-equipped to handle the emotional baggage that prompted her angry comments. Maybe he'd run into her again, here at the wolf sanctuary. If so, he'd make every effort to behave in a neighborly, gentlemanly way.

Period.

He crossed both arms over his chest, determined to keep a safe distance from this feisty young gal. As she tidied stacks of wolf greeting cards, silver jewelry, and wooden plaques for sale in the shop, he straightened the paintings hanging on the back wall while outside, birdsongs, cricket chirps, and the distant yelp of wolf cubs filled the quiet space.

No one was more surprised than Simon when he said, "So, uh, well, what would you say to dinner at the Garden Gate Diner?"

Chapter Two

....

Julia parked beside the buggy and glanced around the Gundens'
front yard. A peek at her watch explained why no one was outside
working. Noon—mealtime on most Amish farms. If she hadn't been
so preoccupied with thoughts of Simon, she would have waited to
visit. Now they'd insist that she join them for dinner. Already Hannah
was on the big covered porch, waving her onward.

"I see you have brought the big black briefcase." One hand on her
blue-aproned hip, Hannah adjusted her white bonnet and aimed a
pointer finger at Julia. "Business will just have to wait until after we eat."

"I can come back later," Julia began, "after—"

The woman clucked her tongue. "Now, now, you have been
around here long enough to know better than to decline an invitation
to join us."

But Julia wouldn't just be expected to sit and chat as they dined.
Hannah, in particular, would be hurt if she didn't pile her plate
high with everything on the table. Smiling, she swallowed a sigh
and followed Hannah inside. At the diner tonight, when she barely
touched anything on her plate, Simon would no doubt think that she
was one of those finicky figure-conscious females who was afraid to
eat. *That'll make it easier to keep him at a distance. A far distance,* she
told herself. Why she'd said yes in the first place boggled her mind.

"I will say it but once," Hannah announced when they entered the
kitchen. "The business of deeds and titles will wait until after our meal."

Julia made note of the loving expression exchanged by husband and wife. "Understood," William said, rising from his seat at the head of the table. He dabbed a bright white napkin to the corners of his mouth. "So good to see you this day, Julia," he said, sliding a chair between Seth and Levi. "Please, sit. And Rebekah? From the cupboard fetch another plate, would you please?"

Blushing, the girl hurried to do as her father asked and returned moments later with flatware and a linen napkin for their guest. Hands folded against her chest, she smiled. "May I bring for you some cool water to drink, Miss Julia?"

She met the girl's bright blue eyes and laid a hand atop her gray-sleeved forearm. "That'd be lovely. Thank you. Thanks to the rest of you, too, for forgiving my bad manners."

" 'Bad manners'?" Seth, at eight, was just old enough to understand adult conversations. He tucked both thumbs behind his suspenders, a much smaller version of his strapping father. "Really now, what bad thing could a nice lady like yourself have done?"

Julia gave him a short sideways hug. "I let my addled brain take control of my good sense, that's what," she said, "and showed up right in the middle of your meal."

Rebekah returned to her seat, directly across from Julia. "Oh, but it is of no bother." She looked at her mother. "Is it, Mama?"

Hannah's face glowed with love as she said, "It is no bother at all." Facing Julia, she smiled warmly. "But it would be ever so nice if someday you would come calling when business is not your reason."

Julia felt the heat of a blush color her cheeks. She couldn't very well tell this delightful family that no such thing would ever happen, or could she tell them why. She was here now, stuck with having to clean a plate piled high with chicken and potatoes, home-canned vegetables, fluffy biscuits, fresh-churned butter, and apple dumplings or fruit pie for dessert. "I'll keep that in mind," she said. Not the promise Hannah would have liked to hear, but at least it wasn't a lie.

"Look, Mama," said five-year-old Levi, "Miss Julia's face is red as an apple!"

Rebekah and Seth hid grins behind their hands, but Hannah and William made no effort to mask their amusement. Again, Julia witnessed the we-share-a-special-secret look that emphasized the beauty of their love.

"Perhaps the apple-red cheeks are from thoughts of the good doctor," Hannah said.

Julia didn't bother to ask which doctor they meant. Her only question was how they'd found out so quickly that she and Simon had met that morning. Did they know about his dinner invitation, too?

"Now, now, Mama," William put in, "we must not interfere. If Simon and Julia are courting, it is no business of ours."

Courting? Julia stared at each Gunden in turn, felt her mouth gaping, and snapped it shut. The merry faces all around the table said what words needn't: They *did* know about the date planned for this evening! Their farm in Paradise was a good half-hour drive from Elm, home of the wolves of Speedwell Forge. Simon lived on the edge of town, just past the Beachy farm—not a long trip, but not a shout across the valley, either. "All right," she said, grinning good-naturedly, "out with it. How did you hear this news already when I only said yes a few hours ago?"

William lifted his bearded chin and said, "Not all kraut is sour."

"And the future," Hannah added, "is but a book with seven locks."

"What fills the heart flows over from the mouth."

"Ya, and 'Every little bit helps,' said the mosquito as he spat into the sea."

Julia, Seth, Levi, and Rebekah followed the volley, heads turning right and left as William and Hannah laughed long and hard with each adage that filled the air. All four giggled, though Julia didn't think the kids understood the quick-witted wisdom any better than she did. "Excuse me, please, Mama, Papa," little Levi interrupted, "but what does it all *mean*?"

In place of an answer, his mother and father roared all the louder. Wiping their eyes on their napkins, they sat back and sipped water from ceramic mugs. "It means," Julia said around a smile, "that the good doctor has been here today."

Levi gasped. "You weren't here. How could you know?"

She pressed her forehead to his. "Two little birdies told me so. I only wonder," she said, eyeing Hannah and then William, "why the good doctor thought the news would interest my Gunden friends enough to—"

"William," Hannah interrupted, "please pass the gravy."

Nodding, Levi narrowed his eyes. "I see. Yes, I think I've figured out the riddle. Doctor Thomas told Mama and Papa that he is smitten with you, and now they think the pair of you are courting!" He sat up very tall, looking quite pleased at having puzzled things out all by himself.

By now, William had regained his full composure. In a quiet voice, he said, "Take care, son, to remember what the bishop taught from Obadiah last week...."

" 'The pride of thine heart hath deceived thee,' " the boy quoted, hanging his head. "I am sorry, Papa."

"Goodness," Julia said, "don't look so glum, Levi. It's only natural that you'd be pleased to have understood all that…those…the, uh…" She looked toward the ceiling as if she'd find answers written there. Exhaling a sigh, she playfully elbowed the boy's ribs. "Well, you're a very smart kid, that's all, and you earned a little pat on the back."

Hannah touched fingertips to her lips, eyes wide with shock at what she considered Julia's blatant disregard of William's warning. Rebekah mimicked her mother's gestures as Levi bit his lower lip and Seth winced, making Julia wonder what could have made them all fear William so, when he'd always seemed like such a gentle man. "If I've said anything to offend you," she told him, "I apologize. I'm not as familiar with the Amish ways as I should be, I'm afraid, but I'll mind my tongue the next time I invite myself to dinner, I promise."

Nodding, William's friendly smile warmed the room. "Time now to be busy with your chores, children." He watched as one by one they happily went off in three directions. The Amish didn't view hard work as a negative experience—that much was evident in their matter-of-fact expressions. Like their friends and cousins throughout Lancaster County, each readily accepted that they must all do their fair share if the farms were to remain self-sustaining, efficient, and on-budget. Julia envied the Gunden kids a little, for the comfort and safety of family life was obvious everywhere she looked in Amish Country. Quite a contrast to her own childhood, moving from one foster home to another.

Self-pity had never made her feel better about her past, so she stood and began stacking plates and gathering flatware. "The missus, she does not mind the womanly work," William said. "Come join me in the parlor so we can get this business of the deed out of the way."

Julia opened her mouth to say that she didn't mind helping Hannah with the dishes. It was the least she could do, she wanted to tell him, after the gracious way they'd welcomed her to their table. Then she remembered her promise to mind her tongue and clamped her jaw tight instead.

Was that a gleam of approval twinkling in William's eyes? Surely he hadn't read her body language and known what had been in her mind….

Without a word, he walked purposefully toward the other side of the house, and Julia followed like an obedient child, stopping to grab her briefcase as she went. In the humbly furnished room, she could choose a straight-backed chair, an unpadded rocker, or one of four long wooden benches that hugged the walls. She chose a bench, thinking it would be easier to spread out the paperwork that William needed to read and sign.

She explained each document carefully and then said, "I need you to sign here"—she pointed—"and here."

William patted his shirt. "May I for a moment borrow something with which to write?" He chuckled and added, "There is little need for a pen in the milking barn or while plowing the fields."

Julia gave him a ballpoint, smiling at the musical Amish way of constructing sentences. "Thanks," she said when he handed it back. "Now then, on Monday, first thing, I'll deliver the paperwork to the clerk's office and get the recording process started. If all goes well, you should have the deed in a few weeks."

Nodding, William said, "This is good." Then folding both arms over his chest, he added, "You will let us know how things go at dinner tonight, ya?"

He'd so surprised her with the question that Julia nearly closed the briefcase on her fingers. "I–I—"

"Doctor Thomas, he needs a good wife, I think."

"And children," came Hannah's voice from the kitchen. "He wants lots of children. He told me so himself many times. How sad that his wife died before she could fulfill her promise to him."

"Ya," her husband agreed. "He has good land, you know, much good land."

"And a big beautiful house," Hannah put in, "with room for many children."

A nervous giggle escaped Julia's lips. "Whoa, you two," she said, hands up like a traffic cop. "Simon and I only just met this morning. All this…this *talk* is very premature, don't you think?"

"What I think," William said, "is that there are only so many hours in a day and so many days in a man's life. God did not make man to live alone, but to share it with a wife, as the Good Lord intended."

"And you are lonely, too, Julia Spencer! William is right, you know. God intended for His children to share their time on earth with loving spouses and children."

Julia had lived on the outskirts of one Amish community or another for most of her life and had never heard of a single instance where the Amish had attempted matchmaking between two Englishers. *Leave it to you to be the first,* she thought. "I'll keep in touch," she said, grabbing her briefcase. At the sight of William's mischievous grin, she added, "On the real estate matter, of course." She was out the door and on the porch in a matter of seconds. "Would you like me to call the Bachmans," she said, standing beside her car, "and ask them to get a message to you about how things are progressing?"

The couple stood side by side on the top porch step. "No need to put them to any trouble," William said. "Just because they got for themselves one of those…those *telephones* doesn't mean we should make use of it."

"Ya," Hannah agreed. "Much better for you to come in person, anyway, so we may see by your pretty face exactly how things are progressing with you and Doctor Thomas."

Now how did they expect her to respond to that?

William and Hannah waved as Julia drove away. *Lord only knows what's behind their silly smiles,* Julia thought. Something to do with whatever Simon had said to William, no doubt. "Thanks so much for the wonderful meal and the delightful conversation!" she said, waving as she drove slowly toward the road.

Thanks to the Gundens' mealtime generosity, it wasn't likely that she'd eat much at dinner with Simon tonight—which meant she'd have plenty of time to find out what information he'd shared with his good Amish friend.

Nearly a dozen items filled her mental to-do list, and having always been the work-before-pleasure type, it surprised Julia that William's documents and other work-related duties came to her mind *after* "What to wear" and "Polish fingernails."

Chapter Three

....

"Sorry I'm so early," Simon said, extending the bouquet he'd bought on his way to Julia's house. "Wasn't sure where you lived and didn't want to start off on the wrong foot by getting here late."

Julia accepted the flowers with a smile that put the pretty blooms to shame. "They're lovely," she said, sticking her nose into the center flower. "How'd you know that daisies are my favorite?"

She stepped aside and, with a graceful sweep of her arm, invited him into the foyer. Simon stood for a second, wondering what to make of the teasing glint in her eyes. In the next instant, he had his answer.

"Did William tell you *that*, too?"

This morning at the wolf sanctuary, she'd told him about the appointment at the Gunden farm, and when he'd stopped by to inoculate the new calves, he'd asked William how long the Gundens had known her, if she'd ever been married, and if she was "involved" with anyone. He pictured the knowing twinkle in William's eyes at every answer.

She had him dead to rights. Simon saw no point in denying it. But he saw no point in acknowledging it, either. "Sounds like *you* had a productive visit to the Gunden farm, too."

One delicate brow lifted as she studied his face. He thought for a minute that she might call him to task for sidestepping her question. Instead she whirled around and headed down the hall, crooking a forefinger over her shoulder. "I'd better put these into

35

water so they won't wilt. Care for a glass of lemonade, since we have time to kill?"

Just an ordinary inquiry? Or carefully disguised sarcasm? Simon didn't know her well enough to tell. Yet. "Sounds good," he said. He couldn't help but notice, as he dogged her heels like an obedient pup, the crisp scent of pine cleaner, the warm glow of dust-free tables, the sheen of hardwood floors. Georgia had been a wonderful wife, but even she freely admitted that "tidy" wasn't a word most people would use to describe her. Surrounded by so much attention to detail, he wondered how much *more* he'd miss her if she'd been a good cook and—

"So how long did it take you," she asked, stretching to reach the vase on a top cabinet shelf, "to get from your place to mine?"

"I would've gotten that down for you, if you'd asked."

Julia turned halfway to face him and fused those pale brown eyes to his face. "I'm sure you would've—if I'd asked." Then, as if suddenly aware of her stern tone, she cleared her throat. "Don't mind me. Guess I've just been on my own too long." Facing the sink, she added, "Too accustomed to doing things for myself."

What a shame, he thought, because something told him that inside this tiny woman beat an enormous and loving heart. Why else would she spend so many unpaid hours at the wolf sanctuary? He watched her fill the vase with water and pop the bouquet into it, plastic sheath and all. "I'll take proper care of these once I've poured your lemonade." Then, "So tell me, Doctor Thomas, do you like ice in your lemonade, or are you a purist?"

"Purist?" Mesmerized by the flutter of her long lashes, the way the late afternoon sun glinted off her hair, and the melody of her voice, he had no idea what she meant.

"Purists," she echoed. "People who don't like anything watered down or altered in any way from its natural form. Anti-changers, y'know?"

He wouldn't have changed a single thing about *her*, but that didn't answer her question. "You mean, like putting steak sauce on filet mignon?"

"Exactly!" She grabbed two sparkling tumblers from the drainboard. "I have to admit," she said, rummaging in the freezer's ice bin, "I don't like steak sauce on filet mignon, but I do like ice in my lemonade." As if to punctuate her statement, she dropped three cubes into one of the glasses.

"So do I." If she kept looking at him in that warm, wonderful way, he'd need more than icy lemonade to cool him down.

She held out a glass, and when he took it, their fingers touched. In that minuscule moment, the soft warmth of her skin sent a tremor from his hand to his spine then straight to his already-pounding heart. "Uh, thanks." He could count on one hand the number of times in his life he'd felt this awkward and clumsy—and have fingers left over. What was going on here, anyway?

Julia snapped off a couple of sheets of paper towels and spread them on the tile-topped table. When had she pulled out scissors and a broad-bladed knife? How had she plopped a big wooden cutting board onto the table without him noticing? He sipped his lemonade, hoping the chilly stuff would wake him up. Hoping that while he'd been off in la-la land, he hadn't gawked like some knock-kneed boy in the throes of his first crush.

"Have a seat, why don't you?" she said. She took the flowers from the vase, slid off the plastic sheath, and laid the flowers on the towels. "Those chairs don't look like much, but they're really quite comfortable."

While she sliced the bottoms from each stem, he plopped onto the tightly woven seat of a ladder-back chair. Man, but she had pretty hands. Tiny and delicate, yet strong and sure and— *There you go again, you big dolt.* Simon cleared his throat. "Nice place you have here. How long ago did your grandparents pass away?"

"Good thing you were early," she said, arranging the trimmed flowers in the vase. "They'll last longer, now that I've had time to snip the stems."

Had she planned to skirt the question, or did it just seem that way? Simon wondered.

"And to answer your question, my grandparents died just over a year ago."

"And you moved right in?"

A small frown etched her brow. *Concentration on the task at hand? Or a discomfiting memory?*

"Not right away. Lots of paperwork to deal with. Figuring out what to do with my place in Lancaster. Trying to decide if I wanted to drive from here to there every day." She shrugged one shoulder. "Just…stuff, y'know?"

There it was again, that strange sadness in her voice, her eyes. He felt like a heel, opening the door to bad memories, which made no sense, no sense at all, because how could he have known that such an ordinary question would wake unhappy thoughts? "Have you been a volunteer at the wolf sanctuary long?"

"No. Didn't even realize it was there until about four months ago." She met his eyes for an instant and winked. "All it took was one visit, and I was hooked. But that's Matt's fault, for introducing me to a new litter of cubs that first day."

Simon nodded, glad that her sunny spirits had returned. "Yeah, Matt has a knack for knowing which volunteers will be good for the wolves and the sanctuary…and which come because it's a novelty."

"I agree one hundred percent. I don't know who hired him to run the place, but whoever it was made a smart choice." Her busy hands hovered for a moment over the arrangement, and she looked at some indiscernible spot over his right shoulder. "You'll probably think I'm crazy, but—sometimes I get the feeling he's…he's almost like one of them."

"I've thought the same thing on a couple of occasions. It's like the guy can read the wolves' minds, and—"

"—and they can read his," they said in unison.

They shared a moment of quiet laughter.

"Great minds think alike?" he asked.

She smirked. "When my grandpa heard anybody say that, he'd pipe up with, '…And fools seldom differ….' "

Simon chuckled again, more because he hoped it would hide his blush than because he'd enjoyed the comment. Part of him wanted to find a dark corner where he could figure out what was happening here. Where he could at least try to understand what was making him act like a six-foot-tall goofball.

He'd done some soul-searching earlier, as he'd showered and shaved and tried on one shirt after another, looking for one that didn't make him seem too fussy or too casual. The process reminded him of Georgia's behavior before any dressy event, when she'd put on a dozen outfits before deciding on the one that would send the right message to their hosts and other guests. While hanging up the stuff he'd decided not to wear, Simon reminded himself to keep a safe distance from Julia and reiterated that her seemingly sad and secret past wasn't something he cared to involve himself in—except maybe as a friend.

But here he sat, sipping home-squeezed lemonade and watching her poke daisies into a vase, as if he'd never spent a second with a grown woman in his life.

"There!" she said, clasping both hands under her chin. "Don't they just look lovely?" She smiled, and for a moment, it seemed to Simon that *he*, not the flowers, had painted that feminine glow on her face. "Thanks, Simon. They brightened my day *and* my kitchen!"

Something told him that if it were within his power, he'd give her the moon and the stars, if they'd make her light up like this. "Glad you like 'em."

Without missing a beat, she said, "And *I'm* glad William told you I would."

Simon nearly choked on his last gulp of lemonade. After a moment of sputtering, he grabbed a napkin from the basket on her table and dabbed his eyes. "Sorry," he croaked. "Must've choked on a seed."

"No way, Jose." She scooted the vase to the center of the table. "I strain my lemons twice before adding sugar or water."

If she looked this gorgeous in the fading light of the setting sun, how much more beautiful would she look in candlelight? Simon finished the lemonade in one long gulp and then got up to put his empty glass into the sink. "Ready?"

"Well, sure."

She stood blinking at him for a moment, as if she'd forgotten that the flowers were a precursor to their date.

Date? If he'd meant everything he'd said to himself back at his place, this was *not* a date. How could it be? Pals didn't go on *dates*. Right?

"Just let me grab a sweater. The weatherman said it might get down to the low forties tonight."

He marveled at her lightfootedness, for she barely made a sound even while running up a flight of wood stairs in high-heeled shoes. He'd doctored pet dogs that outweighed her by more than a few pounds. Odd, he thought, that even as tiny as she was, Julia wasn't afraid to be alone inside the compound gates with nearly wild, full-grown wolves—and yet she seemed wary of *humans*. The only thing William had said on that score was that he believed somebody, somewhere in her past, had wounded her deeply—and he'd pray for the love of God and caring friends to help heal her heart and soul.

The Gundens no doubt were up for the task, but was *he*?

Simon drove both hands through his hair and shook his head. He had a business to run, and it ate up most of his waking hours. That, added to church activities and hours volunteered at the sanctuary, left very little time in his life for…

For *what*? For reaching out to a lonely, hurting young woman? Correction: A pretty and witty and—

"All set!" she said. "Want me to follow in my car so you won't have to come all the way back here after we eat?"

"No way! The drive to and from will give me more time in your presence, m'lady," he said, bowing. *Simon, you're losin' your ever-lovin' mind.* She'd given him the perfect out, and he hadn't taken advantage of it.

If he'd known his response would make her blush, he wouldn't have said it.

Or would he, considering the appealing rosy glow it put into her cheeks?

She headed for the front door, sweater slung over one shoulder, skinny purse strap over the other. "Where are you taking me, anyway? I judge by your outfit that you've changed your mind about the Garden Gate."

How could she have known that he'd decided the diner—while a wonderful place to dine—was far too noisy and crowded for a "getting to know you" dinner? Should he tell her he'd made reservations at the Rainbow Dinner Theatre, or surprise her?

Julia did a mini version of a regal curtsey. "Am I dressed properly for wherever we're going?"

She wore a knee-length aqua sheath that skimmed her curvy little body, adorned with turquoise jewelry and low-heeled black pumps. Standing on the blood red foyer runner, backlit by a beam of sunlight, she looked like a model on a runway. "You look gorgeous," he admitted, opening the door. And before he could ruin the moment with another stupid comment, he stepped outside. "I'll just, uh, fire up the old roadster while you lock up." And just in case she might not know what a roadster was, he pointed.

Man, oh, man, he thought, thumping the heel of his hand to his forehead, *could you* be *any more ridiculous?* How he'd made it from the flagstone walk to the car before she'd even pulled the keys from her purse, Simon couldn't say. But from where he sat behind the steering wheel, she looked even tinier up there on that big wraparound porch, standing on her tiptoes to reach a deadbolt high on the thick wooden door. And when she whirled around and ran down the steps on those dainty little feet, his heart thumped wildly. *Good thing you've got a medical degree,* he thought, because otherwise, he'd worry if the old "heart leaped from my chest" adage had some truth to it.

"What time's our reservation?" she asked, sliding into the passenger seat.

He watched her fiddle with the tricky seat belt and decided to give her a moment to figure it out. Part of him hoped she wouldn't, because then he'd have to reach across the seat and buckle it for her, as he did for Levi and Seth whenever they tagged along on trips into town. "What makes you think we have a reservation?"

A quiet metallic *click* told him that Julia had mastered the belt on the first try, and it was all he could do to keep from groaning with disappointment.

"Well," she said, flicking the blue silk tie draped over the rearview mirror, "guys don't usually decorate their cars with stuff like this." She tapped it with a pink-polished fingernail. "It'll go great with those skinny blue stripes in your pants, by the way."

"Thanks. Got the suit coat on a hanger." He used his thumb to point into the back seat. "Didn't want to overdo it and have you thinkin' I'd gone all googly-eyed on you."

Julia's giggle filled the front seat with energy and joy. He would have reached out and squeezed her hand, would have told her that the last time he'd heard anything as musical was when a mother robin built a nest outside his bedroom window. But Julia chose that moment to adjust the purse on her lap. And tuck her thick cinnamon-colored hair behind her ears. And wriggle deeper into the seat. *Just as well*, he thought, sighing, because if he'd actually squeezed her hand, she'd have seen him as way more than googly-eyed.

Simon backed halfway out of her driveway then braked. "Oh man," he complained, "I don't think I left the porch door open for Windy and Wiley."

"Windy and *who*?"

"My dog and cat. I have this screened-in room behind the house, and the hairy goofballs think it's the same as roaming the great outdoors. Isn't safe to let them run loose, so it's the next best thing." He turned left out of her driveway instead of right toward the Rainbow Dinner Theatre. "Mind if we stop at my place on the way to the restaurant? That way you can meet them in person while I explain their sad and sordid stories."

"Not at all. Might be nice to see this big gorgeous house William and Hannah have talked so much about."

"What did they say?"

"Oh, nothing really. Just that you have lots of—"

She stopped talking as suddenly as if somebody had slapped a hand over her mouth. He was about to ask her why when Julia tugged on the hem of her skirt.

"Aw, don't go and do that," he teased. "You have such cute knees."

Though his focus was on the road, he could feel her watching him. From the corner of his eyes, he'd seen her sit up straighter and could almost see those enormous golden brown eyes narrowing as she assessed what, exactly, he'd meant. He realized he should've waited until he knew her better to crack a joke like that. He certainly didn't want her thinking of him as a wacky pervert!

"It's only about ten minutes from your place to mine," he said, mostly to change the subject. "Nice little drive this time of year."

"Spring is my favorite season," she said. "The colors are so crisp and pure. If I had more time, I'd spend my days painting spring scenes."

"So you're an artist?"

"Oh, I wouldn't go that far. I noodle around with brushes and canvas from time to time, but my work—and it's a stretch to call it that—isn't really 'art.' "

"Beauty is in the eye of the beholder."

"Trust me, the stuff I've done isn't even beautiful in my eyes!" Julia punctuated the sentence with another giggle, sending his heart into overdrive again.

"So remind me. How long have you lived in Paradise?"

"Not long." She sighed. "I almost didn't make the move."

She'd hesitated before answering. Because she felt he was prying? Or because of whatever almost held her back?

"Why's that?"

"I'd been away from my grandparents for years before they died." She shrugged one shoulder. "Hard to keep in touch when the state moves you from foster home to foster home."

Simon's grip tightened on the steering wheel. Did he really want to know *why* she'd ended up in the system? Yeah, he did. Sort of. But he could find out later. Maybe. Tonight, he'd show her a good time. Get her laughing to keep the past at bay. By the time he dropped her off, she might just feel he was trustworthy enough to share a few details, with no prompting from him. Maybe there was hope for them, after all.

He swallowed. Hard.

Hope? For what? The girl was drop-dead gorgeous and, as his grandma used to say, smart as a whip. But with Julia's baggage-filled history? A relationship between them would require work. Hard work, and lots of it. Since Georgia's death, every woman his well-meaning friends had introduced to him had troubles from here to Timbuktu and, frankly, he had neither the time nor the patience—nor the training, for that matter—to help solve them. Ditto, Julia's.

Yeah, he'd show her a good time tonight, so that when they ran into one another—and they were bound to in a community as small as theirs—they'd exchange smiles and polite—

Her quiet gasp interrupted his thoughts. "Is that…is that your house?"

He followed her pointer finger then turned into his winding drive. "Yup. This is the place, all right."

"Oh, Simon," she sighed. "It's…it's just…*beautiful*." She turned in the seat and looked into his face. "How do you drag yourself away every day to go to work?" In what seemed to be one deft move, she unbuckled her seat belt, opened the passenger door, and stepped out onto the gravel. "All it needs is a little snow and some colored lights and it'd look like a Christmas card." She half ran toward the covered porch, giving no thought to her purse or sweater still resting on the front seat. "Well, c'mon, silly, take me inside and show me around!"

And all *Julia* needed was a halo over her head and she'd look like an angel.

Just a good time tonight, he reminded himself. *That's it. Casual friends from here on out. Period.*

In every room, as she oohed and ahhed and commented on the antiques, the furniture arrangement, and the scent of "good old *clean,*" Simon repeated his resolution yet again. But his determination wavered when he opened the door to the sunporch and Windy and Wiley thundered toward them. The dog and cat he'd rescued from abuse and neglect, pets that feared all humans except Simon, went willingly and happily into her open arms.

As he watched in stunned silence, Simon fought the envy that bristled inside him, because more than anything, he wanted to be there, too.

Chapter Four

....

"Wow, that's some welcome!" Julia said, squinting as Wiley licked her cheeks and Windy purred into her face.

"On my honor," he said, hand forming the Boy Scout salute, "they've never done this before. Ever. Not even to me, and I feed 'em!"

"Just call me Snow White," she said. "Everybody does."

"I didn't see any pets at your place...."

"Don't have any." She settled into the nearest chair and was instantly joined by the animals.

"Why not? Allergies?"

"No." She took a deep breath. "I'm just a big sap, I guess. One of those people who gets way too attached, way too fast. And if life hasn't taught me anything else, it taught me that nothing is forever. People leave. Pets die."

Shut up, Julia. Just zip your lip! He already knew more about her than most, thanks to William and Hannah. "So what's the sad and sordid story of how you ended up with these guys?"

"Windy blew into my life about two years ago," he said, "when some heartless fools dumped her and a couple of her littermates on the side of the road. Couldn't save the others, but this one..." Simon bent to scratch between the calico's ears. "This one had a real will to live."

He told her how the cat had sustained deep gashes along the entire left side of her body and suffered a broken jaw when, after being tossed from a speeding car, she'd landed hard on the Route 30.

49

Tears sprang to Julia's eyes when Simon said that to save her life, he'd been forced to amputate half of Windy's tail and two of her toes.

The passage of time hadn't dulled his anger at the so-called humans who'd thrown her away like yesterday's garbage. Fury darkened Simon's face as his green eyes flashed and the muscles of his jaw bulged. Julia didn't doubt for a minute that if Windy's cruel and callous former owners stood before him now, they'd get a taste of their own medicine, doled out by the fists balled tight at his sides.

"And what about this big friendly goof?" she said, hoping Wiley's story wasn't quite as horrifying.

Simon's broad shoulders slumped. "His former owner was a breeder. German Shorthaired Pointer pups routinely sell for a couple thousand bucks apiece because they're excellent bird dogs. Trouble was," he said, crouching to wrap the dog's neck in a hug, "this big friendly goof is gun-shy."

"So the breeder gave him up just because of that?"

Something akin to a growl passed Simon's lips. "Not before he tried to beat 'gun-shy' out of the whole litter." He pointed. "If you look at Wiley straight on, you'll notice that his jaw is crooked, because that…that *beast* broke it. God only knows how. Or with what. And he didn't even bother to rearrange the bones afterward. Same goes for every other part of Wiley that he cracked or smashed—ribs, legs, toes, all healed on their own."

Julia cringed and gasped as her arms joined Simon's in a huge hug for Wiley. "Oh, how horrible!" she whispered. "I can't even imagine how much agony he must have been in." She met Simon's gaze, unashamed for the first time in a long time of the tears that flowed freely from her eyes. "Is he still in pain?"

"Nah. He's on daily megadoses of glucosamine and chondroitin, very good stuff for healing old damage and preventing future wear and tear." Simon kissed the bridge of Wiley's nose and got a big "thank you" lick in response. "I figure all that abuse shaved three to five years off his life. A dog like this oughta last twelve, minimum, so I aim to make whatever time he's got left the best it can be."

Sitting this way, with their arms wrapped around Wiley and their faces were mere inches apart, they were close enough that Julia could see flecks of blue and brown in Simon's sea green eyes. And why hadn't she noticed before that his eyelashes were long and lush and inky black? He must spend a lot of time in the sun, because didn't most blonds have lashes that matched their hair?

Windy chose that moment to join the group and leaped onto Wiley's back. Julia stared into the cat's round golden eyes and sent a silent *Thank you* for the distraction. Something told her that if she had continued looking into Simon's beautiful face a moment longer, she might have given in to the temptation to kiss him. Not a romantic kiss, but one that would tell him what a good and decent man she believed him to be.

When the grandfather clock in his foyer chimed, announcing the seven o'clock hour, Simon got to his feet. "Guess we'd better head out," he said, dusting fur from his trousers, "if we don't want to be late."

"You'll probably think I'm nuts," she said, standing, "but what would you think of having dinner here? If you have eggs, I can whip us up an omelet…."

His brows drew together. "Why would you want to do that? The Rainbow Dinner Theatre is a great place."

"Oh, I know, but"—she glanced at the pets, flanking him like fuzzy statues, looking from their master to his guest, as if they knew what she was about to propose—"but after hearing those stories, I can't ask you to leave them." Meeting his eyes squarely, Julia added, "They need you far more than we need to be entertained by the actors at the Rainbow." She grinned. "But I'll gladly take a rain check on that, because I hear—"

"Julia," he said quietly, "the eggs are in the fridge."

Move, you ninny, she scolded. *Get into the kitchen and start scrambling eggs before he figures out that you don't just* sound *nuts and sends you packing!* But her shoes seemed nailed to the floor, and she couldn't make herself break the intense eye contact that connected her to him, and him to her.

Slowly, he reached out with both hands. To pull her close in a sweet embrace? To bracket her face so he could kiss her cheek? Heart hammering, Julia licked her lips, hoping for either, hoping for both. She wondered about the peculiar expression clouding his handsome face. Hannah and William had explained how, since his wife's death, Simon often spoke of his yearning for a wife and kids to fill this big, beautiful house. Maybe, as the Gundens said, Simon's loneliness and hers gave them a common bond. And maybe—

Gently, Simon tucked her hair behind her ears. "Such a pretty face," he whispered.

She rested her hands upon his thick wrists and took a small step closer.

"Such soft hair, and—"

Two huffy barks and a drawn-out meow put an instant end to the magical moment. When he gave her shoulders an affectionate squeeze, Julia heard the steady *tick-tick-tick* of his watch. She tapped it with a fingertip. "It makes quite a racket for such a little thing."

A chuckle began deep in his chest, bubbling up and out until the delightful notes of masculine laughter filled the room. His mood was contagious, and Julia's tears, shed moments earlier because his pets had endured such pain, now turned to joy. It quickly became one of those "the more you laugh, the more you want to laugh" moments. Weak-kneed, she leaned into him, felt his big arms encircle and support her, felt his warm breath on her cheek. For the second time in minutes, they were close enough to kiss, but this time, rather than hoping it would happen, Julia hoped it *wouldn't*. Instead, she reveled in the pleasant feelings evoked by their harmonious laughter. It felt good. So good, in fact, that she wondered why she hadn't gone searching for reasons to do it a hundred times a day!

Without warning, he went silent and stood perfectly still.

Still smiling but confused by the sudden change in his demeanor, she looked up, searching his face, his oh-so-amazing face…though she had no idea what she was searching *for*. Simon shook his head so quickly that if she'd blinked, she might not have noticed at all. *What's going on in that gorgeous head of yours?* she wanted to ask. *Why are you looking at me as if you just woke from a dream*?

But before she could put her questions into words, he drew her closer—so close that not even the faint spring breeze puffing through the front screen door could have passed between them. Time, it seemed, had stopped. Even Windy and Wiley hadn't moved, hadn't made a sound. If she thought God would listen to her, Julia might have sent a prayer heavenward, asking Him to help her understand what was happening in this amazing moment, and why He'd sent this amazing *man* into her life.

But she'd called out to Him before, in times of fear and fierce turmoil, and He hadn't answered. She had no reason to expect He'd respond to something as silly and unimportant as a budding romance…or whatever this was. Once again, she'd have to rely on her own wits if she hoped to puzzle out the meaning of—

Simon's lips touched hers just then, in the merest hint of a kiss. She felt him tremble, and the tremor traveled from his fingertips to his shoulders. She felt his heart, beating hard beneath her hands. She'd never been in love before. A time or two she'd *thought* she had, only to discover, too late, that handsome faces and pretty words could be deceiving. Disturbing. Dangerous.

The haunting memory of her deepest and darkest secret crashed into her like the foaming surf of a stormy sea, propelling her backward and off-balance, away from the safety of Simon's arms, far from the risk of pain and shame.

She put her back to him and, staring at the plush square pattern carved into the navy area rug, pressed her fingertips into her temples. She shouldn't have come here. Shouldn't have accepted his dinner invitation. Shouldn't have been lured by his kind words and gentle touch. Shouldn't have—

"Julia," he said, planting himself in her path, "look at me." Tenderly, he cupped her chin in a palm. "You look as if you've seen a ghost."

A ghost? *If only!* she thought, unable to maintain eye contact. In time, she might have convinced herself that ghosts didn't exist, that what happened to her had been a hideous nightmare and nothing more. Might have found a way to explain away the grisly images etched deep into her brain and the angry ropelike scars that still glowed on her skin.

She sensed that Simon was a good and decent man. If the way wild wolves, his pets, and Amish friends reacted to him wasn't proof enough of just how good and decent he was, she need only look into his face, brimming now with genuine concern, to know that he'd never harm her. Not intentionally, anyway.

William and Hannah's sentiments echoed in her head: *Simon is a lonely man,* they'd said, *who needs a loving wife, a woman who'd share his life and help him raise a house full of children.*

Her life to date was fraught with misery, her heritage too shameful to inflict on a man like this. She'd known him less than a day, yet she knew Simon deserved a far better woman—one with a pure heart *and* a pure past.

Clearly, she was not that woman.

Windy wove a figure eight around her ankles, reminding her why she and Simon had come here. As if to add to the reminder, Wiley's damp nose nudged her fingertips. She stooped and hugged them both. *Focus on them,* Julia told herself. The dog and cat, like the sanctuary's wolves, offered unconditional acceptance and affection. Even if they'd known every gory detail about that night, it wouldn't have mattered one whit.

Experience had taught her that to dwell on what had happened changed nothing, accomplished nothing, except to open the door to dark, brooding moods. So, yes, she'd focus on Windy and Wiley and on their master, who stood but a foot away, looking worried and bewildered and so concerned that something had upset her.

She had no right to expose him to the memory that had upset her. No right at all. That almost-kiss? It had to be their last. She'd be his friend—if he wanted another—but nothing more.

Julia closed her eyes and took a deep breath, then rose and forced a bright smile. "Wow," she said, dusting her hands together. "Guess that'll teach you not to tell me sad stories about animal abuse!" A nervous giggle escaped her lungs. She took another deep breath to disguise it and grabbed Simon's hand. "Now if you'll show me the way to the kitchen, I'll get busy on that omelet while you cancel our reservation."

* * * * *

He had to hand it to her. Somehow with the meager ingredients in his refrigerator and pantry, she pulled together a hearty, rib-sticking meal. Onions, ham, and cheese made their way into the omelet; half a head of lettuce and two pucker-skinned tomatoes went into a delicious salad; and ordinary white bread, buttered and topped with spices, became crispy garlic toast. And in the short time it took for the omelet to go from yellow to golden, she'd whipped up a pitcher of home-brewed iced tea. Her biggest regret, she'd said, was that he didn't have anything she could turn into dessert.

"Seems only fair," he said once they'd loaded the dishwasher, "that I take you out for an ice cream."

"Frozen custard?"

"Uh-huh."

"You won't have to twist my arm…."

Now, sitting side by side on the weatherworn bench of a hand-hewn picnic table outside the ice cream stand, they lapped chocolate-vanilla-twist cones.

He had let her lead the conversation while she cooked. Gave her control over their dinner conversation, too, because while whatever happened back there in his living room had piqued his curiosity, a mood swing like that…. Simon shook his head, knowing that what little he remembered from college psych classes couldn't provide him with nearly enough insight to help her.

No question about it, Julia was in pain. Did his heart ache for her? Sure it did, and he'd hit his knees tonight—and every night from now on—asking God to heal her. What she *didn't* need was some clown in a lab coat masquerading as a shrink. Oh, he'd check on her now and then, to make sure she was safe. What would that cost him, other than an hour here, an hour there, and a few gallons of gas—

"I used to have a machine," she said, interrupting his reverie, "and a terrific recipe to make this same custard. After one of my moves, I looked and looked but couldn't find them." With a nonchalant wave of her hand, she added, "Oh well."

"How many moves have there been?" The instant the words were out he regretted them, because only God knew what can of worms he'd opened *this* time.

Thankfully, Julia laughed. "You want the list in alphabetical or numerical order?"

"Lots, I take it." Hopefully that would close the door on the topic.

"Eighteen, last time I counted, and that was before Lancaster." Another shrug. "So counting Paradise, lots."

It hadn't escaped his notice that since her trip down memory lane, her smile looked a bit too wide…and never quite reached her lovely eyes. Or that her laughter—while there had been plenty of it—sounded too forced to be completely genuine. While he admired her attempt to cover the tracks left by the strange turn of events back at his place, Simon couldn't help but wonder what was behind it all.

Maybe William or Hannah would know....

And maybe he'd better let sleeping bears lie.

A few years ago he'd vacationed in Alaska, where a pal who worked for the state's Department of Fish and Game had let him traipse along on a "seek and find" mission. A grizzly, fitted with a tracking collar, had gone missing. Their assignment? Find the bear, tranquilize him, and replace the faulty collar. When they finally located the animal, miles from where he'd last been spotted, he was snoring in a shallow cave. Even after a full dose of knockout drugs, the beast had nearly torn the heads from two officers, one who probably still sported scars to remind him of his run-in with the once-snoozing bear.

Some lessons, Simon reckoned, *come to a man for very good reasons.*

"You don't like frozen custard?"

He'd been so deep in thought that her words startled him. "What? No. Sure. I mean, I love the stuff." He frowned. "Why?"

"Oh, I dunno," she said, grinning. "Maybe because you haven't said a word in five minutes, and…" She pointed, indicating his cone.

"Man, oh, man," he complained, grabbing a napkin to sop up the drippy mess his melting ice cream made on the table.

"Guess I'm not the only one who pays occasional visits to la-la land." And to underscore her meaning, she hummed the *Twilight Zone* theme.

He tossed the soggy napkin into a nearby trash can. "I read someplace that deep thinkers like us are smarter than the average bear."

"Really."

He nodded. "Really."

"Well, don't that just beat all."

"What…?"

"I always figured that people who completely zone out were a little, you know…." She drew tiny circles in the air beside her temple. "Not that it's a *bad* thing, necessarily. Though I guess admitting that it's a bad thing would be the same as saying 'I'm loopy as a bedbug! Take me away, men in white coats!'"

She got a kick out of her little joke, so much so that Simon couldn't help laughing, too. Hard to believe how someone so lovely—inside and out—could harbor a secret so haunting it had the power to change the very atmosphere in a room. He'd come *this* close to kissing her. *Really* kissing her.

Who was he kidding? He *had* kissed her. Would've kept right on kissing her, too, if his four-legged interlopers hadn't barged in. And if she hadn't backed away as if he'd attacked her.

He forced himself to focus on the fact that God knew what was best for her—and for him, as well. Simon saw the interruption as a sign from above that the Almighty hadn't granted permission for them to forge a relationship. At least, not of the romantic kind. And so He'd inspired an intrusion to remind them both to ask for divine guidance before embarking on journeys of the heart.

Pity, he thought, grinning to himself, because Julia's lips had tasted every bit as good as they'd felt, and that was saying a mouthful.

Sorry, Lord, he prayed, *no pun intended.*

"You look like the Cheshire cat," she said.

"Who?"

"You know, from *Alice in Wonderland*?"

"You're not gonna believe this, but I've never seen that cartoon."

"Read the book?"

"Nope."

"So in addition to being a la-la land visitor, you're illiterate, to boot."

The rich warm tones of her laughter touched a chord in his heart. As much as he'd loved his wife, he'd never shared goofy jokes with her, never traded teasing barbs, never laughed until his jaws and his sides ached. Not with Georgia. Not with any other woman, for that matter. Was this a sign that he'd misread God's signal about him and Julia?

Julia snapped her fingers. "Earth to Simon, Earth to Simon...."

Chuckling, he said, "Sorry."

"Don't come down to Earth on my behalf," she said. "I think you're kinda cute, staring off into space that way. It's just..." Again she pointed, indicating his ice cream-covered hand. "If you're not gonna eat that thing, well, I've finished mine, so give it to me!" She crinkled her face, as if she believed it necessary to come up with a rationale for her comment. "It's gotta be *some* kind of sin, wasting perfectly good frozen custard."

Grinning, he gave her the cone. She'd earned it, first by digging herself from the pit of painful history, then by making the best home-cooked meal he'd eaten in months, and finally by helping him remember how good it felt to laugh. *If this* is *a sign, Lord, I'd sure appreciate a sign, so I'll know I'm reading Your signs correctly this time.*

The silliness of his thought started a whole new round of laughter.

"What's so funny?"

"Nothing," he said, standing. And wrapping her hand in his, he tugged her to her feet. "Let's take a walk."

"Where?"

"Along Pequea Creek. It's not far from here, and it's a nice night for a walk."

She followed, but he sensed her unasked *why?*

"Maybe we'll hear a whip-poor-will singing in the breeze."

"Y'think?"

"Could be."

"Can't say when I last heard a whip-poor-will."

And Simon couldn't say what inspired him to slip an arm around her waist and pull her close. But he did.

And she let him.

Chapter Five

....

"Tell me," Simon said, balancing an ankle on a crossed knee, "just what does a public defender *do*, anyway?"

Finally, a subject Julia could talk about with no fear of waking sleeping monsters! "Most of the cases I'm assigned require me to represent juveniles whose parents can't afford private attorneys."

"'Require'? You mean, you don't have any say about who you fight for?"

She laughed. "Not if I want to get paid every month."

"So even if somebody's guilty, you're 'required' to go to bat for them."

"Somebody has to."

"Don't know if I could do that."

If she had a dollar for every time she'd heard a similar sentiment, Julia could probably afford that trip to Ireland she'd been dreaming about. "Oh, you'd do it."

On the opposite shore of the Pequea, a young boy sat on a pier. She watched as silvery ripples, stirred when his bare feet sloshed in the water, ebbed to their side of the creek. "You save helpless animals every day of your life, Simon, so you can't tell me you'd turn your back on helpless *kids*."

From the corner of her eye, she saw him nodding then felt him shrug the shoulder closest to her own. "But," he began, "if those kids commit crimes, shouldn't they be punished?"

"Yes and no."

Simon scooted forward on the wrought-iron bench so he could turn slightly to meet her eyes. Milky moonlight gleamed from his blond hair like a silvery halo. "Yes *and* no? I wouldn't have pegged you as a double-talker, Julia."

If she hadn't heard it all before, dozens of times, she might have been offended by his accusatory tone. "Of course criminals should be punished to the fullest extent of the law...*if* they've had the benefit of proper legal counsel and a fair trial."

One brow rose high on his forehead as he tilted his handsome head. "I see your point...I suppose."

It was Julia's turn to shrug. "No shades of gray in the law, I'm afraid. A thing is either right or it's wrong. You'd see that more clearly if a loved one was facing a prison sentence and—"

"I'd be heartbroken, I'm sure," he interrupted, "if someone I cared about broke the law. But there are no shades of gray in the Bible, either. A thing is a sin or it's not."

She tried to think of a single instance when she'd had this argument and won, and not one came to mind. But then, people rarely countered her comments with Bible talk. "I guess it's lucky for me you're such a devout Christian, then."

His frown said what words didn't need to: "I don't get it."

"Didn't Jesus say 'Judge not, that ye be not judged'?" She scooted forward, too, then added, "It's comforting to know that you won't judge me simply because we disagree, wholeheartedly, on this point."

A slow smile spread across his face. "I'll say this for you...."

Julia cringed inwardly as she waited for the proverbial "other boot" to drop.

"...When you're right, you're right."

And one of the things she'd been right *about* had been her judgment of Simon. He truly was a good and decent man, and nothing underscored the fact more than his last comment. If she'd been on a quest to "Find Mr. Right," Julia could have ended her search right there on the banks of Pequea Creek.

But she hadn't been husband-hunting. And she'd already made up her mind to spare Simon—who'd proven "white knight" tendencies by dedicating his life to animals—from having to rescue yet another suffering orphan.

* * * * *

"But enough about me. What made you decide to become a veterinarian?"

If she thought he hadn't noticed her attempt to steer the conversation away from herself, Julia was sadly mistaken. "It's a long, boring story, actually." He'd go along with her wishes…for now. He was under no delusions, though, and had no intention of changing his mind about getting involved with this extraordinary—if not confounding—young woman. Clearly she needed a friend, and Simon believed *that* was why God had introduced him to Julia.

"It just so happens I like long, boring stories. They're my favorite kind."

He'd known her less than twenty-four hours, yet she'd managed to make him laugh more in that short time span than he had in months. It felt good, being in her presence. Not as good as being in her arms, but—

"Okay, since you seem determined to keep your boring story all to yourself, let me guess...." Julia cleared her throat then sat straight and tall, and with hands clasped and resting in her lap, she spoke as if reading a bedtime story to a child: "When Simon Thomas was a little boy—a boy who routinely gave his poor mother fits—he found a baby bird that had fallen from its nest. He looked and looked but couldn't find its mother, so he gently put it into a shoe box. Then he visited his local library to find out what went into the care and feeding of baby birds, and in no time," she said, hands fluttering like bird wings, "the baby grew up and flew away, thanks to its substitute mother, Simon Thomas."

A moment passed, filled only with the sounds of crickets, singing in the distance. "Wow," he said. "Amazing."

Julia's girlish giggle floated around him and hung on the gathering mist. "Oh, c'mon. You don't expect me to believe *that's* the story!"

"No," he admitted. "But you're close. Eerily close, as a matter of fact."

She'd left her sweater in his car, draped over the passenger seat, and the chilly breeze made her shudder and hug herself. If he'd been wearing a jacket, he'd have draped it over her shoulders. Instead he slipped an arm around her back and scooted her nearer to his side. At first, Julia stiffened and then relaxed, content, it seemed, to share his warmth.

"You want me to guess again?"

Chuckling, he shook his head. "It was two baby squirrels, not a bird. And they didn't fall from a nest; I took them when I found their mother dead on the side of the road."

"Oh nooo," she wailed. "Run over by a car?"

" 'Fraid so." It had been awhile since he'd thought of that period of his life, and Simon smiled at the memory. "Had to gather up my courage and march across the street to ol' Mrs. Holt's house." He faked a shiver. "Neighborhood kids claimed the place was haunted and that she was a witch. But rumor also had it she could fix any critter, no matter how broken."

"Kids," Julia huffed, "can be so cruel."

"Just so happened I pulled the short straw that day, meaning it was my turn to sneak under her fence and come back to our clubhouse with something to prove I'd been in her yard." Simon grinned at the memory. "There I was on all fours, heart pounding like a parade drum, expecting to see her stirring a caldron of scary brew…and I caught her red-handed, cooing to a nest of bunnies."

"How old was she?"

"At the time, I'd have said ninety-nine or one hundred." He laughed. "Now? I'd guess midseventies. Behind those Buddy Holly glasses and all that silvery hair, she was nothin' but a big softy. And she bribed me to protect her reputation as a grouch by plying me with hot-from-the-oven sugar cookies and cold chocolate milk. After our snack, she let me help feed her rabbits, chattering the whole time about how important it is to keep babies warm, what to feed them, how much to dole out and how often…." Simon added, "I told her about Boris and Natasha and asked if the same stuff would work to keep them alive." He sighed. "And it did."

Julia reached over to squeeze his hand. "You named them Boris and Natasha?" She giggled. "What a lovely story!" Another squeeze. "Thanks for sharing it." Then, "So what did you bring your friends, to prove you'd entered the 'witch's den'?"

He pinched the bridge of his nose, hoping to forestall the laughter bubbling in his throat. "She gave me a wallet-sized picture of Jesus.

You know the one where He's surrounded by children?"

She threw her head back and laughed, clapping her hands. "She sounds delightful!"

"Yeah," he agreed. "And we stayed in touch right up until her death about six years ago."

She sandwiched one of his hands between her own. "Oh, Simon, I'm so sorry. I'm sure you miss her a lot."

"Yeah, but I think of her every time someone brings an abandoned animal or bird into the clinic."

"Did she have a husband and kids?"

"Nope. Just a bounty of critters."

"And you."

An ash gray cloud passed in front of the moon, shrouding Pequea Creek's edge with shadows that, under other circumstances, would have inspired dread and gloom. But with Julia beside him, Simon's spirit soared with calm content. *Remarkable,* he thought, bearing in mind that he'd resolved to keep things strictly platonic between them.

"Feels like rain," she said, hunching both shoulders and cupping her elbows.

"Looks like it, too." He got to his feet and held out a hand, wondering why it mattered so much that she took it. When at last she did, Simon's heart thrummed with relief.

Her tiny hand tucked into the crook of his arm, they strolled quietly over the cobblestones.

"Very gentlemanly of you," she said after awhile, "to walk so slowly on my behalf."

Another woman might not have noticed that he'd shortened his long-legged strides so she needn't half run to keep up with him. But then, another woman wouldn't have been *Julia*. A good thing that she couldn't read his mind, he thought, because then she'd know her petite stature wasn't solely responsible for his chivalrous pace. He'd been in no particular hurry to reach his car, because getting there only meant he'd have to take her home, and *that* meant spending the rest of the long, lonely night without her. Four and a half hours in her presence were more than enough to make him want four and a half more and another four and a half after that.

"I can't remember when I've enjoyed an evening more," she said, looking up at him.

The clouds chose that moment in time to release their dark hold on the moon, and under its shimmering light, her long lashes cast spiky shadows on her cheeks, making her eyes look even larger than before. Her smile carved a dimple into her right cheek, and he resisted the urge to touch it and then trace the outline of her soft, generous lips.

"I'll bet you're wishing right about now that you'd let me follow in my car."

"Of course not. Why would you say such a thing?"

"Because then you could head straight home to Windy and Wiley instead of driving me all the way to the other side of town."

She'd made a reference to the men in white coats earlier, and if Julia had known how much he dreaded taking her home, *she'd* call them right now. But if he knew what was good for him—and her— he'd better choose his words carefully. At least until he had a chance to hit his knees and find out what in the world the good Lord had in mind for them. "It's only a few miles and a few minutes," he said truthfully. "No big deal."

"Well, still. It's been fun. So thanks…especially for the ice cream."

"And thank you for supper."

"Thank *you* for introducing me to Windy and Wiley. They're… they're grrrreat. And—"

"Thanks for the scintillating conversation."

"—and for the walk along the Pequea and for sharing that delightful 'Why I became a veterinarian' story, and—"

"Uncle," he said, pretending to wave an imaginary white flag. "I give up. It's official: You've out-thanked me."

"Ahh, a man who knows when to quit. You're one of a kind, Simon Thomas!"

No, he thought, you're *one of a kind*. No bigger than a minute, Julia had more energy than five adults and a couple of rowdy kids. She was fun, fascinating, and spunky, with strength of character that belied her petite frame. He'd laughed more in her company than he had in… Simon couldn't remember when he'd had a better time. He frowned to himself, trying to figure out why his brain seemed to be playing a tennis match, lobbing "She's got too much baggage" and "You've gotta get to know her better" over an invisible net.

He couldn't say what had happened between this moment and the one when he'd made up his mind to keep her at arm's length, but as sure as he stood beside her, Simon had done a complete one-eighty. It wasn't like him to change his mind, especially this quickly. But if he got down-and-dirty honest with himself, he'd spent far too many years dragging sad history himself, so who was he to judge? The only thing that could keep him from her now was God, telling him in no uncertain terms to stay away from Julia Spencer. Simon intended to pray like crazy that Julia *was* in the Creator's greater plan for his life. And if he knew what was good for him, he'd better pray, too, that the Lord would give him the courage to accept it in case she wasn't.

Chapter Six

....

"No need to walk me to the door."

"I'd like to see you try and stop me, pip-squeak."

Laughing, she said, "Well, all right. If you insist." Secretly, nothing could have pleased her more. Since she'd decided that tomorrow it would be business-as-usual, Julia wanted nothing more than to squeeze every possible moment out of this wonderful, magical night.

She hadn't remembered to turn on the porch light. "Oh, good grief," she muttered, digging through her purse. "I hope finding the key hole will be easier than finding my keys."

In a heartbeat, Simon aimed the pin-thin blue light of a mini flashlight into her bag. "Does that help?"

"I'll say!" She fished out the key ring. "Wherever did you find that thing?" Julia asked, shoving open her front door.

"One of my patients gave it to me. Nifty gizmo, eh?"

"I'll say," she repeated. *Funny...*, she thought. She usually had no trouble at all in saying good-bye to a date. Which in itself was odd, considering how seldom she dated. But there she stood, fidgeting with her purse strap, trying to decide whether to step inside her foyer or stay on the porch, fumbling for just the right way to end the evening. A short list of possibilities flitted through her head: *See ya around! Take care! Don't let the bedbugs bite!* Julia was about to say, *Drive safely now, y'hear?* when Simon drew her into a hug.

"So what's on your schedule tomorrow?"

73

"I, um…," she stuttered as he rested both hands on her hips. "…I, ah, I have to be in court at nine."

"To defend a murdering, thieving thug?"

"No," she laughed. "Nothing quite that dramatic."

"Well, I'll pray that your side wins."

Julia felt like a dimwit, staring up into his face. *Better back off,* she told herself, *before you get in over your head.* But despite the promise she'd made to herself mere hours ago, she felt rooted to the spot and glued into his embrace. "Thanks," she said.

"Can I call you tomorrow?"

She swallowed. How could she say no? But…how could she say yes? The man deserved a woman who could share everything with him, and Julia had absolutely *no* intention of telling him about the defective genes she'd inherited from her parents!

A thought flashed through her head, and she didn't know whether to laugh or to cry. She'd spent most of their beautiful night together trying to figure out ways to keep him at a distance. How self-centered and arrogant to think he *wanted* more than a casual, platonic relationship! Maybe she'd misread everything, from the way he held her hand to the way he looked deep into her eyes and gently tucked her hair behind her ears. For all she knew, he behaved the same way with kids who brought their dogs and cats into his clinic!

"Earth to Julia, Earth to Julia…."

She had to laugh, for she'd said the same thing to him just a few short hours ago. Part of her felt a surge of relief, thinking that he acted this way with just about everybody in his life. And yet the very idea woke an ache in her that made no sense. No sense at all, since they'd only met that morning!

"So…?"

"So…what?" she echoed.

"So…can I call you tomorrow?"

"For what?"

Simon chuckled and hugged her tighter. "To see whether or not you won your court case."

"Sure," she said on a sigh, "if you like."

"Well, no need to sound so *enthused*." His forefinger traced the contour of her jaw. "All I can say is, it's a good thing I'm not the supersensitive type."

Julia's confused brain buzzed with contradictions, questions, and decisions, and she'd barely heard what he said. "What?" Hopefully his response would fill in at least one of the blanks.

"Never mind."

When Simon wrapped his arms tighter around her, Julia thought for sure he intended to finish that kiss that he'd started in his living room, hours ago. Was *this* what people meant when they talked about love at first sight? Because if she didn't know better, she would've sworn she'd fallen in love with this gorgeous, goofy guy when he'd walked toward her at the sanctuary!

Much to her surprise—and disappointment—Simon's lips touched her forehead, lingering in a sweet, almost-brotherly kiss. *One problem solved*, she thought, trying to hide her disenchantment, *and another born*.

"Good night, Julia."

When he took a step back and released her from the embrace, a bleak chill settled over her, as if a bitter wind had suddenly blown a warm afghan from around her shoulders. *Better get used to feeling this way,* she told herself. And stepping into the foyer, she gripped the doorknob so tightly that her knuckles ached. "Drive home safely."

She couldn't remember a time when it had been more difficult to close a door and bolt it. Couldn't remember missing another human being as much as she already missed Simon, though he hadn't yet driven away. Julia Spencer, known around the office as the newcomer who battled older, wiser men in court—and more often than not beat them—going all soft and squishy over some guy she'd just met?

"Ridiculous," she said, frowning. She flicked on the lamp in front of the bay window and reached for the drapery cord to shut out the night. As she did, Julia saw him, illuminated by his car's dome light, and her heart fluttered. "What you need," she said, heading for the kitchen, "is to slowly sip a cup of mandarin orange tea while you soak in a nice hot tub of bubbles."

After turning on the gas under the chrome kettle, she dropped a tea bag into her favorite red ceramic mug. *Two flies with one swat,* she thought, heading upstairs to pour her bath while she waited for the water to boil. While passing through the living room, she noticed the spine of one book sticking out farther than the rest on the shelf. Her frown deepening, she approached, forefinger poised to push it back into place. "The Bible?" Julia whispered. She hadn't touched it, except while dusting, since moving into her grandparents' house. So how had it gotten out of line in the first place?

Julia grabbed it, thinking maybe one of the paperbacks she'd stored behind it had fallen from the pile and shoved it forward. "Weird," she said, clutching it to her chest, because the novels remained in their orderly stack. One glance at the weathered black leather and worn-away gold lettering was enough to awaken memories of days long gone, when her grandfather read Christ's parables instead of bedtime stories. Even at four and five, as she sat on his knee, Julia understood that he and her grandmother wanted to heal the wounds inflicted upon their only grandchild by their daughter and son-in-law. They'd welcomed her into their home and done their level best to care for her—until illness and old age made it impossible. That day when the social worker came, Julia only needed to remember Granny's pitiful sobs and the tears clinging to Gramps's face to know that it had been as hard for them to let her go as it had been for her to leave.

"Take my Bible," Gramps had said, pressing it into her hands. "Keep it with you always, so you'll never forget how much we love you…how much *God* loves you."

Julia sat in the very chair where he'd recited from the Good Book, one palm pressed to the supple cover and the other resting upon her chest. How different her life would have been if their failing health hadn't forced her to join an already-overcrowded foster-care system.

But thoughts like that, she'd learned, were as useless as the tears now puddling in her eyes. Swiping them away with the heel of one hand, Julia opened to the first page, where Gramps had listed the births, marriages, and deaths of family members. He'd left this miserable world long before her mother and father, so their names remained on the blue-scribbled list of the living. How a couple as warm and loving as her grandparents could have spawned a daughter as selfish as her mother was something Julia would never figure out. As if drugs and the petty crimes that funded her addiction weren't injurious enough, her mother married a career criminal to ensure her steady supply of heroine. "You're the only good thing that came of that union," Granny used to say. But the kind and loving words could not overpower Julia's belief that *as* the product of that union, she was defective.

Amazingly, she'd obediently dragged the Bible from foster home to foster home. Just as amazingly, it was no worse for the wear. But then, Julia had only opened it on Gramps's or Granny's birthdays, or her own, to stare at two dog-eared photographs: a wedding picture of her parents and one of Granny and Gramps, side by side in matching rockers on the covered porch. Gently, she pinched her gold locket and closed her eyes, the oh-so-familiar *zzz-zzz-zzz* sound floating into her ears as she slid it left and right on its dainty chain. *How ironic,* she thought, *that though I own a paid-for car and a mortgage-free, fully furnished house, my most treasured possessions are right here in my hands.*

She scooted to the edge of the chair and tossed the old King James Bible onto the coffee table. It landed with its pages open to Psalms. "*What time I am afraid,*" she read, "*I will trust in thee.*"

Trust? Julia nearly laughed out loud. "Trust, indeed."

Disgusted—with her so-called parents and especially with God who, in her opinion, allowed every bit of the misery that brought her to this point—Julia harrumphed and shoved the Bible. And when she did, it opened to the book of John: "*...the Father hath not left me alone.*"

If that were true, she demanded, *why do I feel unloved, too tainted to be worthy of sharing my life with a wonderful man like Simon?* Exasperated, Julia reached out to slam the Bible shut. Instead she missed, and it fell open yet again, this time to Job. Julia remembered Gramps sharing that God's obedient servant was rewarded for his faithfulness after many losses, indignities, and pain with an abundant life filled with peace and joy.

Her own life hadn't exactly been blissful, but then she hadn't suffered as Job had, either. She really had very little to complain about, because despite the muddled mess that was her past, she'd become a strong, capable woman—had chosen a career path that made her a champion for those unable to fight for themselves. She identified closely with every client—even the truly guilty ones—because, like her, they were alone, unloved, misunderstood…and abandoned by God.

"Enough of this nonsense!" she said. On her feet now, Julia grabbed the Bible and carefully tucked the photographs inside to protect them. After slamming it shut, she marched purposefully back to the bookshelf and thrust it into its proper place between *The Song of Roland* and her grandfather's favorite, *The Complete Collection of Shakespeare*.

The teakettle's shrill whistle caught her attention, and she headed down the hall to silence it. No longer in the mood for the romantic candlelight and warm bubble bath that would have evoked memories of her wonderful night with Simon, Julia poured angrily boiling water into her mug. "Seems you don't even deserve a gently steeped cup of tea."

Aware she'd been wallowing, Julia knew she wouldn't stay long in this dark, dangerous place. Later, as she fought the nightmares and bad memories that threatened to deprive her of sleep, she'd beat down the defeatism swirling in her head and heart. But for now, she'd give in to it, because didn't a tainted woman with no family—and no hope of creating one—deserve just a *little* self-pity?

Julia stirred sugar into her cup. "Oh, get over yourself, you big whiny baby," she said as the spoon clattered into the sink. With her tendency to throw herself into her clients and their cases, a husband and kids would feel neglected at best—unwanted at worst. She'd lived a lifetime feeling unloved and would *not* inflict that pain on another human being.

The self–pep talk began in earnest:

She'd done quite well in life, considering her roots.

She'd achieved everything by dint of her own hard work.

She'd gained the respect and admiration of peers and superiors alike.

And she'd accomplished it all without Mr. Right at her side.

Julia was the first to admit that she had much to be thankful for. But that didn't stop her from wishing there was hope for her. Hope that someday she'd share her life with Prince Charming and a gaggle of Little Charmings.

* * * * *

Julia hadn't seen Simon since the night they'd walked along the Pequea, but he'd called every few days. Their chats had been short but lighthearted, always ending with a promise to find time to get together again soon. She might have done a better job of getting along without him if not for those fun and friendly phone calls....

After a light breakfast of cornflakes and sliced peaches, Julia headed out for the Gunden farm. Her nine-o'clock hearing had been rescheduled, meaning she had plenty of time to deliver William's deed. He'd been uncharacteristically impatient during the title search and had surprised her with a bellow of joyous laughter when she told him that no liens or other encumbrances would stall his land purchase. She could hardly wait to see his reaction when she handed him the deed that gave him full ownership of the parcel.

She parked her little sedan beside the Gundens' buggy and returned Levi's wave. "My, but it's quiet around here today," she called, grabbing her briefcase. "Where is everybody?"

"They are in the killing room, helping Papa with the pigs."

Julia froze, one foot on the bottom porch step, the other on the gravel walk. "The…killing room?"

Nodding, Levi pushed a hand-carved wooden tractor back and forth across the flaking white paint of the porch floor. He barely flinched when a single shot rang out, cracking the quiet morning, but Julia did. "Goodness!" she gasped, one hand clasped to her throat. "What *was* that?"

"Papa has shot the first pig," he said matter-of-factly.

Staring across the vast lawn, Julia's gaze settled on the shedlike building attached to the silo.

"I do not help," Levi said. "I do not like job."

"Can't say as I blame you," Julia said, laughing nervously. She sat on one of the whitewashed rockers that flanked the front door. "Does it take long?"

He'd been kneeling but stood to adjust his suspenders. "Oh, yes. It takes all morning. Sometimes more." Scratching an itch at his hairline, the boy added, "It depends how many pigs must be slaughtered. And *that* depends on how many people in town have ordered one."

Julia glanced at her watch. She could wait around for a while and still make it to court for her one-thirty arraignment.

"You can go down there if you want. I am sure they will be happy to see you."

Grimacing, Julia swallowed. "No way. I'll just wait here with you."

"Would you like to play trucks with me?" He grabbed the smallest vehicle from among the half dozen lined up on the floorboards and held it out to her.

"I'd love to, Levi," she admitted, "but if I kneel down, I'll scuff my shoes and wrinkle my skirt, and I have to be in court this afternoon."

On the floor once more, he said, "What is 'court'?"

"It's a place where people go to settle arguments."

Levi nodded. "And what argument are *you* taking to court?"

"I'm not going for myself," she said, smiling. "It's my job to argue on behalf of someone else."

He aimed that bright-blue-eyed stare at her. "Who?"

How would she explain the intricacies of a legal proceeding to a five-year-old Amish boy? "Well," she began, settling back into the rocker, "a teenaged boy has been accused of stealing, and I'm going to try to keep him out of jail."

Levi's blue gaze held her own. "What did he steal?"

"Potato chips, sodas, candy bars…silly things, really."

A frown crinkled his smooth forehead. "Why would anyone want to put him in jail for that? If he was hungry, why didn't his parents just *feed* him?"

Julia laughed a little. She didn't have the heart to tell Levi that the boy came from one of Lancaster's best families. How would she make innocent little Levi understand that most people didn't steal because they were hungry or that this client's file bulged with police reports, counselors' assessments, and judges' rulings.

Nodding, Levi tilted his head, giving the matter serious thought. "I think I understand." He squinted one eye. "This boy… he has been bad before."

Julia hoped that, in her attempt to answer his questions in a friendly, casual way, she hadn't stolen some of his innocence. "What makes you say that?"

Arms out and palms up, he shrugged. "It seems very simple to me. You would not have to go to court today to keep this boy out of jail if he *once* stole a little food."

Levi was close enough to hug, and so she did. "You're pretty amazing for a little guy, you know that?" Julia mussed his thick blond curls and popped a quick kiss to his freckled cheek. Oh, to have a child like this of her own! She'd be a good mother, attentive and loving and—

Reality, like a cold slap, interrupted the warm moment. *Why torture yourself with silly notions like that?* she thought, turning him loose. If William didn't return soon, she'd write a note to leave beside the deed and put both inside. No doubt Hannah would have a crock of flowers on the kitchen table to keep the papers from floating away on the breeze.

"I can fetch Papa if you like," Levi offered.

She could tell by his crinkled nose and hunched shoulders that the last thing he wanted to do was head for the killing room, where he might witness the slaughter. Another peek at her watch told her she could wait a few minutes more. "No, no, I wouldn't ask you to do that."

In a dramatic gesture, Levi drew fingertips across his forehead. "Whew!" he said. "Am *I* relieved!" Then, after a little shiver, he added, "I would not like to have Papa's job."

Julia smiled. "And why is that?"

Sitting cross-legged, Levi rested an elbow on a knee and balanced his chin on a fist. "Because first he has to trap the pig, and that is not easy. They know what is to happen, I think, and it makes them run around like crazy. Then he has to shoot it, right in the head. Terrible," he said, clapping a palm over his eyes, "the way they kick and squeal, even after they're dead."

Levi stared in the direction of the killing room and swallowed. "Then Papa picks it up—not an easy thing, with an animal as big and heavy as a pig—and dumps it into a tub of boiling water to soften the hair." He pinched his nose. "And, oh, what a stink!"

Julia caught herself grimacing and hugging herself and consciously sat up straight.

"And *then*," the boy continued, drawing out the word, "he skins it. By the time he has finished, he will be all covered in the pig's blood. And if—"

"I get the picture," Julia interrupted, holding up one hand. "I don't think I'd like to be your papa, either." She thought of the packages of bacon and pork chops in her freezer and suddenly had very little desire to cook them up.

"You would not want to be Mama, either, then."

Julia was afraid to ask why.

"She has to *hold* the pig while Papa skins it."

One hand to her stomach, she asked, "What about Rebekah and Seth? Do they—" She gulped. "Do they help, too?"

"If there are many pigs to slaughter, yes. Papa says it is all part of doing their share to keep our farm going." Levi shrugged. He leaned forward and, looking left and right, whispered conspiratorially, "Soon

Seth will take Mama's job, and I will take on Seth's chores." Groaning, he slapped both hands to the sides of his head. "Makes a boy like me want to never grow up, I tell you!"

Laughing, Julia got to her feet. "And I'll tell *you*, Levi Gunden, you must keep your family in stitches all day long with stories like that!"

His expression went stonily serious. "Oh, it was not a story, Miss Julia." Hand over heart, he said, "Every word is true." Then, cocking his head slightly, he added, "You know, of course, that stitching is for girls and women…."

Julia was about to admit she didn't get it when he explained, "I have never sewn a stitch in my life. And I never will, unless I must repair a wound on a cow or a horse." Eyes wide with pride, he clasped both hands in his lap. "I watched Papa do that once, when an Englisher hurled a stone and cut one of our horses' legs. He sewed up the big bloody cut, good as any doctor, I tell you. Not as good as Doctor Thomas, but good!"

She knew better than to ask for details about the horse's injury. All too often, the locals—annoyed by the slow pace of carriages— took their frustrations out on the Amish and their horses. The bigger problem, sadly, was vandalism to buggies, the direct result of ire which was sometimes fueled by tourist-attracting ordinances that encouraged the Amish to tether their quaint carriages in front of stores…forcing townsfolk to park much farther away.

Digging in her briefcase, Julia withdrew a slip of "Note from Julia" paper, the Christmas gift from last year's office Secret Santa, and scribbled a message to William. After paper-clipping it to the envelope that held his deed, she stood. "Is it all right if I leave this inside for your father?"

"Of course!" Levi said, exposing a missing lower tooth when he grinned.

She opened the creaking screen door and entered the hushed house, where the scents of simmering stew and fresh-baked bread hung in the air. Placing the envelope on the kitchen table, Julia tiptoed out. And, after patting Levi on the head, she grabbed her briefcase. "Have a good day, my little friend," she said, descending the porch steps.

"What is jail like, Miss Julia?"

The question brought her to a sudden stop. "What is…what is *jail* like?"

When he looked at her as if to say, "Are you deaf, or merely dense?" Julia smiled. "I guess you'd say jail is like a cage."

"Like the one where I keep my bunnies?"

She'd seen the rabbit hutch, which was fashioned from chicken wire and wood. "Sort of like that, only bigger, with fat iron bars and cement walls and floors."

Blinking, Levi said, "How very sad." He pursed his lips. "I will pray for the boy who stole the food. Maybe God will choose not to punish him in a cage." He shrugged. "But maybe a lesson as harsh as that is just what he needs."

Oh, from the mouths of babes, Julia thought.

Levi went back to playing with his trucks. "Tell him that, not far away, someone is praying for him." He shot her the gap-toothed grin again. "I think that will make him happy."

She'd known young Michael Josephs for many months now, more than long enough to predict that, if she shared Levi's promise, it would be met with ridicule and smirks instead of joy or gratitude.

Julia might ask the help of the Almighty, too, if she thought it would do a bit of good. But experience had taught her that prayers for herself fell on deaf ears. God may indeed answer the pleas of good people like Levi and the rest of the Gundens, but He surely didn't waste time performing miracles for people borne of drug-addicted felons.

She fired up her car and waved through the open window.

"I will pray for you, too," Levi called as she backed down the drive. "I will pray that God makes you get married to Doctor Thomas. Like Papa says, you two will make a handsome couple, and together, a good strong family, too!"

Maybe since the prayers would come from an innocent child, loved completely by God, He'd see fit to answer them.

"A girl can dream," she said, picturing Simon's handsome face.

Chapter Seven

....

The creamy white sweater had been on his front seat for weeks when Simon decided that enough was enough. Every time he'd moved it, his calloused, clumsy hands had left tiny snags in the tight-woven knit. Worse, its scent and softness reminded him of Julia's silky hair. He'd done his best to exercise patience, waiting for the Lord to let him know "go" or "no go." But it hadn't been easy.

He wondered why last week, when he hadn't needed diversions, the clinic had all but overflowed with sick and injured pets. His surgery schedule had rarely been fuller, and he'd seldom gone home more exhausted. The past few days, having to concentrate on putting a dachshund on a diet or curing a calico's ear infection would have been welcome distractions from thoughts of Julia.

Today he'd return the sweater, even if it meant tucking it into a plastic bag and leaving it on her porch. Even if it meant he couldn't see her gorgeous face or hear her pretty voice. "I'm not good at being left in a holding pattern, Lord," he muttered. "I'm all for doing things Your way, but please, can't You meet me halfway?"

"What's that, Doctor Thomas?"

Wincing, he kept his back to the counter. "Nothing, Debbie. Just thinking out loud, I guess."

Man, but he missed Alice. Not only had she organized every aspect of his clinic until it ran like a well-tuned engine, but she'd never poked her nose where it didn't belong, either. Debbie performed her duties well enough, but in the month since she'd taken Alice's place, things had fallen through the cracks. Debbie never picked up the phone by the second ring like Alice did, never put away the files before leaving for the day. She didn't call patients or their owners by their names, wouldn't tidy magazines on the waiting room tables, and refused to wear scrubs. *You're just spoiled,* he'd tell himself every time she did something to annoy him. Which was often. Admittedly, Alice was a hard act to foll—

"You know what they say about people who talk to themselves…."

Debbie giggled. Not a merry, musical sound like Julia's, but a high-pitched twitter that set his nerves on edge. He didn't trust himself to ask what "they" said. Instead, Simon grit his teeth and waited, knowing she'd tell him whether he liked it or not.

Flipping long blond hair over one shoulder, she tilted her head. "That's one way to make sure somebody's listening," she singsonged, batting her false eyelashes.

Forcing a grin, Simon nodded. "Ahh," he said.

She thrust out one hip and propped a fist there. "I hope you'll take this in the spirit of which it's intended…."

Every muscle in him tensed. If he had a lick of sense, he'd fire her on the spot. Send her packing, right this minute, with a month's pay and a promise to provide a great recommendation. But she was his cousin's neighbor, and he'd agreed to give her a chance. "That bum of a husband of hers walked out," Casey had explained, "left her high and dry and with a kid to take care of." It had been Simon's bad luck that the news came on the same day Alice handed in her resignation. And though she'd agreed to stay one week, to help train her replacement, Simon made no secret of his doubts that Debbie *could* be trained.

"She'll do great," Casey insisted. "Debbie was Dean's secretary before they got married, see, so she can walk right into the job!"

Simon surely didn't condone that the man had abandoned his wife and child. But he thought he understood what might have driven him to it.

"You're really, *really* handsome when you smile like that...."

Groaning inwardly, Simon pretended to busy himself by flipping through a file. Too bad Casey hadn't mentioned that Debbie never learned to type or balance a checkbook. That she didn't know how to file in alphabetical order or take a proper phone message. At the close of her first week in the clinic, when Casey inquired how Debbie had fared, Simon had put it as gently as possible: "I don't know if this is gonna work, Case. She ought to have found her sea legs by now."

"Aw, give the girl a break," Casey had said, winking. "She hasn't worked outside the home in years. She'll pick things up. Just be patient."

How much patience is a guy supposed to exert in one lifetime? he wondered. Wait for Georgia to say "okay" to parenthood. Wait for God to give him the go-ahead with Julia. Wait for Debbie to blossom into a top-notch secretary. Wait for—

"...so you really, *really* ought to do it more. Lots more." She giggled again, as if to underscore the point.

Now just how was he supposed to react to *that*? If he said thanks, she'd think he liked the way she so blatantly flirted with him—all day, every day. Simon decided to err on the side of caution and merely nodded. "Phone's ringing," he said absently.

"Oh, so it is." Another giggle. "Guess I oughta get that."

He watched her half run, half skip back to the front counter. *Maybe some guys would find a woman like this attractive—sexy even— but not* this *guy*, he thought. Then he pictured Julia, petite and curvy, a lady in every sense of the word, with a smile that could melt butter and eyes as big as—

"It's Casey!" Debbie hollered. "Silly me, I thought he called to talk to *me*. Shows you how well I understand men."

Simon reached for his phone…just as the blinking light went out.

"Oops," she said. "Looks like I cut him off." And shrugging, she added, "No big deal. If it's important, he'll call back, right?" And with that, she plopped onto Alice's stool and inspected her fingernails.

He had to ask himself if Debbie really was infuriating or if she just seemed that way in comparison to Julia. Hands behind his head, he leaned back in his desk chair as her image floated through his mind. Rocking forward, he grabbed his cell phone, scrolled to her number, and hit SEND. As it rang, he whispered, "Let her answer, let her answer, let her answer…."

Debbie suddenly appeared in the doorway, startling him so badly that he nearly dropped the phone. "What's that, Doctor Thomas?"

Simon pointed at the phone.

"Oops," she repeated. "Sorry."

As she backed out of his office, he said, "Close the door, will you please, Debbie?"

From her shocked expression, the casual observer might have guessed he'd given her a good dressing-down. She closed the door, all right, with an unnecessarily loud slam. Using his free hand, he massaged taut muscles in his neck and grumbled under his breath. "You've got to do something before she drives you outta your ever-lovin'—"

"Hello!"

Instantly, Simon relaxed and smiled. "Hey there, pretty lady," he heard himself say. "Are you missing a sweater?"

* * * * *

Rats! he thought, listening to the rest of the message. Must've been a godsend, getting her answering machine instead of the real thing. Because if her *recorded* voice made his palms sweat and his ears hot, he could only imagine what would have happened if she'd actually picked up the phone.

They'd been talking, a few minutes here and a few minutes there, a couple nights a week since their date. So why was he feeling so nervous *this* time? Especially considering that he had her sweater to use as his excuse for calling....

Simon hung up then sat back and fished through his wallet for the business card she'd given him at the wolf sanctuary. JULIA L. SPENCER, ASSISTANT PUBLIC DEFENDER, in embossed black Times New Roman font, appeared beneath the Lancaster County seal. *Wonder what the* L *stands for?* On the back of the card, in large feminine script, she'd written her home and cell numbers, along with her address. Something told him her middle name, like Julia herself, was anything but ordinary.

Before Wiley came into his life, Simon hadn't given much thought to anti-lawyer cracks and quotes. Then the prosecutor's office called on him to provide "expert testimony" against the creep who'd tortured the dog. In addition to Simon's professional opinions, the prosecuting attorney entered frightening photos into evidence and called on the man's neighbors, who recounted terrified howls of agony that woke them night after night. The defense attorney argued that without eyewitness testimony or other evidence to prove the breeder had inflicted the hideous injuries, the judge had no choice but to let the bully off with nothing but a stern warning.

That's when Simon's opinions of defense attorneys had changed.

Talk about irony, he thought, his hand hovering above the phone. There he sat, trying his best to find a loophole in his self-imposed "wait for God's guidance" rule so he could deepen his relationship with a gorgeous lady lawyer. A defense attorney, no less.

With a sigh and a shrug, he lifted the handset. While he waited for Julia to pick up, Simon propped one foot atop the other on his desk. "Public Defender's Office," said a gravelly voice.

"Uh, Julia Spencer, please."

"She's in court. Any message?"

"No." Simon looked at her cell phone number. He'd call and record a message there as soon as he got rid of this short-tempered guy. "But thanks."

The man hung up without another word, underscoring Simon's not-so-positive opinion of public defenders. Life experience had taught him to trust his instincts. Dozens of times it had saved him from scratches and bites at the clinic. Almost as often it kept him from second dates with women, lined up by well-meaning friends, who had no more in common with him than…than Debbie.

His gut told him Julia was an okay gal. If she behaved a little weird from time to time, if she acted like a woman with a secret, well, Simon hadn't been born yesterday. People with no skeletons in their closets were few and far between. But with God on his side, he could handle anything her past might throw at him.

In college and med school, he'd aced every math and science exam and earned stellar grades in English and history. But subjects that delved into the human psyche? Simon considered himself lucky to have squeaked by with high Cs. He credited the so-so scores to his "pull yourself up by the bootstraps" mentality. And his attitude for folks who needed shrinks? He had no patience for the self-involved who sought counseling and therapy every time they spotted a zit in the mirror.

He stared at her business card, but instead of the county's seal, he saw her big, long-lashed golden eyes and the smile that glowed with beautiful innocence, despite her chosen profession. Did he *really* have what it might take to get her through some tough emotional times? Or was he letting himself be fooled by her lovely face?

More reason than ever to pray for God's input. Simon tucked her card into his lab coat pocket and tossed his stethoscope onto the desktop. His forehead leaning on both fists, he closed his eyes tight. "Lord," he prayed, "You've read my heart, so You know how much I've come to care for Julia in this short time. Show me the way, Father, because I get the feeling she's survived lots of disappointments, and I sure don't want to be yet another—"

"Are you okay in there?"

Simon opened his eyes and saw Debbie's silhouette through the opaque glass of his office door. Slapping one hand over his eyes, he whispered, "Lord, grant me patience…."

"Hello? Doctor Thomas?"

"I'm fine, Debbie," he said, maybe a little louder than he should have.

He watched as her shadow turned toward the waiting room. "We're done for the day. With scheduled appointments, that is. Okay if I leave a little early?"

He wanted to ask if she'd done the filing. If she'd written checks for the statements that had arrived that morning. Wanted to find out if she'd taken any messages while he sat behind his closed door, pondering the sanity…or the craziness…of pursuing Julia. "Sure, go ahead," he called instead. "See you in the morning." Once she'd gone for the day, Simon would check on all those things, and if they needed to be done, he'd do them himself. Same as he had yesterday. And the day before. And every other day since he'd hired her. It wasn't like he had anything better to do. "Man, do I miss Alice," he said, standing.

"What's that? Hard to hear through the closed door…."

Chuckling, Simon hung his head. "Go home, Debbie," he all but shouted, "and have a wonderful, *wonderful* evening!" Would he ever get used to her, after years of Alice's efficiency?

One glance at the untidy stack of patient files on the corner of his desk answered his question. If God aimed to teach him a new lesson, He was off to a dynamite start. Because if Simon didn't learn patience working with Debbie? Well, then, he simply wasn't capable of learning it at all.

"See you in the morning," he heard her say as the entrance doorbell pinged. And even before the door hissed shut, his right hand wrapped around the phone's earpiece as the fingers of the left dialed Julia's cell phone number…and he prayed that God wanted her to answer every bit as much as he did.

Chapter Eight

....

"I tried to call," he said when she opened the door. "Guess you haven't had time to check your messages."

Julia stood, one bare foot trying to warm the other, in the slightly open doorway. "I was in court most of the day," she admitted. *What on earth is Simon doing here,* she wondered, *especially at suppertime?* "Have you eaten yet?"

He ran a hand through thick blond waves. "Nah. I'll grab a hot dog or something at the convenience store. I just didn't want another day to go by without making sure you got this back."

She glanced at the sweater draped over his right forearm. "Thanks," she said, taking it. "It's one of my favorites." She clutched it to her chest. "It's white. And white clothes match just about everything else in the closet, you know?"

Julia watched one brow rise on his forehead and concluded that he had no interest whatever in whether or not clothes matched. But if that was true, why did he look so well-put-together himself? With his hair fluttering in the breeze and wearing a slanting grin, faded jeans, and a white shirt cuffed to his elbows, he could just as easily have been on a *GQ* cover instead of her front porch. And those amazing, gorgeous green eyes that she'd pictured every time they talked on the phone....

Simon shifted his weight from one sneakered foot to the other, hinting that she'd stared a tad too long.

"Well, now that you've got your favorite sweater back, guess I'll hit the road." He pointed over one shoulder.

One broad and muscular shoulder.

But thankfully he made no move to leave. Instead, Simon pocketed both hands and jangled loose change and car keys. The sound reminded her of Gramps, whose palsied hands couldn't be stilled even when buried deep in his own trousers pockets.

He reminded her of Gramps in other ways, too, starting with the way he stood, feet planted shoulder-width apart, to the straight-backed way he walked…like a man who knew where he'd been and where he intended to—

"It's been great seeing you again, Julia."

The resonant tones of his voice roused her from her reverie. "Sorry," she said. "Sometimes after a day like this, I tend to zone out. Makes me seem spacey, I know, but really, it's just me, running through the events of the day, trying to figure out if I've dotted all the i's and crossed all the t's." Shrugging, she tucked in one corner of her mouth. *There you go again, you little ninny,* she scolded, *rambling nonsensically.* Surely Simon's day had been just as harrowing. What made her think he wanted a blow-by-blow of hers? "Good to see you, too."

He headed for the flagstone walk, and when he hit the bottom porch step, he threw up a hand. "See ya, Julia," he said without turning. "Have a nice evening."

Wait, she wanted to say, *don't go!* "Haven't you heard? Hot dogs are bad for your health," she said instead.

Now he stood with one foot on the flagstone, the other two steps up, and balanced a forearm on his knee. "I hope that's an invitation to share whatever smells so good in there…."

"Spaghetti," she said, smiling. "I always make more than I can eat, which is downright weird, since I've never had to cook for a crowd."

Simon patted his flat stomach and, in three long strides, stood in front of her. "Don't you worry, little lady," he said, "I'm more than happy to be your crowd."

Taking a step back as he passed, she kicked her high heels aside. "Don't mind the mess," Julia said, grabbing her suit jacket from the newel post. "I only got home about fifteen minutes ago and went straight to the kitchen to put the sauce on to warm up. Saturday is my big cleaning day and since it's only—"

"Shh," he said, smiling, as he laid a finger over her lips. "Your house looks super, just like you."

If she stood there blinking and staring much longer, she'd have no one to blame but herself when he suddenly "remembered" a previous engagement. Why in the world would he want to share his supper with a full-grown woman who behaved like an addle-brained teeny bopper? "I'll just run upstairs and put this stuff away. Make yourself at home," she said, collecting her shoes and bounding up the steps. "I'll only be a minute."

She quickly changed into jeans and a T-shirt, stuffed her feet into clean white socks, and raced back down the stairs, tucking her hair into a loose ponytail as she went. Simon wasn't in the living room as she'd expected. Instead, she found him at the stove, where a big pot of water steamed beside a pan of simmering sauce. He held its shining stainless lid in one hand and a big wooden spoon in the other.

"What brand is this stuff, and where'd you buy it?" he said, smacking his lips. " 'Cause I've gotta tell you...it's the best I've ever tasted!"

"You can't buy it," she admitted. "I made it myself."

"From scratch?"

"Well, not exactly. I start with canned tomato paste and stewed tomatoes."

Simon rinsed the spoon under hot water then dropped it into the sink. "If that isn't 'scratch,' I don't know what is," he said, drying his hands on a red-and-white-checkered towel. "What do I have to do to get your recipe?"

Just keep standing there, looking all big 'n' brawny, she thought, grinning to herself.

"Wow," he said, brows high on his forehead. "I didn't realize I was hungry till I took a taste of that stuff. Now my stomach is growling like a grizzly. Bet you can hear it from there."

She didn't trust herself to speak, so Julia walked to the fridge and stacked lettuce, tomatoes, green peppers, butter, and unsliced bread in her arms.

"Can I help?"

Her first instinct was to say "No…just relax." But he looked so much like a wide-eyed eager-to-please kid that she said, "How 'bout you set the table while I make the salad and get the garlic bread ready for toasting."

Rather than asking where she kept the plates, Simon opened and closed cabinet doors until he found them. After sliding the top two from the stack, he rummaged in the drawers for flatware. He distributed them as if dealing a hand of cards, and Julia wanted to say "Napkins on the right" and "The knife goes next to the spoon." But she merely smiled and dumped a box of angel hair spaghetti into the boiling water.

"One of these days soon," he said, dropping ice cubes into tall tumblers, "I'm gonna have to take you *out* for dinner…."

She sensed that he hadn't completed his sentence and resisted the urge to ask what he meant.

"Otherwise," he continued, "you're bound to think I'm some kind of cheapskate."

No way she would turn around and let him read the excitement and relief that was no doubt written all over her face. "I can always cash in on that rain check to the Rainbow Dinner Theatre…."

Laughing, Simon fiddled with the dials of the under-cabinet radio. "What kind of music do you like? Easy listening? Country? Broadway tunes?"

"Music is music," Julia said. But secretly she hoped he'd find a classical station, because few things better soothed her after a long, hard day than the quiet strains of Beethoven or Tchaikovsky. As if he'd read her mind, the enchanting melody of Bach's "Brandenburg Concerto Number Four" floated into the room.

"You want to say grace, or should I?"

"Go ahead," she told him. What would he think if he knew she hadn't "said grace"—except to fake it for so-called Christian foster parents—since leaving this house nearly twenty years ago?

Wrapping her hand in his, Simon closed his eyes and bowed his head, his voice a near whisper as he prayed: "These simple words, Lord, come from a simple heart that overflows with awe at Your goodness. Bless this house, Father, and the humble servant who lives here. We ask that You bless us as we eat. Bless this food and the hands that prepared it. May it nourish our bodies, just as Your Word nourishes our souls. Help us to be mindful of the needs of others. We thank You, Father God, for sending Your Son into the world to save us."

He gave her hand a little squeeze then said, "Amen."

"Amen," Julia echoed. "That was lovely, Simon. Thanks."

"Don't thank me," he said, aiming a thumb at the ceiling. "He puts the words on my heart. All I do is open my big yap."

She laughed along with him, but Julia knew better. Often, when Gramps prayed, Granny said that all men could pray, but few had a gift for touching hearts and moving spirits. It seemed that Simon, like Gramps, had a special talent for talking with God.

She laid the napkin across her lap as Simon ladled a generous portion of spaghetti onto her plate.

"I'm so glad you're not a 'sauce on top' kind of gal."

"Granny was full-blooded Italian, born on the shores of the Adriatic Sea. She said her people did it this way to make sure no one left their table hungry."

"I would've loved your granny." Then, "Is this her recipe?"

Julia nodded. "Sort of. Hers starts with tomatoes fresh from the garden. I rarely have time for that, so I have to make do with canned stuff."

"Well, for a guy who's never had the pleasure of eating 'from the garden' sauce, this is a little taste of heaven."

Julia loved the sound of his voice and thought she could listen to it nonstop without ever tiring of the full-bodied baritone. She encouraged him to talk about his day and learned that his office manager had resigned to nurse her husband back to health after a bad fall. Simon had offered to pay for an in-home caretaker, but Alice wasn't having any of that. " 'My place is at his side,' " he quoted her. "And, much as I miss her, I know she's doing the right thing."

"Guess that's what comes from being too good at your job," Julia observed. "Nobody can take your place."

Simon laughed. "Oh, you don't know the half of it!"

She listened in quiet amazement as he described Debbie's ineptitude for office duties. *Amazing,* she thought, *that he managed to complain without ever really saying anything negative about the woman*. Another item for her "Reasons to Like Simon" list.

"It's good you're such a patient man, Simon. Just think of all the good you're doing her and her son." Julia shrugged. "If she's been out of the workforce as long as your cousin says, of *course* it'll take awhile for her to get unrusty."

He covered her hand with his and laughed. " 'Unrusty'?"

Julia felt the heat of a blush creep into her cheeks. "I don't know what inspires me to make up words that way," she said, hiding a giggle behind her free hand. "I've tried changing. Just not hard enough, I guess."

"Do me a favor?"

"If I can…"

"Pay attention to Billy Joel."

"I…" Julia snickered nervously. "Billy Joel?"

"Don't change. Ever."

Julia wondered if it was possible for a person's face to explode under the pressure of a seriously deep blush. A part of her wished he'd turn her hand loose so she could hide behind it. A very small part, admittedly…

It seemed serendipitous, the way the music changed in tone and tempo just in time to save her from having to respond. But had the song just started, or had the sweet intimacy of the moment distracted them?

Simon used his fork to spear another slice of garlic bread. "Now which composer is *that*?"

She leaned toward the radio. "Vivaldi."

"Are you sure…?"

"Of course I'm sure. Nobody wrote piano-violin concertos like that dude."

Simon laughed. "Don't think I've ever heard anybody call him a *dude* before." Just then another melody began. "Okay, smarty pants, who wrote that one?"

Julia listened for a moment. "Schutz, from the Baroque era."

And so it went, back and forth, one naming Chopin, the other Handel…Puccini, Weiss, Mendelssohn…both of them laughing until their sides ached.

"Sorry I don't have anything for dessert," she said as they loaded the dishwasher.

"Hey," he said, hands up in mock surrender, "I would've had to pass, anyway. I'm stuffed to the gills. That was some meal, kiddo." As she tucked the last of the leftovers into the refrigerator, he stared out the window above the sink. "Hey, is that a chiminea I see on your porch?"

She'd bought the miniature furnace weeks ago at Bargain Mart, thinking it would be nice to sip hot chocolate or tea while watching the flames dance inside its round clay belly. So far Julia hadn't had time to test it. "Yes," she told him, "but I don't know if I have enough kindling or—"

Simon hunched his back and, arms dangling, grunted, "Me find wood, make big fire for Julia…."

Before she could agree or object, he was out the door. In the dwindling light she could see him gathering twigs and sticks that had blown to the ground during last week's spring thunderstorm. He dumped a small armload of wood on the porch then disappeared into the shed and came out carrying a small saw. Next, he'd removed several long-dead limbs from an ancient oak tree and cut each into two-foot lengths. In no time, Simon had everything necessary to start and maintain a cozy fire.

Julia couldn't have him thinking she'd been watching him the whole time, so when he started for the back door, she quickly opened the refrigerator door.

"Got a match?"

"In the drawer under the toaster."

"What about cocoa?"

She pointed to the cabinet above the stove.

"Milk?"

"Bought a half gallon just yesterday."

"And sugar?"

"The canister's full."

"When was the last time you enjoyed a cup of homemade cocoa?"

Granny used to make it every Saturday. "Movie Night" she called it. Julia, snuggled between her grandparents on the couch, held a big bowl of popcorn as they watched old Westerns on TV and sipped the sweet-smelling cocoa. "It's been years," she admitted.

"Then you're in for a treat, pretty lady."

"Is that so…?"

"Soon as I get the fire started, I'll whip up a batch of the best cocoa you ever drank."

His enthusiasm was contagious, and Julia grinned. "I dunno. My granny's was pretty special stuff…."

"Hmm," he said, rubbing his chin, "never competed with a grandmother before…." Brightening, he added, "Not to worry. It might not be as good as Granny's, but it'll warm your innards." He paused then added, "Do me a favor?"

"Another one?" she teased.

Chuckling, Simon winked. "Four cups of milk in a saucepan," he said. "Warmed, not scalded. If I'm not back before it starts to bubble gently, holler. Okay?"

And with that he was gone, leaving her alone to do as he asked… and eavesdrop as he talked himself through the process of building a fire. Humming, Julia acknowledged that he'd transferred his upbeat mood to her. Oh, but he was charming. And funny…and easy to be around…. She'd love nothing better than to enjoy his company on a daily basis, if only…

Suddenly sadness tapped at the fringes of her joy as she reminded herself that while spending more time in his presence would be wonderful for *her*, it would be grossly unfair to *Simon*. She didn't think it was mere coincidence that a specific Bible verse came to mind just then: *"Be ye not unequally yoked together with unbelievers: for what fellowship hath righteousness with unrighteousness? and what communion hath light with darkness?"* Everything about him, right down to the brief but heartfelt prayer before dinner, proved how deeply he believed. And while she had been a follower, too many years, too many disappointments, too many prayers unanswered had convinced Julia that she was not among His chosen ones. And so she'd given up. *Better not to ask at all*, she'd decided, *than to know you aren't worthy of His answer.*

But right now, watching him putter on the porch, listening to him whistle merrily as he went about his chore? If Julia thought for an instant that God would hear her, she'd ask the Almighty to allow her to share the rest of her life with this wonderful man.

* * * * *

Simon couldn't remember a time when he'd been more clumsy.

First he'd spilled cocoa while mixing it into the small bowl of warm milk and vanilla. Soon, sugar crystals joined the brown powder that dusted her countertop. Completely nonplussed, Julia laughed good-naturedly as she wiped up every drop that slopped over the bowl's rim while raving about his hot chocolate, claiming it was at least as good as her grandmother's. True or not, Simon loved her for saying it.

Fact was, he loved a lot of things about her. It made him want to know what had happened to cause the light to dim in her otherwise bright golden eyes and what made her beautiful smile wane ever so slightly from time to time. He'd pray on it, that very night, Simon decided. He'd ask the Lord to provide him with discernment, so he'd know what to ask Julia—and when. And then it dawned on him—he could probably find out most of what he wanted to know from William and Hannah, who both seemed to know a lot about Julia.

He'd promised to stop by their farm in the morning to check on an ailing cow. During his last visit, he'd told William that if the heifer's infected udder hadn't cleared up by week's end, antibiotics would be necessary. As he conducted the exam, made the diagnosis, and doled out the proper medications, he'd ask, and if they didn't have the answers to his questions, maybe they'd direct him to someone who *did*.

Leaving Julia earlier had been harder than anything he'd done in months. The ache of loneliness reminded him of how he'd felt those first bleak days after Georgia's funeral. They'd had their share of hurts and disappointments during their marriage, but Simon had held onto the belief that in time, they'd work out those kinks, together. Surprisingly, Georgia had endured the pain and indignity of cancer with quiet acceptance, telling him repeatedly that she expected him to remarry.

Oddly, Julia's face, with its dancing eyes and bright smile, flashed across his mind at the thought. And that voice…why, it had the power to warm him right to the marrow of his bones. In her presence, he felt powerful. Energized. Young and enthusiastic about life. And he hadn't felt that way since…

…since the moment before the doctor told him in quiet, somber tones that Georgia's chances of beating the cancer were nonexistent. The man might as well have clamped vise grips around Simon's heart. He'd decided right then and there that he'd never love another woman.

He'd focused on the sounds of nurses' shoes squeaking down the polished floors between the OR and the waiting room. Once the double doors had hissed shut, he'd slumped into the nearest chair, held his face in his hands, and wept. Simon didn't know how much time had passed before his sobs subsided. He only knew that when he looked up through bleary eyes, the world was not the same place.

How could God have allowed this to happen to a woman who'd tirelessly devoted herself to him, her parents, their church? As miserable as he'd been, Simon knew he must pull himself together for Georgia's sake. He'd put on a brave face to make her last days as pleasant as possible. He went to the men's room and splashed cold water on his face then headed for her room. Sitting beside her, he'd pressed kisses to her hands. "I'll never love anyone as I've loved you," he'd whispered. "Never."

Despite the tubes and electrodes attached to her frail frame, Georgia beamed up at him. "You're a sweet, sweet man, Simon

Thomas, but you're silly as silly can be." Something akin to a weary giggle popped from her lips. "How can I enjoy heaven if I know you're down here pining away for me? You're barely twenty-eight years old, for the love of Jesus. You have a whole lifetime ahead of you. Of *course* you'll fall in love again. It's what I've been praying for ever since I learned—"

The nurse had told him that she'd refused her last dose of morphine, and at that moment, her frail body trembled and her jaw clenched with pain. Whether she'd stopped speaking because of it or because she'd been forced to admit that the cancer had won, he'd never know. But how could she think he'd replace her?

"Shh," he'd said, patting her hand. "Just try and get some rest, will ya?"

She'd looked deep into his eyes and, with a clarity he hadn't seen in days, held his gaze. "It's time, Simon," Georgia rasped. "I can't take it any longer." She squeezed his hand with a strength that belied her condition. "I want to go home. To Jesus." A lone tear oozed from one eye, leaving a shining trail as it rolled down her pale cheek. "I'm sorry to leave you, but—"

"Hey, now," he'd interrupted. "I said hush, didn't I?" He tried desperately to stanch the tears that threatened to spill from his own eyes. "Be quiet and rest now, you hear?"

But Georgia had sighed and shook her head. "It hurts so bad, Simon. So so bad…"

"I know, I know. You want me to call the nurse? Maybe she can give you a shot or something."

"No. I want to be awake. And alert. Because what I'm about to tell you is important. Very important." She laid a hand atop his. "Yes, it hurts. I've never been in such pain. But I won't leave you. I'll hold on and endure it until you promise me…"

He could see the agony glinting in her eyes, tightening her lips. She wore it like a badge of honor, and it made watching her suffer even tougher. "Anything, honey. Tell me what you want me to do and I'll do it."

"Someday love will come knocking at your heart again, and—get that 'No way Jose' look off your face, Doctor Thomas, because this is serious stuff—and when it does, I want you to be open to it."

If he could have run from the room at that moment, Simon would've bolted for the door like an Olympic sprinter. He wanted God to perform a major miracle right then and there—wanted one of His angels to descend and announce that Georgia's cancer had been cured, that she'd live a long, productive life and they'd end up gray and wrinkled, side by side on their porch swing, watching their kids and grandkids—maybe even *great*-grandkids—frolic in the yard.

"You won't turn away when it happens?"

The harsh reality of her words made him realize that she'd finally given up hope. Swallowing a sob, he had stared into her watery eyes and taken a deep breath. If he had to tell lie upon lie to make her last moments more comfortable, so be it. "All right, if that's what you want."

"It's what I want." Her taut muscles relaxed, and her peaceful smile shimmered in her eyes. "Now say it."

"What?"

"Out loud, in plain English, so I know you're not just trying to humor me."

To this day, he believed the miracle of that day came when he found the courage to say in a calm, sure voice, "I won't turn away if love comes knocking." And in a last-ditch effort to bring about a miracle of a different kind, he climbed onto her bed and lay beside her, cradling her in his arms and whispering, "How 'bout a little nap now? Who knows—maybe when you wake up, your doctor will come in here with good news about—"

She expelled a trembly, exhausted sigh. "Don't, Simon. Please don't." She stiffened then added, "I can't go until I know you'll be all right."

And she'd wanted to go. Everything from the edginess in her voice to the tension in her fragile body made that clear. Simon was beyond asking God for last-minute help. He'd dropped to his knees so many times that his trousers had all gone threadbare, yet Georgia continued to wither like a flower left too long in the sun. He hadn't wanted to let her go, but Simon hadn't wanted her to suffer, either. It killed him to say it, but he forced himself to speak the words she so desperately needed to hear. "All right…no more treatments. No more hospitals. No more pain. Let go, and don't you worry about me. I'll be fine, just fine."

She closed her eyes and sighed then reached out and smoothed a wrinkle in his shirt. "Wish I'd taken the time to teach you to use the steam iron." One side of her mouth lifted in a wry grin as she tugged his wrinkled shirt collar. "Life just ain't fair, is it?"

Then, wearing a mere whisper of a smile, she left him.

Simon had buried his face in the crook of her neck and tried to ignore the ear-piercing one-note of the monitor that had counted her heartbeats. "I'll never love another woman as I loved you," he'd sobbed. "Never."

Time alone had eased his pain and dimmed the anger he'd harbored toward God for allowing Georgia to get sick, for allowing her to suffer—but time hadn't cured his never-ending, aching loneliness. Every time kids came into the clinic, worried sick about one of their pets, Simon watched as parents doled out comfort and encouragement. He'd never have admitted it to another living soul, but *he'd* wanted the white-picket-fence life every bit as much as anyone who dreamed of "happily ever after" endings!

Though he'd tried hard to mask his feelings, some of that yearning must have shown. Why else would married friends and family members introduce him to a long line of available females? For a year or so, he'd given it the old college try, as the saying goes, in the hope Casey had been right when he'd said, "Who knows? Miss Right might just be the caboose of the Girl Train!"

Sadly, not one of the dozens of women he'd escorted to church socials, weddings, movies, and plays woke even a shred of interest in him. Some had been model-gorgeous, others downright brilliant, and a few funny enough to earn a living at stand-up comedy. But not one quickened his heartbeat. He'd never committed to memory the sound of their laughter or the touch of their hands. He'd begun thinking that Georgia, God love her, had been out of her ever-lovin' mind when she'd insisted that new love would come knocking.

But he'd been wrong. It *had* come knocking. And on the other side of the door?

Julia.

Simon popped up the footrest of his recliner and toed off one shoe and then the other as Windy hopped into his lap. Wiley propped his chin on the chair's armrest, waiting for a thorough head patting. "So, did you guys have a nice evening?"

A quiet *woof* and a soft purr answered his question.

"*I* sure did," he said, grabbing the TV remote. "Sat by the fire sippin' cocoa and chatting with the cutest little gal east of the

Mississippi, while every other sane man was downing iced tea and fanning himself to stay cool."

Windy snuggled down beside him and Wiley lay at his feet as Simon admitted that the thought wasn't accurate *or* fair—why limit it to this side of the Mississippi?

He traded the remote for his Bible, let the book fall open on his lap, and then repeated the process that had long been part of his evening devotions by praying about whichever verse first caught his eye.

" 'He who finds a wife finds what is good and receives favor from the Lord,' " he read aloud. Heart soaring, Simon's gaze moved deeper into Proverbs: *"Listen to advice and accept instruction, and in the end you will be wise. Many are the plans in a man's heart, but it is the Lord's purpose that prevails."*

Simon closed the Bible, marking the page with his forefinger, and said a silent prayer that the verses were signs from God telling him that it was okay to pursue something more than a friendship with Julia.

Chapter Nine

....

Of all the places she'd lived—an admittedly considerable list—Julia loved Paradise best. Clean and cozy, its welcome started at the border and spread across each street and every shop. One of her favorite spots in town was the Cackleberry Café. Cute and quaint, locals and tourists alike gathered for down-home meals, fresh-baked goods, and creamy ice cream…the special treat she gave herself whenever a difficult case produced a winning outcome.

Although a balmy early summer breeze blew as she left the courthouse and she had succeeded in keeping Michael Josephs out of jail, Julia didn't feel much like celebrating. As she stood outside the café's front door, she pictured the boy's smug reaction to the outcome, and it left her with an eerie, unsettled feeling. Some might chalk up his cocky demeanor to immaturity, but Julia sensed that something malevolent lurked deep in the overweight, bespectacled teenager's soul.

Thanks to a faulty surveillance camera and a blind cashier, the police and prosecutor hadn't had a legal leg to stand on, making it frighteningly easy for Julia to get all charges against Michael dropped. But having the letter of the law on her side did nothing to ease her conscience. The boy was guilty. She'd known it the instant her eyes first met his. While packing up her briefcase, Julia quieted her guilt by rehashing all the times when her job helped bring about true justice.

And then Michael's father stepped up, grinning as he grabbed her hands. "I knew you'd get the kid off," he'd gloated, pumping as though he expected water to trickle from her fingertips. "I don't know what the county pays you, but you're well worth every penny and then some." When he swaggered away, badgering his son for being stupid, for getting caught, she found herself wanting to wash imaginary slime from her hands.

Now, as she sat on the bench just outside the Cackleberry's door, Julia tried her best to divert herself from imagining what Michael might do in a week, a month, a year, with this win shining in his head as some sort of proof that he was above the law. A shudder passed through her as she acknowledged that his next offense might not be filed under "petty crimes."

"Hello, Miss Julia."

"Levi," she said, brightening. "How nice to see you!"

"You look so serious," Hannah interjected. "Is everything all right?"

Standing, Julia smiled. "Everything's just dandy. Just going over some stuff that happened in court this morning, that's all." Over Hannah's shoulder, she saw William tying Matilda to the hitching post across the way. Stooping to make herself child-sized, she laid both hands on Levi's shoulders. "And what brings the Gunden family to Paradise on this beautiful day?"

"Mama is here to deliver a quilt she made for a lady in town."

Hannah beamed. "I must guard against false pride," she said, hiding her grin behind a work-hardened hand. "My sewing grows more and more popular."

"May I see it?" Julia asked, taking a step closer to the cloth bag dangling from Hannah's wrist.

The woman opened her cloth satchel, and Julia peered inside. "Oh, it's just lovely, Hannah." With any seamstress this talented, she might have poured on the compliments. But to do such a thing with Hannah was to guarantee a thick, brightly colored patchwork quilt on her own bed…and her Amish friend would consider it an insult if Julia offered to pay for it. "Where are Seth and Rebekah?"

"At school, of course," Levi answered. And with a playful grin, he added, "Where else would they be?"

"Mind your manners," Hannah scolded gently. And to Julia, she said, "William must go to the hardware store for nails and things. Are you planning to stay in town awhile?" Julia hesitated just long enough for her to add, "Could I maybe leave Levi with you while I deliver the quilt?"

"I'd love that! Is it all right if he and I share some cookies from the café—or maybe an ice cream? The servings are always so huge, and I hate to waste food…."

Levi leaped into the air, clapping his hands. "Oh, may I, Mama? I will not dirty my shirt, I promise."

Laughing, Hannah touched a finger to the tip of his nose. "I think that will be fine. Just be sure you leave something for Julia to eat." Tucking the quilt back into the bag, she said to Julia, "I will be just down the street at the gift shop, in case you need to leave before I am back." And, waving, she left them on the sidewalk.

"So what are you in the mood for, my little friend? Cookies? A slice of pie? Ice cream?"

"Oh, that is a very easy choice!" he exclaimed. "Mama makes cookies and pie every Sunday. But ice cream…" Eyes closed, he licked his lips and rubbed his tummy. "Ice cream would be a wonderful treat."

She opened the door and held it as he entered the café. "Do you have a favorite flavor?"

"Chocolate chunk, I think."

"You *think*?" Julia echoed, stepping up to the counter.

"Well, I got strawberry three times in a row, because it is Mama's favorite. She likes it, I think, when she has someone to share her favorite things with. Seth and Rebekah like chocolate, and Papa always gets vanilla." He shrugged. "So this time, I think *I* will have chocolate."

"In a waffle cone or a bowl?"

"Oh, a cone. Definitely." He leaned forward and, looking up into her face, whispered, "I think you get more that way, for the same price!"

Smiling at the thought that a boy of five had already accumulated such money sense, Julia put in their order. As the counter girl prepared their cones, Julia asked Levi if he'd rather eat inside or outside.

Winking one eye, he tucked in one corner of his mouth. "Inside, I think, because at our farm, except for when we sit down to eat, we are outside from the minute we open our eyes until it is time for bed. Besides," he added, "not quite so many people will stare at me in here." He rolled his eyes and pretended to be a tourist. " 'Oh, look, a little Amish boy.... Isn't he *cute!*' "

Laughing, she let Levi choose a table.

"You have very pretty eyes," Levi said when she sat across from him. "One of our barn cats has eyes that color." He studied her face for a moment and then asked, "What is it called?"

"Hazel."

Levi snickered. "Hazel. Do you know that, just last week, my cousins were all talking about how they got their names? The only one who didn't know where hers came from was…"—he licked the cone and took a moment to properly dispose of a hunk of chocolate—"Hazel!" Another chuckle. "My cousin Hazel is what Papa calls a runt. Smaller than the others her age. Rebekah has told me that some of the older boys tease her at school. They call her *Carrot*."

"Carrot! That's a funny name!"

"Well," he said haltingly, "she *does* have hair the color of a carrot." Frowning, Levi said, "But I suppose that is no reason to call her such a name, ex-*pish*-illy when they know it hurts her feelings."

Julia nodded in agreement. "You are a very smart and sensitive boy, Levi Gunden."

"Yes," he said matter-of-factly, taking his first bite of the cone, "I know. Mama says the same thing *all* the time."

Oh, what a joy this child was! Julia found herself secretly hoping it would take Hannah an hour.

"You are quite pretty, you know."

"Why, thank you, Levi."

"So I do not understand it…."

Blinking, Julia grinned. "Don't understand what?"

"Why you have no husband." He gave her a sidelong glance. "Is there something wrong with your teeth?"

"Why, no!" she said, laughing.

"Your feet, then?"

"My feet are just fine, little nut."

"Then I truly am confused." He ate the last bite of his cone then sat back in the chair. "Papa says people do not buy horses or cows that have bad teeth or feet. These are signs an animal is not healthy—but I am sure you know that—and no farmer needs that kind of expense."

Julia had never been compared to livestock before. The notion tickled her so much that her laughter caught the attention of diners at nearby tables, but she couldn't stop long enough to apologize.

"I made a joke?" Levi asked.

"It appears you did…."

The deep voice had come from directly behind her, and Julia would have recognized it anywhere. Blotting tears of laughter from her eyes, she turned toward him. "Simon," she said, unable to quiet her enjoyment, "how long have you been standing there?"

He scooted out the extra chair at their table and spun it around. "Long enough to wonder if my veterinary degree would get me in to see your dentist. Or your podiatrist." He straddled the chair's seat and rested both forearms across its back. "So which is it?" he said to Julia.

She expelled a long end-of-giggles sigh. "Which is what?"

"Bad teeth? Or bad feet?"

"If you ask me," Levi put in, "I would say it is the tall, skinny heels on those shoes she wears. They can*not* be good for the toes." He gave a serious nod. "You can easily see when she smiles that Miss Julia has very pretty teeth."

Laughing, Simon said, "You're a pretty smart kid."

"Yes," Levi sighed, feigning boredom with yet another compliment, "I know…."

When Simon's brows rose in response, Julia explained. "His mother tells him that all the time."

"Ahh, I see…"

My, she thought, *but he looks handsome in this light.*

But never more handsome than when he reached out and gently chucked Levi's cheek. It all but broke her heart to admit it, because it was a bit more proof what a wonderful father he could be. No doubt he'd make a wonderful husband, too.

* * * * *

"Are you here for ice cream, too?" Levi asked.

Giving the boy's shoulder an affectionate squeeze, Simon said, "No. I've been invited to dinner at my cousin's house and promised to bring dessert. Trouble is, I can't decide between cake and pie." He shrugged. "Which do you recommend?"

Levi rubbed his chin, making Simon wonder what the boy would look like in twenty or so years, after he'd married and started his own traditional Amish beard. "Mama bakes all our desserts, you see." He cut a quick glance at Julia. "But I have always liked cakes better than pies."

"And why's that?" Julia asked.

Hiding a giggle behind one hand, Levi said, "Because there is no icing on pie, and I *love* icing."

Simon nodded. "So what's your preference—chocolate?"

"Oh, it truly does not matter"—Levi slapped his thigh—"as long as there is plenty of it!"

Julia's pleasant laughter rode a warm air current right into his ears. *Just look at her,* he thought, *beaming like a proud mama at Levi's ability to hold his own in a conversation with two full-grown adults.* Wisps of her shoulder-length hair had escaped her ponytail and fluttered in the breeze of the ceiling fan. Every time she raised a hand to brush it from her eyes, Simon was reminded of the house call he'd made on his way into town. As he'd inoculated a prizewinning 4-H calf, its little-girl owner wished aloud for eyelashes even half as long and luxurious as her heifer's. The notion made him chuckle as he wondered what Julia would say—after questions about her feet and teeth—to being compared to a baby cow.

123

They'd been so tuned in to one another when Simon entered the café that neither had noticed his approach. A relief, he acknowledged, because surely it would have flustered her to know he'd overheard Levi, wondering aloud why a pretty young woman like Julia had never married. He'd asked himself the same thing a time or two since meeting her. But the question died a quick death as another idea percolated: twice in as many minutes, Levi and Simon had compared her to livestock.

Still grinning, Simon got up from the table and stepped up to the bakery case.

"Hey, Doctor Thomas," said the girl behind the counter. "What can I do for you today?"

He'd helped Carrie adopt an orphaned calico several months back, and the overprotective "mama" had brought the cat into his clinic four times in the short while since. "I'll take that one," he said, pointing at a white-frosted cake. "Is it chocolate?"

"Yep," she said. "With a raspberry filling that's positively to die for."

"Perfect," he said, grinning. While he waited for Carrie to box it up, Simon turned and leaned on the counter's thick, rounded glass, arms folded and one ankle crossed over the other. *Isn't she a sight to behold?* he thought, watching Julia's animated discussion with Levi. Either she'd deliberately deleted her name from the "eligible ladies" list, or every single guy in Lancaster County needed their eyes examined. And their heads.

"Here you go," Carrie said, holding a pink cardboard box by crisscrossed twine. She rattled off the price, and Simon turned and reached into his back pocket, nearly losing his footing on the polished linoleum floor.

"What'sa matta, doc?" said an elderly man as Simon regained his balance. "You fallin' for little Carrie back there?"

"He ain't my type, Mr. Hobbs," Carrie said, grinning. "I like my men old and rich, half-blind and hard of hearing." She winked playfully. "Like *you!*"

Hobbs wiggled both bushy white eyebrows. "Don't think the missus would approve, dearie. But you've made my day, for sure!"

Laughing, Simon paid for the cake as Hannah entered the shop, her broad, merry face alight with mischief. "I hope you left some ice cream for other customers, Levi Gunden."

"Yes, Mama," he said, standing to hug her. "Did you deliver your quilt?"

"I did," she said, bending to kiss the top of his head.

Levi cupped a palm beside his mouth and whispered to Simon, "She makes quilts for all of Lancaster County but will not sew one for *my* bed. Now, what do you think of that?"

"He thinks," Hannah said in Simon's stead, "that you are plenty warm enough without one!" And without skipping a beat, she took her son's hand and led him to the door. "Thank you for minding him, Julia."

"My pleasure," she said. "Did William find my envelope?"

Hannah nodded. "He did. We are so grateful for all your hard work. Come see us soon to get your money, and I will feed you well!" And with a smile and a wave, the Gundens were gone.

Julia gathered the used napkins and tossed them into a nearby trash can. After picking up her purse, she headed for the door. "After you, pretty lady," Simon said, holding it open.

Had Hannah's invitation made her blush? Or was it his simple gesture that inspired it? All Simon knew was that the heightened pink in her cheeks only made her eyes look even bigger and more golden. "So where are you parked?" he asked as she passed by.

"Up the street," she said, heading for the intersection.

"It's a nice day, so I can't say as I blame you. Mind if I walk with you?"

It seemed to Simon that she'd hesitated just a bit, so relief surged through him when she said, "That'd be right nice."

"'Right nice'?" He chuckled. "I didn't know you were from the South."

"I'm not, but one of my foster families was."

One of her foster families? Another reminder that she'd lived a hard life. Julia's quickened pace, together with the frown etched on her face, made it clear that she regretted having let the fact slip. "Got a court case this afternoon?"

"Deposition," she said, digging in her purse. "By phone, no less. I hate those."

"Why's that?"

"I've never been a fan of any conversation where I can't look somebody in the eye." She looked up at *him* just long enough to add, "And in a legal proceeding? It's imperative." Julia withdrew an overloaded key ring. "So where are you headed? Back to the clinic?"

"Yeah." And raising the cake box a tad, he said, "And then it's off to dinner at Casey's."

"Casey?"

"My cousin. His little girl turns four next weekend, and since I can't make it to her birthday party, his wife invited me to a pre-party of sorts."

"That sounds nice. I'm sure you'll have—"

"Hey, you wouldn't have time to help me pick out a little present for Cassie, would you?" Simon didn't want to say good-bye to Julia just yet. *Be honest, ya big goof*, he thought, *you don't want to say good-bye at all.* "I don't have a clue when it comes to gifts for little girls. Big girls, either, for that matter," he added, laughing. "But she's such a special kid. I'd hate to disappoint her."

"I'm sure whatever you bring will be just fine."

"You don't have time, then…."

Julia glanced at her watch, setting her keys to jangling. "Well, I have a half hour or so before—"

"That's rough on your ignition, you know."

When she looked at him like that, all wide-eyed and innocent, he could just kiss the stuffing out of her. But Simon resisted the urge and pointed at the key ring instead. "All that weight can damage the ignition cylinder. See…the keys dangle and bobble back and forth as you drive, and the stuff inside the switch is made up of plastic. So, in time, the parts can wear out."

Julia wrinkled her nose. "I thought that was a myth."

"So did I…till I learned better—the hard way."

Shrugging, she palmed the keys. "Guess I *could* get rid of a few of these. Truth is, I don't remember what half of them open."

A wistful, faraway expression settled over her face as he realized that her car was parked just across the street. If he didn't get her to agree soon to help him shop for Cassie's gift, he'd have to say good-bye. "So what do you say…?"

"Okay, I—"

"Terrific!" he all but shouted.

"Easy, big fella," she said, giggling. "If a few keys, more or less, makes that much difference to you, well, you need to get out more!"

"No, no," he said, stepping out in front of her. "I didn't mean the *keys*. You absolutely ought to lighten that load, but what I meant was, what do you say to helping me pick a present for Cassie?"

At first, Julia seemed a tad perturbed that he'd blocked her path. Then she tucked in one corner of her mouth, making that adorable dimple of hers appear like magic, and blinked up at him. Why hadn't he noticed before that a collection of freckles dotted her nose and cheeks? He'd been close enough to kiss her that night in his living room.... And why hadn't he seen the blue and green flecks that gleamed in her tawny eyes?

"As I was saying," she overpronounced, "I've got about a half hour."

"You're a lifesaver!" This time he didn't fight the urge to give her a big one-armed hug. When he felt her stiffen, a twinge of longing pulsed in Simon's heart. Difficult as it was, he turned her loose. "So which shop do you recommend?"

She took a deep breath and licked her lips, making him wish he'd thrown caution to the wind and kissed her while he had her close.

"She's four, you say?"

The best he could come up with was a slow nod. It had been a long, long time since he'd felt this way about a woman—so long that Simon didn't quite know what to make of the flood of emotions rumbling inside him.

"How much do you want to spend?"

He heard himself say "Money's no object" in a far-off voice he didn't recognize as his own.

"Have you been to Zooks'?"

"They sell toys? I thought they just carried crafts and hex signs and stuff like that."

"I saw the cutest little doll in there last time I went in." Julia commenced walking again and headed up the street. "She's dressed like a little Amish girl," she chattered over her shoulder, "pretty blue dress, high black boots, one of those long-brimmed caps, and the tiniest black-button eyes."

"If she looks half as good as you make her sound, Cassie will be cuddling her tonight."

They spent a few moments browsing in the store before she locked her sights on the doll she'd described. "Here she is!" Julia announced. "Isn't she just the most precious thing you've ever seen?"

Simon pocketed both hands and shrugged.

"Oh, pardon me, Mr. Macho," she teased, giving him a playful shove. "I should've known better than to foist a sissy word like 'precious' on a big strapping man like yourself."

"I'll admit, it isn't exactly part of my regular vocabulary." *But it could be*, he thought, *if it promised to bring out the sparkle in her face that way*. Simon wanted to say more but held back. If he didn't want to mess things up, he'd better watch his p's and q's and figure out how to read the *precious* woman who stood before him.

"They do a beautiful job with wrapping," he heard her say.

"Huh?"

"You know," she said, pointing at the doll, "for Cassie's present?"

"Oh. Gift-wrapping," he echoed. "Yeah. Guess I'd better get them to do it. Last time I tried, the package turned out looking like something a baby chimp had done—with his toes."

She treated him to another peal of pleasant laughter. "Well," she said, "now that you've got your gift, I'll be on my way." As she neared the door, Julia stopped at a rotating card rack and, after looking at the options, chose a card and handed it to him.

Simon glanced at the pink-hazed cover: the back shot of a tutu-clad little girl posing before a tall, gilded mirror. Just last week, when he'd stopped by on his way home from work, Cassie had been on the front lawn practicing dance moves. "Look, Simon!" she'd crowed. "I can do an arabesque penchee. Mrs. Marketa will be so proud!" He'd rewarded her with a big hug and a kiss to the cheek, and she'd returned his affections with equal fervor. He grinned a bit at the memory. It surprised him that he'd remembered the name of the ballet move. Even more surprising was how much she resembled the little girl on the card. Simon opened it, hoping the verse would be half as perfect as the cover. "Aw, rats," he said, frowning. "It's blank inside."

"Precisely. So you can write something in it that tells her what she means to you. She'll love it."

"Really? She's only four...."

Julia's ponytail danced as she nodded. "Girls are *born* sensitive," she said, smiling. "Trust me. Cassie will put that card in her keepsake box and save it forever."

"Keepsake box?"

"I never had one, of course, but I always wished I did. It's something every little girl wants."

"But...what if she doesn't have a—"

Julia walked halfway across the shop and came back a few seconds later holding what looked to Simon like a cigar box wrapped in padded pink satin and embellished with shimmering pearls that spelled out MY SECRET TREASURES. When she put it on the counter beside the doll, he teased, "You're gettin' mighty good at spending my money, pretty lady."

For a moment, he feared he'd overstepped his bounds and said something to rile her or hurt her feelings, because her big eyes got bigger as those perfectly arched brows rose higher on her forehead.

"Oh, please." She patted his hand. "Haven't you heard?"

Less than a second ticked silently by as he watched her smile widen.

" 'You can't take it with you,' " they quoted together.

Julia gave his hand a final pat and headed for the door. "Have a good time tonight," she said. "Be sure to take pictures—lots of them— so I can see Cassie's reaction to the doll. And the keepsake box."

Before he could respond, the cashier started ringing up his order; and when he turned around again, Julia was long gone. If she'd stayed, he would have asked her to join him tonight. Casey and Joanna had spent the past two years trying to find the Miss Right that would suit him. If he'd been a betting man, Simon would've bet the clinic that the pair of them would welcome Julia with open arms even if they hadn't chosen her themselves.

Maybe he could catch up to her before she disappeared with her car.

Maybe he'd drive to Lancaster and, using the business card she'd given him, find her office.

Maybe he'd march right up to her desk and tell her how much he wanted Casey and his family to meet her—tonight.

And maybe he'd better retreat, pray harder, think things through.

"Way to go, General Pemberton," he muttered, putting the gifts and the cake onto the pickup truck's backseat. And as he fired up the motor, Simon added, "Good thing Casey doesn't live in Vicksburg."

Chapter Ten

....

Julia couldn't wait to get home, kick off her shoes, and settle on the porch with a nice cup of herbal tea. Like Gretel from the fairy tale, she'd left a trail through the house with her purse, shoes, and jacket. And like Scarlett O'Hara, she'd worry about the mess tomorrow.

She loved the changing seasons and appreciated each for its particular traits. Springtime had always been her favorite. As the trees grew full and lush, new life flooded the world with buds and blossoms, baby birds and bunnies. It was a happy season, ripe with promise and hope. But summertime? Life seemed to move more slowly as temperatures soared, and the season's laid-back, easy pace was hard not to like.

Smiling to herself, Julia snuggled into the cushions of the Adirondack chair after dinner and rested her stockinged feet on its matching footstool. Never in a million years would she have thought, one short year ago, that she'd have a home of her own, one filled with antiques and mementos that evoked beautiful memories. Soon, she'd sit in this same spot, warmed by Granny's crocheted afghan as she stared out at the inky, star-studded sky.

How much nicer it would be, she thought, *to have a cat that would purr in my lap or a dog to curl up at my feet. Or both!* She'd meticulously avoided pets because moving from one foster-care home to another had taught her how painful saying good-bye could be. There were no good-byes in her future. She loved this house and

Paradise and everybody in it and had no intention of leaving, ever. Maybe this weekend she'd pay a visit to Simon's clinic to have a look at the animals that were up for adoption.

Golden lamplight, filtering through the dining room window, illuminated the white-painted porch. The tall shadows of potted houseplants stretched across the floorboards, spilled down the wooden stairs, and puddled on the flagstone walk. Her gaze followed the path from its origin at the bottom step to the quaint little toolshed Gramps had built so long ago. Back then, it had been the playhouse where Julia had hosted tea parties with stuffed bears and doll babies, where she'd played games of hide-and-seek with Granny and napped on hot summer afternoons.

The faint scent of newly-opened roses wafted to her on the soft breeze. Soon they'd put her limited gardening skills to the test. She'd learned a lot, working beside Granny all those years ago. Years of neglect hadn't been kind to the gardens, but Julia felt a certain kinship with the plants that had been her grandmother's pride and joy. Closing her eyes, she took a deep breath of sweet night air.

"I wish I had a camera…."

The pleasant baritone startled her, but only a little. "Simon," she said, sitting up straighter. "What are you doing here?"

One foot on the flagstone, the other on the bottom step, he shrugged one shoulder. "I was just in the neighborhood and thought maybe you'd like a slice of Cassie's cake." He climbed onto the porch and stood in the beams of lamplight. "Joanna wouldn't let me leave the leftovers. She's on a no-sugar campaign with the kids."

"Except for birthdays and special occasions," Julia put in. And as he nodded, she added, "That's a lovely name…Joanna."

"She's a lovely woman. You're gonna like each other."

Julia didn't quite know what to make of that. When a man brought a woman home to meet his family, didn't it mean he—

"Stay put," he interrupted, hand in the air. "I know where things are. I'll hack us both a slab of cake and deliver it before you can say 'good idea!

She climbed out of the chair. "I need a refill on my tea, anyway, so I'll join you."

"I did what you asked," he said, flipping on the overhead light.

Julia shook off the unhappy thoughts. "What's that?"

He slid two plates from the cupboard. "Pictures," Simon said, opening the cake box, "lots of them. On my digital camera."

"I can't wait to see your cousin and his family," she admitted.

Simon had just lifted the cake from its box and put it onto a platter. Rinsing frosting from his fingers, he said, "No time like the present!" Then, after drying his hands on a blue-and-white-checked towel, he pulled the camera from his shirt pocket and stepped up close.

She felt as small as a child, standing in white-socked feet beside him. He leaned down a bit and squinted at the little screen as he worked to bring the photos into view. Julia heard the sounds of his starched white shirt crinkling beside her ear. Inhaled the slight trace of his woodsy aftershave. Felt the subtle warmth emanating from his muscular arm.

Not so long ago, that arm had draped across her shoulders in an attempt to fend off the night's chill air. She remembered it as well as if it had been an hour ago, and the memory made her heartbeat quicken.

"That's Cassie," he said, pointing, "after seeing her dolly." Chuckling, Simon added, "I thought she'd lose her voice, the way she squealed."

"Oh, Simon," Julia sighed, "she's a beautiful child."

"That's her baby brother there," he said, scrolling to the next frame. "Josh. And Casey with Joanna."

"Such a lovely family. And I love the way the kids' names start with one parent's initials."

"Huh." Simon took a half step back and looked into her eyes. "I hadn't even noticed." He winked. "Guess it's that 'women are sensitive' thing you were talking about at Zooks' gift shop?" He didn't wait for her to comment. Instead, Simon leaned in and showed her the rest of the pictures. "I'm nuts about those kids," he admitted as he put the camera on her table.

Had she imagined it, or did Simon hold back from saying "I can't wait to have a couple of my own"?

"You must've had a hard day," he said, plopping cake onto the plates.

Julia refilled her mug, filled a second with steaming water, and added a tea bag to each. "What makes you say that?"

One big shoulder rose in a half shrug. "Oh, I dunno...maybe 'cause you seem quiet and subdued tonight."

"No harder than usual."

"Well, then," he said, leading the way to the back porch, "it's my professional opinion that you're suffering from fever." Simon waited until she'd walked through the door then added, "And I've got just the medicine for that."

She returned to her chair as Simon leaned against the porch railing. "Is that so?"

"Mmm-hmm," he said around a mouth full of cake. "Bicycles."

"Bicycles!"

"Nothin' cures fever better than a long ride in the woods." He speared another piece of cake. "We could go this weekend. Stop on the banks of the Pequea for a picnic of fried chicken, lemonade, apple pie. My treat."

She'd intended to ask him about adopting a cat or dog—and wanted to get the flower beds ready for planting. That, added to routine household chores, would leave little time for a daylong bike ride and picnic....

"Something tells me you already have plans."

"Sort of." The look of disappointment on his face made her want to jump up and promise she'd go anywhere with him. Instead, Julia said, "I've been giving a lot of thought to the dogs and cats at your clinic. The ones with no families of their own?"

His expression brightened. "You want to take one home?"

"Possibly."

"I have clinic hours from nine to noon on Saturday. Stop by around one, and we'll see which one chooses you."

Julia giggled. "Chooses *me*?"

Using his fork as a pointer, Simon assumed the stance of a college professor. "Oh, make no mistake, dear lady. Ninety-nine percent of the time, pets choose their people, not the other way around."

A sobering thought, Julia decided, because in her mind, it sounded a bit like foster families and the kids they take in.

"If a dog or cat picks you," he continued, "you won't want to run right home with it. You'll need supplies…food and dishes to serve it in, toys, a bed, a collar…not an inexpensive proposition."

"It's a major commitment; I realize that. And a life-changing one, too."

"If only everybody knew that, going in. I can't tell you how often somebody comes into the clinic and convinces themselves to take home one of the critters, only to discover they don't have the time or the temperament for it." He heaved a sad sigh. "It's heartbreaking, I tell you, to have to put those animals back into kennel cages after they've had a taste of what life with a family could be like."

"I know exactly how that would feel."

One brow rose on Simon's forehead, and she gritted her teeth, hoping he'd let the comment die a quick death.

"Just how many foster care homes were you in, Julia?"

Oh, how she wished she'd kept her lips zipped! "Too many." She grabbed her mug and took a long sip, hoping to hide behind it.

"Do you mind telling me what happened to your parents?"

In a flash, she imagined his reaction to the news that her mother had died of a drug overdose, that her father had been murdered in prison by a fellow inmate. No doubt he'd run to his car so fast that he'd pull the paper napkins into his wake. Julia came out from hiding to say, "Actually, I mind very much."

Simon's fast-blinking eyes were proof that her answer had been harsher than she'd intended…harsher than he'd deserved. "Sorry if that sounded blunt," she continued. "It's just…" She took a deep breath. "Why dredge up stuff like that, you know?"

His gentle, understanding smile warmed the space between them. "Okay." He popped the last bite of cake into his mouth then said, "Next time I pry into your personal business, you've got my permission to smack me."

Julia felt more than a little silly keeping the facts so closely guarded. But maybe the information would come in handy down the road, if she ever needed a story to convince Simon he deserved far, far better than the likes of her. The idea made her sad, but rather than dwell on it, she got up. "My tea's cold. I'm going to fix myself another cup." She held out her hand. "Can I warm yours, too?"

Instead of giving her his mug, Simon wrapped his hand around hers. "I'd like that…if you'll let me help." Then he turned her loose and gathered their plates and forks in one hand and held the door open for her with the other.

Every rational thought in her head screamed, *Tell him! Tell him every gory detail, right now!* It dawned on her, as the bright florescent light on the kitchen ceiling flickered on, that despite her best intentions, regardless of the promises she'd made to herself, she'd gone and fallen in love with him, anyway. She might have cried at the admission…

…if he hadn't chosen that moment to wrap her in a comforting embrace.

Chapter Eleven
....

Though the skies grew cloudy as a storm rolled in, Julia hadn't wanted to sit inside. "Soon it'll be even more hot and humid, and we won't want to fire up the chiminea," she'd said. So once again, he gathered wood and built a roaring blaze in its fat belly.

Now they sat side by side in wide-armed wooden chairs, quietly talking as they stared at the thunderheads roiling on the horizon. "Such a shame," she said wistfully, "that the stars and moon are hiding."

He reached across the small space separating them and grabbed her hand. "Aw, what do I need with the moon and stars when I've got your big sparkly eyes to look at?"

She gave his hand a little squeeze. "Simon, I declare. You must lie awake at night thinking up ways to make me blush."

Oh, he lay awake many nights thinking of her, all right. But looking for ways to make her blush hadn't been the reason. "I think pink cheeks become you."

"Now see?" A giggle punctuated her question. "Stuff like that embarrasses me!"

"The truth shouldn't embarrass you, Julia."

She stared straight ahead as a slow smile spread across her face.

"I wish I could paint," he admitted, staring at the floorboards.

"I've been meaning to sand and paint it. It's on my to-do list."

"Not because of the porch floor," he said, laughing. Scooting his chair closer to hers, he added, "If I had any artistic talent at all, I'd paint *you*."

"Oh, good grief. I think between the frosting and the sweet tea, you've overdosed on sugar!"

"Why?"

She shook her head, sending a lock of shimmering hair spilling over one shoulder. He wanted to run his fingers through it.

"See over there," she asked, "between those clouds?"

He looked in the direction she'd pointed. "Mars," he said, nodding. "And if you think you can distract me that easily, you're mistaken."

From the corner of his eyes, he saw her shoulders lift in a girlish shrug. "Can't blame a girl for trying."

"I'll humor you, though. Just give me a minute to think of something other than your pretty profile to talk about." He let a moment of silence tick by then added, "So what *are* your plans for the weekend?"

"I thought I'd clean up some of these flower beds. They've been neglected far too long."

"I think your grandmother would like that."

She twisted her upper body in the chair and faced him. "Tell me, Simon, what sort of pets are on the 'adoptable' list at your clinic?"

He blew a stream of air through his lips. "Let's see…there are a half dozen cats, two flop-eared rabbits, a gerbil, a hamster, and three dogs."

"With my erratic schedule, I probably ought to get a cat, don't you think, since they're more independent than dogs and—"

"You're home every night, right?"

"Sure."

"And once a week or so, you come home for lunchtime, right?"

"Yeah…"

"And didn't you tell me that sometimes you work from home all day?"

She nodded.

"Then I see no reason you couldn't have a dog, if that's what you want." He chuckled. "Or a cat *and* a dog."

"Whoa," she said, her free hand in the air, "don't you think I oughta get my feet wet first? I've never had a pet of my own before. I might stink at it!"

"What? *You?* No way. If God had made me a dog, I'd hope for a nice lady like you to take me in. You've got a heart as big as your head! You'll be a natural. I can tell."

"You can? How?"

She seemed so happy at his assessment, so eager to please, that he wished the chairs were closer still so he could gather her up in a reassuring hug. "Well, for starters, let's take the way you talk with Levi as an example. When you're with that boy, your focus is on him one hundred percent."

"That's hardly a fair comparison. He's…he's adorable."

And so are you, Simon thought. But he pressed on. "I saw the way Wiley and Windy took to you. Why, I was a little afraid they'd follow you home that night! No question in my mind, you'll be a natural." He held up his free hand to stall her objection. "Hey, as the only veterinarian here, I'm the resident expert on this porch."

Julia laughed. "How silly of me to second guess you, *Doctor.*"

"Seriously? If somebody wants to be a good pet owner, that's just what they'll be. Love has a funny way of dictating people's actions."

"Still, it might be best if I start with just one pet. Make sure it's happy and well-adjusted before adding to my little family."

"See there?"

She leaned forward and looked into his eyes. "See what?"

"Already, you're considering what's best for the pet, even before you've chosen one."

Settling back into her chair, Julia sighed. "Then I'll see you on Saturday at one o'clock sharp."

Simon had a feeling he'd end up counting the hours between now and then. "Wow. Did you see that?"

"The lightning, you mean?" He nodded. "I noticed it earlier, too. It's getting closer."

"And the wind's kicked up, too."

"Guess we'll have to go inside."

"Guess so."

"Either that," he said, standing, "or we could be brave. You could show me where you plan to put all the posies tomorrow." He put their mugs on the railing and held out one hand. For a moment, it looked as if Julia wasn't going to accept it, that she intended to cite a dozen reasons why his idea was half-baked at best. Much to his delight, she let him help her up and lead her onto the lawn.

Two minutes into the tour, she stopped under an ancient oak. "Isn't it amazing," she said, fingering the thick ropes that dangled from its gnarled branches, "that this old swing is still here even after all these years? You'd think the hemp would have dry-rotted by now."

Simon gave the ropes a hefty tug then leaned all his weight on the swing's wooden seat. "Somebody put a lot of time and effort into making sure it had lasting power," he said, sitting on it.

"Gramps," she said. "His motto was 'Good enough never is.' "

Simon pumped his legs a time or two and set the swing to swaying. "I'll bet as a kid, you felt like you could touch the sky with your toes when you got this thing going."

"How'd you know?"

"Hey, I was a kid once, too, you know." Then, after a pause, "Ride with me."

"Oh, I couldn't!"

"Don't worry, the rope's solid. It'll hold us both."

"Until it doesn't…," she pointed out, looking toward the loops securing it to the branch overhead.

"Where's your faith, pretty lady?"

An expression darkened her face at almost the same moment as thunder rumbled in the distance. He patted his thigh. "Humor me."

Hands on her hips, she stepped closer then planted both tiny sneakers between his big loafers and eased herself onto his lap. In no time, he had them swinging eight, twelve, fifteen feet off the ground. The wind of each forward motion blew the hair away from her face…and directly into Simon's. Eyes closed, he inhaled the aroma of peaches. Or coconuts. Or apple pie. Something sweet and delicious that made his heart pound and his palms sweat…. "Julia," he said, digging both heels into the earth to stop the swing. Though she made no move to get up, he wrapped both arms around her.

"Mmm?"

"You know I like you, right?"

"Mmm-hmm…"

"And you know I like being *around* you, right?"

"Uh-huh…"

Help me out here, Lord. My brain turns to mush when she's this close. "You know I'd never do or say anything to hurt you…."

Julia nestled closer, and he read that as a "Yes."

"So if I kissed you right now, would that…would it upset you?"

He heard her swallow, felt her shrug, then turned her until she faced him. He guided her face closer, so close that her image blurred. Closing his eyes, he pressed his lips to hers, slowly, softly. When a quiet murmur escaped her throat, he wondered if maybe the swing had flung him right into heaven. *Easy*, he cautioned himself, *you don't want to scare her now that you've finally made a little progress.*

He opened his eyes a slit and froze, surprised to find her staring at him. "You don't have a romantic bone in your little body, do you?"

Julia grinned. "What?"

"You're supposed to close your eyes when I kiss you." With a wave of his hand, he added, "You know, so you can…sorta commit the moment to memory."

"Ahh, is that how it's supposed to go?"

"What were you looking at, anyway?"

She bracketed his face with both tiny hands and tilted her head. "You," she whispered.

And just as quickly as it had been born, the magical moment died. Julia got to her feet, brushed imaginary lint from her skirt, and tucked her hair behind her ears. "I felt a raindrop," she said, hugging herself.

"Me, too." He grinned and stood beside her. "But unlike you, I'm not made of sugar. No chance I'll melt if I get wet."

She ran a few steps ahead then stopped. "Better get out from under there," she warned as the wind picked up and the rain teemed. "Lightning is attracted to trees."

Like I'm attracted to you? he thought, joining her in the downpour. Simon only intended to slide an arm around her slender waist and run with her to the protection of the porch. He didn't know why he pulled her to him, instead, and held her tight. "Julia," he said huskily, staring into her sweet rain-slicked face, "as God is my witness, I never thought I'd feel this way again. I thought when my wife died, that was it for me."

Lightning sizzled and thunder roared, startling her enough to wrap her arms around his neck. Simon buried his face in her soggy locks. *Too early to say "I love you,"* he wondered, *and admit she's the answer to your prayers?*

She started to shiver and, reluctantly, he released her. But not before looking one last time into those delightful dazzling eyes. "Better get you inside."

Nodding, Julia darted for cover, leaving his arms and hands and chest suddenly empty and icy, and he shook off the chill.

"C'mon," she said, waving him nearer. "I'll make us some nice hot tea." And extending one hand, Julia added, "I did a huge load of laundry just the other day…things I dragged out from my grandfather's closet so I could donate them to charity."

As Simon stepped onto the porch, she cupped her chin in a palm and gave him a quick once-over. "He was about your size, so if you don't mind that the clothes are a bit old-fashioned…." Darting into the house, she said, "Go ahead into the powder room and get out of those wet things. I'll leave the stuff right outside the door, and by the time you're changed, I'll have our tea ready."

She was halfway up the stairs before he could agree or object. "And she worried she wouldn't make a good pet parent," he mumbled, stepping into the tiny bathroom. Simon might have laughed out loud if he hadn't caught sight of a small black-and-white photo displayed on a glass shelf—a little girl, dressed like a fairy princess, right down to the sparkling wand in her tiny hand. Long hair draped her narrow shoulders like a gleaming cape, and a glint of sunlight sparkled from the toes of black Mary Janes. And though she'd smiled for the camera, Simon saw no joy in her eyes.

He began to unbutton his shirt but found himself unable to take his eyes from the big haunted ones in the picture. What sort of childhood had she lived? Why had she been sent to live with her grandparents? Better still, why had she been taken from them and forced to live in one foster home after another?

Guilt panged in him as Simon remembered the day they'd met— when he'd decided not to get involved with her. Shaking his head, he admitted that time had changed things dramatically, because he'd gone from being a guy who feared having to take care of her to a man who would have done anything to turn her painful past into a dim and distant memory.

A soft knock startled him, and Simon banged his elbow on the towel bar. "Here you go," she sang through the door.

"Thanks," he called, wincing and biting back a quiet "Yee-ouch." He waited until he heard her rummaging in the kitchen then cracked the door just enough to grab the tidy stack she'd placed on the floor.

The shirt and pants, though slightly worn, fit as if they'd been sewn just for him. Julia had even thought to bring thick socks to warm his feet until his loafers dried out. If this thoughtful, loving little gal was still carrying emotional baggage, he'd gladly heft a case or two!

She wore black sweatpants and a long-sleeved white T-shirt and had pulled her hair into a high ponytail when he padded into the kitchen. If he didn't know better, Simon would have sworn she hadn't yet celebrated her sixteenth birthday.

"I thought maybe you'd like some cookies with your tea," she said, gesturing toward the plate near his mug.

"Chocolate chip?"

Julia nodded.

"Homemade?

Another nod.

"I thought earlier that I must've died and gone to heaven." He pulled out a chair and sat then grabbed a cookie. "Now I'm sure of it."

"When?"

"When what?"

"When did you think you'd died and gone to heaven?"

Dare he admit it had been when he'd kissed her, out there on the swing, and she'd returned it? *No, too soon,* he cautioned, *way too soon.* "When I slid into this flannel shirt," he fibbed. "It's as soft as bunny fur."

Her entire being brightened at the mention of her grandfather. "Gramps liked it, too. In fact, that's one of his favorites. *Was* one of his favorites, that is."

"Well, I appreciate the loan. I'll get it back to you tomorrow." His fingers formed the Boy Scout salute. "On my honor."

She sat across from him and smiled. "Were you a Scout?"

"You bet," he said around a mouthful of cookie.

"No wonder you're so good at starting fires."

"Speaking of which," he said, using a half-eaten cookie as a pointer, "want to go back out there, near the chiminea?"

Julia shook her head. "No, this is just as nice. And warmer."

"Drier, too." He didn't understand the stream of small talk. It seemed they were talking just for the sake of filling the silence.

Simon hoped his kiss hadn't caused that, because he'd quickly grown fond of that particular mode of communication. "Tired?"

"A little. You?"

"Yeah, I guess." He washed down the last of his cookie with a gulp of tea. "Will you be in court tomorrow?"

"No. Thankfully, I'll be in the office all day."

"Want to have lunch with me?"

"I'm supposed to stop by the Gundens," she said, "to explain the paperwork I dropped off the other day."

"You lucky stiff."

One brow quirked in response.

"You get to see Levi."

At the mere mention of the boy's name, her demeanor changed. Julia sat up straighter and her eyes widened. "Oh, but he's a dear little boy, isn't he?"

"The dearie-est." He chuckled. Simon took another cookie. "I was there the day he was born."

Simon proceeded to tell Julia how, nearly six years earlier, William had mentioned that he'd be taking Rebekah to Ohio, to attend his mother's funeral, leaving his very pregnant wife home alone with Seth. Though William assured Simon that Hannah would be fine on her own, Simon found reasons to hang around. As a veterinarian, he knew the signs…and her time was near. "She may have had an easy labor and delivery with the other two," Simon told Julia, "but that wasn't the case with Levi."

He bit into the cookie then sipped his tea. "She was worried what the bishop might say if they knew I was there while William was out of town, so I parked my truck in the barn and spent three nights in the hayloft, running through the shadows so I could check on her every couple of hours. My part in Levi's birth has to remain a carefully guarded Gunden family secret." Finishing off the cookie, he dusted his hands. "Bet you didn't know that his middle name is Simon, did you?"

"No, but it makes perfect sense." She ran a finger around the rim of her mug until it emitted a quiet hum. "I'm sure the other Amish would have understood, under the circumstances," Julia said, "but your secret's safe with me, all the same."

Suddenly she gasped and flashed a big bright smile. "Hey, now it all makes sense!"

"What does?"

"The way you look at him—as if he's your very own child."

"If wishes were fishes." Simon winked. "I don't mind admitting, I couldn't love that kid more if he *was* mine. I have to work hard to keep Seth and Rebekah from thinking that Levi's my favorite. But to be honest, he *is*."

"You're a pretty amazing man, Simon Thomas."

He felt the heat of a blush creep into his cheeks and hid it by faking a big, exaggerated yawn. "You know," he said when it ended, "maybe I'll make good on that promise to take him to the wolf sanctuary, since you're busy this weekend."

"Oh, Simon, I'm sure he'd love that!"

"He'd like it better if you came with us."

"No, you boys should go alone. It'll be good for you both, I think." She tilted her head and smiled sweetly. "Can I ask a personal question?"

"Sure. You've endured plenty from me, so it seems only fair that you get in a few jabs."

"It's so obvious that you love kids, so…so why don't you have any of your own? Wasn't your wife able to—"

"No, no," he said, waving the comment away, "we were *able*. It's just that Georgia wanted to wait so we could adjust to being a couple first, and travel and furnish the house just the way she wanted it… stuff like that."

"Oh," she said quietly, staring at her hands.

"You don't know how many times I've wished I'd pushed harder to have kids. That way, when she—" Simon cut himself off. The last thing he wanted to do was burden her with the long, sad story of his loss. Instead, he drank the last of his tea and glanced at the clock.

"That way," Julia finished for him, "you'd have the children to remember her by."

"That, too, I guess. But mostly, I'd just have them." He shrugged. "Gets mighty lonely, rattling around in that big old house all by myself."

"It would be a great place to raise kids. All those rooms. All that space. That big back ya—"

"Julia," he interrupted, "can I ask *you* something?"

"Sure."

He didn't fail to notice the note of wariness in her tone, and it made him smile. "Remember, I gave you permission to smack me if I got too personal…."

"Ah, yes. I'd almost forgotten."

But the twinkle in her eyes told him she hadn't. "Why aren't you married? I mean, even Levi knows it isn't your feet or your teeth." She giggled quietly as Simon counted out her qualities, one finger at a time. "You're gorgeous, smart, loving, and kind, easy to be with, a great cook, an excellent housekeeper…." He frowned. "All I can figure is, every guy you've met is as dumb as a bag of doorknobs."

"There you go again," she said, fanning rosy cheeks.

"And there *you* go again, trying to distract me from the question at hand."

She took a deep breath before saying, "I know it's tough to believe, considering how *perfect* I am and all"—Julia laughed, a hearty, happy sound that echoed through the cozy kitchen—"but, honestly? Nobody's asked!"

Had she wanted someone to ask? he wondered. Simon didn't want to dwell on that. He slapped the table. "Just as I suspected. Dumb as a box of hammers!"

She gave him a long, intense look, one he couldn't read. Rather than press the issue, he looked at the time again. "For the love of Pete, how'd it get to be ten fifteen?"

"Time flies when you're having fun?"

Simon got up and walked around to her side of the table and helped her to her feet. "So you had fun tonight?"

"Yes, I did. Very much."

And God help him, his stomach churned and his heart flipped as if he were a teenage boy in the throes of his first crush. "So what about lunch tomorrow?" he asked, heading for the front door.

"I have to—"

"Oh, right. The Gundens." He tapped his temple. "Sorry. Blame the hour for my thickheadedness."

"Wait right here...."

She dashed down the hall and, after several metallic thumps and bumps, came running back, carrying a plastic bag. "Your clothes," she said, "all dried and folded."

"When did you have time to do that?"

"I grabbed them while you were fixing us that cup of tea. You didn't see me slip by, leaving a drippy trail behind?"

"No," he admitted, amazed at his own lack of attention to detail.

"Well, good."

"Good?"

"A girl needs to keep a few mysteries about her…."

"A *few*?" he echoed. "You're one big giant ball of mystery!" But it was way too late in the day to get into that. "Guess I'd better hit the road. The cookies were delicious."

"When I bake another batch, you'll be the first to know."

"Soon, I hope."

Again with the small talk. What gives?

Side by side, they walked to her gravel drive, where he'd parked the pickup. One hand on the door handle, he said, "You're quite a woman, you know that?"

"Simon, stop. You're embarrassing me."

He slid in behind the steering wheel. "I told you, the truth shouldn't embarrass you." He hadn't even left yet and already, he was trying to think up ways to see her again. Already he missed her. He crooked a finger, beckoning her near. "I think maybe you have a flaw after all."

She bent at the waist, putting her face mere inches from his, and feigned annoyance. "I beg your pardon?"

"You're too easily embarrassed."

Grinning, she said, "Perfection is boring."

Reaching through the window, he stroked her cheek. "I don't think you're the least bit boring."

And with that, he drove away.

Simon watched her reflection grow smaller in the rearview mirror until she all but disappeared from view. And when he nearly mowed down a mailbox alongside the road, Simon blinked himself back to attention.

Because now more than ever, he wanted to live a long, healthy life.

Chapter Twelve

....

Good thing you live so far from the neighbors, she thought. What would they have said if they'd seen her waving at the diminishing glow of Simon's taillights as they were swallowed up by the ravenous rainy darkness? Hugging herself against the early summer night's chill, she hiked up her long, winding drive, smiling at the memory of him snapping off a smart salute as he drove away.

Julia took her time cleaning up the dishes, remembering as she stored the last slice of cake that he'd seemed as reluctant to leave as she'd been to let him go. Something was happening between them, she admitted, tossing her own rain-soaked clothes into the washing machine—something grand and glorious and good. All her best intentions to keep a safe distance from Simon had fallen by the wayside…thanks in no small part to his guileless charm.

If she had a lick of decency in her, she'd gather her courage and stick to her initial convictions, because while her feelings *for* him had changed immensely, her belief that he deserved better than her had *not*.

Julia hurried into her favorite cotton nightgown and climbed into bed, cuddling under the thin, fraying afghan Granny had sewn so many years before. In the not-too-distant future, she'd have to part with this love-worn memento, for it would never survive another laundering—no matter how mild the soap or how gently she rubbed and rinsed—and the thought made her heart ache.

Even in the dark, Julia knew where to find the sole minuscule stain, hidden in the petals of a rose, and remembered how it came to be: The loud jangle of Granny's clunky black phone had startled her, making Granny prick her finger as she stitched one colorful scrap to another. Tears stung behind Julia's eyelids as she pictured her grandmother popping the needle-stuck digit into her mouth and mumbling, "Nothing worthwhile comes without a price."

She wondered what price Simon would pay for his association with her....

Rolling onto her side, Julia faced the windows and watched the wind riffle the limbs of the tree just outside. Silhouetted by silvery clouds, witch-finger branches tapped softly against the glass, interrupting the flow of rain that sheeted down each pane. How odd that Simon had wanted a tour of her yard *after* seeing lightning in the distance. Odder still that he shared her sense of wonder at the raw, unbridled, sometimes dangerous power of nature…something no one but Granny had ever understood about her.

As she'd moved from one foster home to another, Julia had tried hard to forget Paradise, Pennsylvania. Leaving the pleasant memories in the past had been easier than missing the two-story farmhouse with its fuzzy blue sofas, bright Priscilla curtains, and footpaths worn onto wood floors by years of living. Mostly she'd needed to stop missing the man and woman who'd welcomed her into that house when her own parents were deemed unfit by the Commonwealth of Pennsylvania.

Julia remembered the story Simon had told her about helping Levi come into the world. Clearly he loved the boy. But she'd seen him with other children, and it had been just as clear that he loved them all. Julia loved kids, too, but despite a years-old ache to have her own, she couldn't rid herself of the notion that to fulfill that dream would be an act of selfishness equaled only by her parents'. What if she'd inherited her mom and dad's self-destructive inclinations? Their risky behavior? Their tendency to cling to dangerous habits? No way she'd subject even one innocent child to the miserable kind of life she'd lived!

All these years she'd dedicated herself to the law, because at least that way she could *help* a kid or two. Seemed rather pointless to embark on a husband hunt, knowing that a family would never be in her future. Far better—and easier—for everyone concerned if her sorry history remained a well-hidden secret.

Julia had learned the hard way what happened when others stumbled onto information about her past, and from her unique perspective, the Amish had nothing over her when it came to shunning. Why, even her foster siblings, who'd come from similar backgrounds and situations, felt superior enough to distance themselves from her once the ugly truth came out.

Time, a hard-earned college education, and success on the job had all helped to dull the sharp edge of loneliness, but Julia never quite managed to shake the concept that she was somehow tainted. And for proof, she hadn't needed to look further than yearbooks and family photos that pictured her mom and dad as successful, well-adjusted, happy individuals who'd become a successful, motivated young couple.

Whether she'd been colicky or allergic to formula or simply one of those babies who couldn't be satisfied, Julia would never know. But one fact was inescapable: Her birth had put them on the path to perdition. She'd been around finicky, fussy babies and tantrum-throwing toddlers, and neither had the power to drive normal, sane people to despair. So it was clear. Her parents were weak and immature, defective somehow, and she simply would not risk that she'd inherited their weaknesses.

She'd taught herself to count her blessings and learned to be content with what she had rather than torment herself with dreams of things that could never be hers. Life hadn't been all *that* bad, after all. She'd never gone without a meal or lacked warm clothes in the wintertime. And how many other orphans had grandparents like hers? When Julia learned all they'd sacrificed to ensure that their only grandchild would someday have a home and a little money in the bank, her heart ached with love and gratitude.

Still, Julia—feeling contaminated and undeserving—left the money untouched as the house went fallow. If not for a long, stern scolding from Gramps's good friend Judge Sullivan, she might never have come to her senses. And when finally she did, Julia had yet another reason to be grateful: She'd been deeply loved, surely and completely by her grandparents.

It had taken several months working as a public defender to realize that not *all* foster parents were contemptuous phonies, as a few of hers had been. But even with this surprising information, Julia remained suspicious, particularly of those who professed to be born-again, for they'd been the most cruel and twisted of all—especially when compared to good Christians like Gramps and Granny. She built a wall of anger and resentment around herself, and while hiding behind it, Julia didn't have to concern herself with disappointment and rejection.

So the girl who'd moved from place to place with just four personal items and an odd assortment of hand-me-down clothes to her name now owned a fully furnished four-bedroom house on three beautiful acres in what tourist brochures called "God's Country." *Let them call it "God's Country,"* she thought. Julia would not thank Him for any of what she had, because what had *He* done to make any of it possible? She owed everything she had, everything she'd become, to Gramps and Granny. And maybe just a little to Judge Sullivan, whose advice and guidance had helped her become a lawyer.

Julia stroked the quilt's butter-soft satin trim and sighed. If she got hit by a bus in Lancaster tomorrow, who would *she* leave it all to?

The question brought Simon to mind. Tomorrow, first thing, she'd draw up her own will, stipulating that he could use whatever funds came from the sale of her house and land to provide for unadopted pets. He'd come to mean a lot to her, and so had his many "causes."

She dreaded the day he found out about her mother and father, because then he'd know what the kids from her past knew: Julia Spencer had been born of drug-addicted thieves. Just because she could never enjoy a happy future as his wife didn't mean she couldn't count him as a friend, as one of her blessings…however temporary.

The wind kicked up as the rain beat down, conjuring images of her whimsical hours with Simon. Now, an hour into her sleepless night, Julia smiled, realizing that if she had to write up a "Reasons to Like Simon" list, she'd get writer's cramp. Besides being compellingly handsome, he'd proven time and again that goodness and decency were as much a part of him as his teasing green eyes and gleaming blond hair. She'd be hard-pressed to think of a person with a greater talent for making others laugh. He fearlessly cracked jokes, sometimes at his own expense, to the delight of those around him— like the funny faces and silly sounds he'd made at the café to coax merry giggles from Levi. If anyone needed proof of how much the guy loved kids, all they'd need to do is watch him with that one.

And if they wanted proof of Simon's innate kindness and generosity? Both could be found in his chosen life's work and the now-happy and well-adjusted pets he'd welcomed into his home.

He'd befriended the Gundens and dozens of other Amish families in Lancaster County and often provided free veterinary services to any Paradise family in need. And what about all the hours he dedicated to the wolf sanctuary?

Julia made a mental note to get over there as soon as possible; hopefully the litter of cubs, born shortly before her last visit, would be old enough to hold by now. The caretaker had promised she could hold them—"If you don't mind a few nips and bites…," he'd said.

No, she didn't. She'd earned a scar or two, putting in volunteer hours around the sanctuary. Not as many as she'd noticed on Simon's hands and forearms, but then he spent no fewer than forty hours a week with a wide variety of clawed and toothed creatures at his clinic. No reason to believe the beautiful wolves had inflicted *every* injury.

The day they'd met, when she'd first noticed him from the corner of her eyes, Julia admired his natural, easy way with Casper. Then, when he spotted her playing with Fawn, he'd ambled closer, instantly inspiring the same reaction from the she-wolf…and herself.

Yes, there certainly was much to admire about the man. What Julia couldn't figure out was what Simon saw in *her*. And there was no doubt in her mind: He saw something. She'd have to be an idiot not to have noticed that he liked her, liked her a lot. A certain joy settled over her as she thought of the way he'd so tenderly held her, as if he believed God had crafted her of delicate porcelain. Even more wondrous, the sweet yet solicitous way he'd kissed her—proof, in her mind, that Simon's passion was tempered by respect and a genuine concern for her feelings.

All this from a man who made no secret of how much he'd enjoyed married life enough to want to marry again and, this time, raise a family. And though he hadn't said it in so many words, Simon's actions made it clear he'd like *Julia* to share that dream with him.

Knowing that a man like Simon cared for her—and cared deeply—touched her as few things in her life had. But then, he only knew the public Julia, whose reserved behavior was meant for the office and the courtroom or meandering through the quaint shops in Paradise. A time or two she'd unintentionally given him a peek into her past and let him catch a glimpse of memories that had the power to cast ominous shadows on her present. The brief visit into her history awoke the hero in him, and Julia instinctively knew that he wanted to protect her not only from things that had hurt her long ago, but from anything that might hurt her now and in the future, too.

Lying on her stomach, Julia punched her pillow then buried her face in the crook of one arm. *How many single women live in Lancaster County?* she wondered. *How many would count themselves fortunate to have a man like Dr. Simon Thomas interested in them?*

Every last one, she admitted.

And how many needed rescuing?

Very few, she thought—spawning the idea that his interest in her might be likened to his "save the helpless critters" tendencies. The very thought made her wince. She'd fallen hard and fast for Simon, and Julia had experienced just enough close calls to know the difference between what merely *felt* like love…and the real thing.

Trouble was, knowing the difference opened a whole new can of worms. Because love stirred the protector in *her*, too, prompting a reaffirming of her decision to spare him from herself.

That decision that would prove to be the toughest of her life.

* * * * *

A whopping case of "missing Levi" woke him earlier than usual, inspiring Simon to pay a visit to the Gundens' before opening the clinic. His pickup hadn't even rolled to a complete stop when Levi raced up to the driver's door, tears streaming down his face.

"Doctor Thomas," he cried, "come inside, quick. It's Mama…she is very, very sick."

Instinct made him grab his doctor's bag from the passenger seat. "What is it, Levi? Did she fall?"

"No," the boy wailed. "Papa says something is wrong with the baby."

Baby, Simon thought, racing toward the house, *what baby?* He hadn't heard that Hannah was pregnant….

William met him at the door, white-faced and wide-eyed. "God must have sent you," he rasped. "Hannah is in a bad way, Simon. I have never seen anything like it."

The man had brought dozens of farm animals into the world— some breech. Things must be terrible indeed to paint that look of fear on his face. "Where is she?" Simon asked, stepping up to the sink.

"Upstairs in her bed," Levi said as Simon dialed 911 on his cell phone. And then he prayed, because he knew from experience it would take no fewer than fifteen minutes for EMTs to arrive. Meeting William's gaze, he said, "Blood?"

"More than I have ever seen," he answered, running a trembling hand through his hair.

Simon barked instructions and information to the dispatcher, then snapped the phone shut and dropped it into his shirt pocket. Raising and lowering the pump handle, he started a stream of cool clear water. Grabbing a bar of homemade soap from the counter, he began vigorously scrubbing his hands.

"Where are Seth and Rebekah?"

"At the schoolhouse," William said on a shaky breath.

Good, Simon thought. Now if only he could think of something to occupy and calm Levi while he ran upstairs to see what he could do for Hannah until the ambulance showed up. A knock at the door startled all three in the kitchen, and Levi ran to it. "Oh, Miss Julia!" he sobbed, flinging himself into her arms.

When she made eye contact with Simon, her expression registered concern and confusion.

"Mama is very sick," Levi blubbered. "Very, very sick."

Simon had never been more relieved to see anyone in his life. "God must have sent you," he said, quoting William. Then, turning to the Amishman and his son, he added, "You two get down to the end of your drive, in case the ambulance needs help finding your house." To Julia he said, "Grab my bag and follow me, will you?"

Instantly, she snapped into action. "What happened?" she whispered, racing up the stairs behind him.

"Not sure yet. Levi said something about a baby, and William says there's lots of blood. Sounds like a miscarriage." He stopped on the landing. "Now, we don't know what we're gonna find in there," he said in a low, grave voice, "so do your best to stay calm and try not to look so terrified, okay?"

Julia took a deep breath then nodded.

Simon strode confidently into the room and tried to ignore the huge puddle of blood that surrounded Hannah. One hand over her stomach and the other pressed to her forehead, she grimaced with pain.

"So what's the big idea," he said around a tense smile, "keeping this pregnancy a secret from your friends?"

"I wasn't even sure myself yet," Hannah said. Opening her eyes, she spotted Julia at the foot of the bed. "I prayed God would send a woman," she rasped. "I am so glad He sent you."

Julia returned her smile and then knelt beside the thin mattress, taking Hannah's hand in her own "How far along do you think you are?"

"Not far." A tear escaped the corner of one blue eye. "We were so looking forward to another child."

"This is far from over, Hannah Gunden," she said, patting the hand. "Keep a good thought."

"You are right, of course." Hannah managed a feeble grin. "Will you pray, Julia?"

He could almost read her mind. Eyes wide and lips parted, the idea scared her nearly as much as Hannah's condition. *Lord God*, Simon prayed, *give her the words that Hannah needs to hear....*

He watched as Julia licked her lips and straightened her spine, listened as she took a deep breath and cleared her throat. "O Lord our God," she began, "be with us now and bless us with Your strength. We trust that You will watch over Hannah and her baby as You correct whatever is causing Hannah's pain, as You put an immediate stop to her bleeding. We know that You are all-powerful and wait with hopeful hearts for You to answer this prayer...."

"Amen," Hannah whispered. "Amen."

The composure that seemed to flow from Julia filled the room, reminding Simon that he'd almost forgotten his purpose here. "Would you hand me my stethoscope," he said to her, "and see if you can find a couple of clean sheets and towels around here somewhere?"

She was on her feet in a heartbeat, hurrying around to his side of Hannah's bed to place his doctor's bag on the night table. "Are the linens in the dresser, Hannah?" she asked, handing Simon the stethoscope with one hand and pointing at the tall many-drawered bureau against the far wall.

The woman answered with a slight nod, and in no time Julia was back again, carrying neatly folded sheets in her arms. After putting them beside his bag, she grabbed a washcloth. "Be right back," she said quietly. "I'm just going to the kitchen to dampen this. Maybe if I wash her face…"

She was gone before Simon could tell her what a good idea it was, and he wondered how many women would handle a crisis like this with her level-headedness. Especially considering that Hannah's pulse was thready and her heartbeat far faster than normal.

"Who would have guessed," Hannah said, her voice soft, her words slow, "that she could pray like that."

"Who would have guessed," he echoed. "Now you be quiet, Mrs. Gunden, and conserve your strength, you hear?"

She gave the barest of nods as the hint of a smile curved her lips upward. "Yes, Doctor."

Hannah slipped into unconsciousness just as the blare of sirens raced up the drive. "What Julia said, Lord?" he prayed. "Ditto."

* * * * *

The doctors agreed to let Hannah go home from the hospital only if she promised to stay off her feet for at least a week. "And remember," Levi said as he helped Hannah into the kitchen, "no climbing the stairs!"

Seth and Rebekah hovered nearby, chattering about how they'd prepared for their mother's return. "Seth and I brought our beds into the parlor," her daughter said. "You'll sleep on Seth's and I'll sleep beside you, in case you need anything, anything at all."

"But where will Seth sleep?" Levi wanted to know.

"In your bed," said his older brother, "with *you*."

Levi groaned. "Oh, that will never work. You are a blanket hog!"

Seth chuckled. "And you are a pillow pig, so we are even."

After inhaling a huge breath, Levi shook his head. "Oh, I suppose I can stand anything for a week, since it is for Mama."

Julia would give anything to have children like these! But this was neither the time nor place to dwell on her own sorry past. "I'm making your supper tonight," she announced.

"Such a good friend," Hannah said, sinking gratefully onto the bed where she'd spend the next seven nights. "You came to see me every day I was in the hospital and came to take me home, and now this?" She bit her lower lip. "We will be all right, if you have something else to do."

"You'll be doing me a favor," Julia said.

William stacked pillows behind his wife's back. "How are we doing *you* a favor, Julia?"

"You're my guinea pigs." She flapped a recipe card in the air.

"It's the first time I'm making this casserole."

"Is there enough for one more?" said a voice through the screen door.

"Simon!" Levi squealed. "Have you come to welcome Mama home?"

"Indeed I have," he said, scooping the boy into his arms. "How are you, Hannah?"

"Very well," she said around a wan smile.

But Julia knew better. She'd been at the hospital when the doctor came in to say that Hannah had lost the baby. She didn't think she'd ever seen a woman cry harder. When the tears had subsided, the woman wiped her eyes and blew her nose and said "Gottes wille," and not another word was spoken of the miscarriage. Though Julia didn't see eye to eye with the "God's will" theory, she did hope that if she were ever put to such a test, she'd carry herself with the same grace and dignity.

Supper that night was a festive event. Instead of mourning their loss, the Gundens chose to celebrate Hannah's recovery. Halfway through the meal, Simon was called to the clinic to perform emergency surgery on a dog that had fallen from a second-story window. Julia stayed to help Rebekah with the dishes, then bid them all farewell and headed home to study a brief for her court case the next day. "But I'll be back tomorrow," she promised, "with another recipe to test!"

When she arrived an hour earlier the next day, Hannah looked much more like her old self. Not quite the robust, rosy-cheeked woman she'd been before the miscarriage, but far healthier than when Julia and Simon waited with her for the EMTs to arrive. Julia brewed a cup of herbal tea for the two of them and perched on a wooden bench beside Hannah's temporary bed in the parlor. "I cannot sip from a cup while lying down," Hannah protested. "I am well enough to sit quietly at the table." And with that, she marched into the kitchen.

Julia followed dutifully, carrying a steaming mug of tea in each hand. "All right," she said, placing one mug in front of her Amish friend, "but if I even *start* to see signs that you're feeling poorly, it's back to bed for you!"

Chuckling, Hannah nodded. "You would have made a good nurse, I think." Easing onto a chair, she said, "You keep to yourself far too much. God did not intend for His children to be alone."

Julia sat a little taller. The comment had come from out of nowhere, leaving her wondering how—or if—she ought to respond. It would have been disrespectful to say "Mind your own business," especially considering what the married mother of three had just survived. And although, according to Levi, his mother was only three years older than Julia, Hannah had always seemed much older and wiser than that.

"I hope my honesty does not offend you, Julia, but I have always felt closer to you than the others in town."

Smiling, Julia sighed, knowing that by "others," Hannah meant "not Amish." "And I'm sorry if it sometimes seems as if I'm standoffish and withholding."

"If I could, I would bring some tea to William," she said absentmindedly. "He has been hard at work in the killing room all morning."

"Again?" Julia asked. And remembering the lessons about slaughter little Levi had given her, she tried not to wrinkle her nose.

"More pigs means more customers," Hannah said matter-of-factly. She gave a slight shrug. "But as I was saying, I have been watching you closely this past year. I would have to be blind not to see the sadness in your eyes." One hand over her heart, Hannah shook her head. "No one would argue that our lives are very different, yours and mine, but I *am* your friend, you know."

"I'm touched, and I'm honored," Julia admitted. And, not knowing what else to say, she took a sip of the tea. "Delicious…"

"Tell me, Julia Spencer, just who are you, anyway?"

"Goodness," she said with a laugh. "What a question!"

A deep furrow appeared between Hannah's eyebrows. "I know that you live just down the road a bit in the house built by your grandfather. I know that your work puts you in Lancaster every day, where you do many important legal things inside the courthouse." She tilted her head. "But where did you go, all those years ago, Julia? And *why* did you leave Paradise?"

Where to begin? Julia wondered. And then she sat back, clasped both hands on top of the table, took a deep breath, and confessed everything to the woman who now seemed more like a sister than a friend. She started with the gloomy Tuesday morning when a counselor delivered a frightened three-year-old to her grandparents' house, to the Saturday last summer when she came back to it again, scarred by her parents' abandonment and the sexual abuse that had happened in between. As Julia spoke, Hannah's blue eyes filled with tears.

"Oh, Julia, I admire you so, for having survived it all without even more bitterness."

Even more *bitterness?* Julia's mind echoed.

Hannah dabbed at her eyes with a corner of her white apron. "Life has inflicted many wounds upon your heart, and God our merciful Father has given you many years to heal." Wrapping both hands around her mug, Hannah spoke slowly. "But…why do I get the impression that you blame *Him* for all the sadness of your past?"

"Well, it's kinda hard *not* to," Julia admitted. "He's supposed to be all-powerful. Loving and merciful. 'Ask, and ye shall receive' and all that, right? But it isn't true. At least, not all of the time. Not for some of us, anyway." She was rambling and knew it but seemed incapable of stopping now that she'd started. "I asked for His help. Believe me, I asked. Plenty of times! Not unreasonable, silly things, mind you. Yet never, not *once*, did He answer. I can't help but think—"

"Your parents did horrible, regrettable things. I cannot argue with you about that," Hannah interrupted, "but you had no part in any of it." She gave Julia's hand a light tap. "They made poor choices, but admitting that they could not care for you? It was not one of those poor choices. *That* was a good-for-you choice."

Dozens of times, Granny had said as much before the Commonwealth took Julia away, though back then, little-girl Julia had no concept of what it meant. Now Julia watched as Hannah fiddled with her bonnet ties, half wishing she'd exercised more self-restraint and kept her sordid story a secret.

"Do you know why Amish women wear hats all the day long?"

"Of course I do," Julia said. "It's because you believe that, in order to pray, your head must be covered. And since you never know when you might be called to do just that…"

Laughing, Hannah said, "I am impressed. How did you learn this?"

"What I didn't learn from watching you, my friend, I learned from life itself. I've lived on the outskirts of Amish communities most of my life. In fact, one of my foster fathers was born Amish."

"Ahh," the woman said. "Shunned?"

Words like "outskirts" and "shunned" had always awoken unpleasant feelings in Julia. No surprise, really, since that's how she'd felt most of her life.

"You often come into my mind, Julia, and when you do, I pray for you."

Julia cleared her throat. "I…well…thank you…."

"May I be blunt?"

Julia grinned, because it seemed to her that Hannah had already been blunt! "I suppose."

"Ah, there it is again…the wary look of a nonbeliever." Hannah took a deep breath. "To tell you the truth, I would expect someone with so much book learning to be smarter." She didn't wait for Julia to respond. Instead, Hannah launched into a full-blown lecture:

"You may have inherited the eye color of one parent or the height of the other, but inside"—she patted her own ample bosom—"inside, you are not like them at all. This I know from watching closely when you are with my own children." She leaned in and narrowed one eye. "I always know that I can trust you with any of them, because you have a good head and a good heart and good instincts, too. So this…" Hannah waved her hands. "So this 'I might not be a good mother' nonsense…" She slapped the table. "That is what it is…just nothing but nonsense!"

Julia knew it, too…on a conscious level. She'd taken the required psych courses in college, studied about misplaced hostility and other destructive behaviors. But book knowledge and what a person believed, she'd learned, were two entirely different things. "Feels good to know you care." And it did, right down to the soles of her shoes.

Hannah shook her head then folded both arms across her chest. "Make no mistake, Julia, my words were not intended to make you feel good." Shaking a maternal finger, she added, "God put this little speech on my heart months ago, and ever since, I have prayed that He would tell me just when to deliver it."

Julia's watch beeped. "Goodness. I'd better get supper started. Your family will be in soon, hungry after their hard day."

But Hannah seemed not to have heard the chime or Julia's words. "Will you be seeing Simon tonight?"

The question came from out of nowhere, flustering and confusing Julia, who couldn't understand why her heart began pounding at the mere mention of his name. "No…no, I don't think so. It'll be late by the time I get back and—"

"You know, don't you, that God does not approve of wastefulness."

Julia could only sit blinking. "Wasteful—"

"He has brought you two together for a reason. Nothing He does is without a reason. Don't you see?"

"I don't mean to be obtuse, but I'm afraid I—"

On the heels of an exasperated sigh, Hannah said, "Simon will make a good husband, and he will be a good father. Do not waste this opportunity!"

How could Hannah possibly know what prompted the tough decision she had made, days ago, to spare Simon a lifetime of heartache? "What might seem a good opportunity for me," she said, "might not be so good for poor Simon."

Hannah clasped Julia's hands between her own. "Poor Simon, indeed." Hannah clucked her tongue. "You already know, I am sure, that he had a wife?"

Julia nodded.

"Her name was Georgia. A very elegant lady with very fancy tastes. She did not want babies, though Simon would have moved the mountains to change her mind. He decided, I think, to be satisfied with a life that did not include children and put everything he had into pleasing her." Hannah groaned. "He told me not long after her funeral that his biggest mistake as her husband was not being stronger, especially on that important subject. At the time, I did not know what he meant. But when he began hanging around here more, to be near Rebekah and Seth and especially Levi after her passing, I figured it out: If she had given him a child or two, he would not have felt so alone once she was gone."

Julia made no effort to hide her disapproval. "Now really, what kind of loving and merciful God would tear Simon's world apart like that? Why didn't God save her? If Georgia had *lived*, she might've changed her mind and given—"

"Spoken like a true Englisher," Hannah said matter-of-factly. "God called her home because her work here was done." She shrugged. "Would she have taken children as God's blessings, had she not died?" Another shrug. "Only God knows, but I do not believe so."

Julia wanted to say that things weren't that simple, but something told her Hannah would have disagreed wholeheartedly.

"God loves you, Julia. I believe it saddens Him to know you have so little faith, so little trust in Him."

Though Julia failed to see what her faith—or lack of it—had to do with her relationship with Simon, she said nothing.

"You have told yourself the same lie so many times that you believe it yourself!" Hannah blurted.

Lie? What lie? Julia prided herself on being honest, on telling the truth....

"You think that because of what your parents were and how they died, and because a very sick and sinful man attacked you, you do not deserve a man like Simon!" She slapped the table again. "It is rare that I give in to frustration, but I'm ready to give up!"

"Um, sorry," Julia whispered.

"If only it were as plain to you as it is to me. Any man would be blessed to have a wife like you. And the children God would grant you? *They* would be blessed, too." Suddenly Hannah was on her feet, heading for her makeshift parlor bed. "I am tired," she said, "and I feel the need to pray."

It didn't take a genius to figure out that Hannah hadn't exaggerated when she'd said their conversation had frustrated her. *Should have kept your big mouth shut*, Julia told herself. Baring her soul might just have cost her a dear and beloved friend.

Halfway across the kitchen, Hannah paused and pulled Julia into a big, warm hug. "You are such a dear, dear young woman, Julia." She held her at arm's length and gave her a gentle shake. "Your life could be so different, so wonderful, if only you would trust in our God! Promise you will pray on it?"

Relief at knowing that Hannah wasn't angry prompted instant agreement from Julia. It had been a long time since she'd spoken with the Almighty on her own behalf, so long that Julia didn't have the faintest notion where or how to begin. But amazingly, for the first time in many years, Julia wanted to try. "You'd better lie down before you fall down," she said, smiling. "Before I start supper, I think I'll see if William and the children would like a cool glass of water."

Hannah laughed. "Just take care," she warned, "that they do not talk you into helping with those pigs!"

Chapter Thirteen

....

During a previous visit to the Gundens', Simon had arranged to take Levi to the sanctuary. And though both Hannah and William had hesitated at first, he'd convinced them to agree by saying the boy might learn things he could put to good use on the farm. Besides, he'd told them, what better way for a boy to spend a summer day? But when he arrived, Levi sat alone on the top porch step, his chin resting on a fist as he stared at the horizon. "Hey, big guy," Simon called from the pickup truck, "why the long face?"

"I am punished," Levi said on a sigh. "Again."

Simon sat beside him. "Uh-oh. What did you do…this time?"

Levi heaved a huge breath. "It was not what I did, but what I said…I guess. Papa claims my mouth is fresh…but I do not know what that means."

The boy shrugged as Simon slid an arm over his slender shoulders. "My dad used to say that, too. It means you've spoken out of turn or said something disrespectful." He gave the boy a sideways hug. "Or both."

"I got mud and dung on Mama's clean kitchen floor," he explained. "I got thirsty, doing chores, and went inside for a drink."

"And forgot to wipe your feet?"

Levi nodded. "And when Mama chased me with the broom, I told her she took God's Word too seriously."

Simon hid a grin. "I don't get it."

"Do you know the Bible, Doctor Thomas?"

"Not as well as I should," he admitted, "but I can recite a verse or two."

"I heard the bishop say once, 'He that spareth his rod hateth his son, but he that loveth him chasteneth him betimes.' That is from the book of Proverbs."

"Uh-huh…"

"I asked Papa what it meant, and he said that parents who love their children cannot be afraid to punish them. So I told Mama, 'A broom is not a rod, and besides, is mud on a clean floor really a beating offense'?"

Chuckling, Simon hid his eyes behind one hand. "Oh, wow, kiddo, you sure know how to pluck your parents' nerves, don't you?"

Levi met Simon's glance and, blinking bright, innocent blue eyes, said, "It seems that way." Another deep sigh, and then, "Can you keep a secret?"

"Sure I can."

Levi leaned closer and, looking left and right to make sure the "coast was clear," whispered, "They were just looking for a reason to keep me home, if you ask me."

"Oh?"

"They did not want me to go with you today."

Simon had gotten the same impression.

"They are afraid, I think, that if I see too much of your world, I will not want to live Amish."

"Oh, I don't know about that," Simon reassured. "You're a little young yet to make a decision that big."

"I am old enough to know I would not like living English. This life is plain and simple, and I like it just fine." He pursed his lips, as if searching his young mind for words to back up his statement. Instead, Levi said, "Maybe Miss Julia will go with you to visit the wolves."

It was Simon's turn to sigh. "That's what I'd hoped. But she has gardening chores to catch up on."

"Can you keep another secret?"

"You bet, kiddo."

"There is a bigger reason I am punished today. A better reason than dirtying a floor." He clasped and unclasped his tiny hands. "Mama caught me eavesdropping, you see, and…and when she caught me at it, I fibbed."

"Bummer," Simon acknowledged, nodding sympathetically.

"Miss Julia was here, and I heard her tell Mama all about her life as a little girl." He scratched his head. "Did you know her mother and father got rid of her when she was just *three*?"

Simon wanted to hear more. "Is that right…?"

"Just like the Englishers who drop cats and dogs from their automobiles to run free on our farm!"

"Sad, isn't it, how cruel people can sometimes be."

"Her grandmother and grandfather took care of her for a while, but only until some teacher in town decided that it was not good for Miss Julia to live with forgetful old people who could burn the house down." Levi's eyes filled with tears. "I do not know who is worse," he said around a quivering lower lip, "the mama and papa who threw her away…or the Englishers who took her from her grandparents."

Simon had said dozens of times that Levi had an old soul, and it never seemed truer than at this moment. That he could so completely grasp the gravity of the situation at his young age was amazing enough, all by itself. But for the boy to have put himself in Julia's shoes? "You're some kid, you know that?"

But Levi seemed not to have heard the compliment. "Poor, poor Miss Julia." After knuckling his eyes, Levi drew his shirtsleeve across his nose and sniffed. "Good thing Seth is not here."

"Why's that?"

"He would call me a baby if he saw me sitting here crying."

"That's only because he's a little jealous that you're so wise and so sensitive."

"I am sad for her. For Miss Julia, I mean."

"Me, too," Simon admitted.

"I can almost see her as a little girl, crying because she had no mother and no father, and then some mean lady she did not even know came to take her from the only people she *did* know and brought her to live with strangers."

Memory of the photo Simon had seen in Julia's powder room flashed in his mind…a tiny, pretty little thing in ruffly socks and hair bows…. It was enough to make even a grown man cry.

"I do not wish to live English," Levi said quietly. "And I suppose parents only punish their children because they love them."

"Definitely. Your mom and dad love you a ton. You're one lucky kid."

"Definitely," Levi echoed. Then, "Do you know what I think?"

Simon grinned. "What do you think?"

"That you should marry her."

The sudden conversation shift shocked Simon so badly, he couldn't help but laugh. "Think so?"

"She needs a family," he said, holding out one palm. "And you need a family," he added, extending the other. "I am just a child, but even to me it seems like a good solution to both of your problems. And besides, you are both English. What could make more sense?"

Simon would have agreed without hesitation, would have jumped up and headed for her place, if he believed she'd agree, too.

Logic, common sense, caution, and reason combined to throw doubt on the idea. Nice as sharing his life with her could be, Simon didn't have the foggiest notion of how to go about making it happen. Or if it should, for that matter, since he still wasn't certain of God's intent for the two of them.

"Well?" Levi said, interrupting his reverie.

"Do you think if I had a word with your folks, they'd change their minds? About your punishment, I mean?" He hoped that Levi's powers of concentration weren't as lax as his own and the abrupt change of subject would steer the boy in a different direction.

"Ha!" Levi said, cupping his chin in a palm. "Not a chance. No, I am in deep trouble this time. Up to my knees, as Papa would say." He aimed a mischievous grin at Simon. "But thank you for wanting to try."

"Hey, what're friends for?" Simon got to his feet and ruffled Levi's hair. "Maybe we'll go to the sanctuary another time."

"Maybe." Levi stood, too, and mimicked Simon's spread-legged stance. "Are we really friends, Doctor Thomas?"

"'Course we are. What a question!"

The boy's smile lit up his whole face. "Thank you. I am honored."

"Me, too." And Simon meant it. On the day this delightful kid was born, he'd locked eyes with Simon the moment he drew his first breath…and smiled. Gas? Couldn't have been when the baby hadn't had a meal yet! Yes, Levi Simon Gunden had been a special kid right from the get-go. "Well, guess I'd better head out. Tell you what, I'll take some pictures at the sanctuary and show 'em to you the next time I stop by." Which would be soon, if Simon had anything to say about it.

"I would like that." Levi took his place on the top step and, hugging his legs, buried his face between his knees. "I would like it very, very much."

As he steered the pickup onto the highway, Simon had a feeling that, for days, he'd see that adorable face every time he blinked.

* * * * *

It had taken stubborn determination, but after a half hour of struggling, Julia managed to open the shed's rusted padlock. Once inside, a look at shovels and rakes that weren't in any better shape forced her into town to buy replacements. And the minute she unloaded her car's trunk at home, Julia hauled every bucket and mud-caked garden glove from the ten-by-twelve-foot structure and gave it a thorough cleaning, right down to the eight-pane window on the back wall. Now, with huge sacks of bark mulch lined up along every garden bed, she set about the arduous task of removing years of thick weeds from around the foundation.

At noon, dirty, sweating, and exhausted, Julia headed inside for a quick sandwich and something cool to drink. She'd just sat down when the phone rang. It rang again a second time as she decided whether or not to answer, and by its third shrill peal, she grumbled an annoyed "Hello?" into the receiver.

"Hey, pretty lady."

The breath caught in her throat as her heart hammered. "Simon," she said, trying to hide the tremor in her voice. "How've you been?" She couldn't help being happy to hear from him. And couldn't help feeling bitter regret about what she had to tell him—the sooner, the better.

"Excellent. Just got back from the sanctuary. They've got a passel of cubs over there. You would've loved 'em…."

"Oh, wow, that's right. Matt said last time that they'd be old enough to cuddle this week. So, tell me, are they fat and adorable?"

The delicious sound of his laughter filtered into her ear. "Yeah, guess you could call them fat and adorable…and not too happy with me right now."

She couldn't imagine anyone or anything not being overjoyed to spend time in his company. "Why not?"

"Exams, vaccinations, ear cleaning, worming…not pleasant stuff for little critters, especially wild ones."

"Wish I could've been there."

"Me, too."

Had he read her comment to mean she'd wanted to see *him*? "I could've helped out," she said, hoping to sound convincing.

"Oh. That. Yeah. An extra set of hands would have been useful."

She heard him clear his throat.

"So did you finish your yard work?"

"Good grief, no. Between rusting locks and rusting tools and a filthy shed, I've barely made a dent."

"Bummer," he said. "I was hoping you'd join me for lunch."

The wall clock read 12:25. "I just took a break, as a matter of fact, and sat down for a good old-fashioned ham on rye when the phone rang."

"Oh. Sorry," he muttered. "Want me to let you go so you can eat?"

"Don't be silly. I mean, it isn't like you're going to talk all afternoon, right?"

"Right. No. 'Course not." He cleared his throat again. "So how about dinner, then? As I recall, you've still got that rain check to cash in…."

Everything in her wanted to scream, *"What time should I be ready?"* Instead Julia said, "I'm a filthy mess, with at least three hours' work left to do outside…."

"Bummer," he said again. "Guess you'll have to take a rain check on that rain check, huh?"

"Or we could have dinner at seven or eight instead. I should be finished and reasonably presentable by then." Julia wrapped the phone cord around her forefinger, wondering what on earth had prompted her to say that. Nothing even remotely like it had been in her mind. At least, not in her *conscious* mind.

"You've made my day."

Suddenly, planting the bright yellow magnolias and red zinnias she'd splurged on at the nursery didn't seem quite as important. Ditto for pulling the weeds. "I'll leave the mowing for first thing tomorrow. That way if that beat-up old machine has sat idle for too long, I'll have time to drive into Lancaster for a new one."

"I have an extra one in my barn. It's yours if you want it."

"It's awfully nice of you to offer, but—"

"You'll be doing me a favor. It's just in the way out there. I'll throw it in the bed of my truck as soon as we hang up. Just remind me it's back there when I get to your place, so I remember to off-load it for you."

"Are you sure?"

"Positive."

"At least let me pay you for it…."

"Don't be ridiculous. Like I said, you're doing me a favor by taking it off my hands."

Her brain warned, *You're gonna think of him every time you use that mower,* but her heart countered, *Exactly, and won't that be great!*

LOREE LOUGH

His voice ended the argument. "See you at seven thirty, then?"

"Okay."

"Good luck in the yard."

"Thanks."

She didn't want to hang up, and it appeared that neither did Simon.

"Careful not to overdo it."

"I won't."

"First time in the yard can raise ugly blisters. Ask me how I know...."

Okay, she'd play along. Anything to prolong their good-bye. "How do you know?"

He chuckled. "Well, now you've caught me flat-footed."

"Flat-footed?"

"It's been years since I worked outside. I hire a neighborhood kid to mow and trim. He's pretty handy with a planting spade, too."

"Well," she said with a smile, "I'll be careful all the same." The last thing she wanted were ugly red blisters ruining the fun if he decided to hold her hand. *Don't be an idiot,* scolded her brain. *Have you already forgotten your promise?*

Oh, let her enjoy his company just once more before it's over, her heart chimed in, *you killjoy.*

"Will you be wearing those little sandal-like shoes you had on the other night?"

"The black pumps, you mean?"

"I have no idea what shoe genre they fall into. All I know is, they're cute as can be on those itty-bitty feet of yours."

The heat of a blush crept into her cheeks. "You know," she pointed out, "one of us has to be first to hang up."

"You."

187

"No, you."

"Why me? Obviously, you're the mature one in this relationship."

Relationship? Julia bit her lower lip. "I could argue the maturity point, but that would only extend the conversation. And I'm burnin' daylight over here."

"Okay, on the count of three."

"Agreed."

Together, they said, "One, two, three."

Silence. Then Simon said, "Hello?"

"So much for mature, eh?" If it was this hard to hang up on him, how much harder would it be to tell him she could never see him again…except as a friend?

"G'bye Julia."

"Bye."

"I mean it."

"So do I."

He snickered quietly. "Seriously. I'm hanging up now."

"Well, I should hope so."

"Seven thirty…"

"Seven thirty."

When the dial tone buzzed in her ear, Julia's shoulders sagged as Hannah's words rang in her ears. *"Talk to God,"* she'd said. Maybe, somewhere amid the hoeing and planting and watering, she'd put in a word or two with the Big Guy.

Couldn't hurt, said her brain.

Couldn't hurt, her heart echoed.

With a sigh and a grin, Julia headed outside, wondering if

maybe the problem all along was that God sometimes grew weary of listening to ditzy, silly females like herself.

* * * * *

Since he had time to kill, Simon decided to spend it on the Internet trying to find out all he could about Julia's past. Clearly she had no intention of sharing any of the details. If he wanted answers to his questions, well, he'd just have to get them himself.

An hour into his investigation, Simon still knew nothing. Frustrated, he dialed Casey's number.

"You want me to *what*?" his cousin said.

"You don't really expect me to explain the whole thing again, do you?"

"No. Just stalling," Casey said, "so I can come up with a legitimate excuse to say 'Go take a hike.' "

"Very funny," Simon said, laughing. "Now, seriously, how long will it take you to get here?"

"What makes you think I can dig up more on the poor girl than you did?"

"You're always bragging about what a computer geek you are. Time to prove it."

Chuckling, Casey said, "No can do today, Simon. I'm on kid duty till six. Joanna is at a baby shower."

"I'll bring my laptop over there, then."

"And I'll put on a pot of coffee. The kids are napping. We're good for an hour, at least, so I'll see ya in ten."

Simon gathered up the few notes he'd taken, grabbed his keys and laptop, and headed for the door. "You guys be good, ya hear?" he told Wiley and Windy. "I'll bring you a special treat to make up for leaving you alone so much lately."

The cat and dog sat side by side, staring at him as he turned on the TV. "Aw, don't look at me that way. You met her. Do you blame me?"

Wiley yawned and Windy bent in a long, low cat stretch. "Man, curb your enthusiasm," he teased, punching the remote's numbers to select the Animal Channel. "I won't be late," he said, heading for the foyer. "Promise."

Simon closed the door behind him just in time to catch a glimpse of their "yeah, right" grins. It wouldn't surprise him to find out that, while he was gone, they had long, deep discussions about his parenting skills.

An hour and a half later, Simon shoved back from Casey's computer desk. "This is *it*? How can that be?" he asked, scratching his head.

"You've got a lot, if you ask me. I don't know anybody else whose—"

Simon paged through the printouts. "You haven't read a word of this stuff, *cousin*, so how do you know what I've got?"

"Judging by that stack of papers, it looks like a lot." He added in a thick British accent, "Perhaps you can hire Sherlock Holmes to conclude the investigation."

"You know, that's actually a great idea."

Casey leaned back in the desk chair. "You're kidding, right?"

"Serious as a heart attack."

"What's wrong with exercising a little faith?"

Simon frowned. "Faith?"

"You like her, right?"

"Yeah…"

"So go with your gut. What's the worst that could happen?"

She could break my heart, Simon thought.

"You think maybe she's an ax murderer?"

"Of course not."

"Bank robber?"

Simon blew a puff of air through his lips. "Knock it off."

Drawing quotation marks in the air, Casey whispered, "Lady of the evening?"

"With that innocent face? No way."

Shrugging, Casey held out both hands. "They say Delilah had an air of innocence about her, and look how Samson ended up."

"I never did like guys with long hair."

"Okay, I'm just sayin'…"

Casey was the closest thing to a brother Simon would ever have. A cutup by nature, the man had proven over the years that he had a trustworthy, dependable side, too. Maybe he'd made a valid point and the secret to the mystery of Julia was faith, pure and simple.

"You think maybe she has a long-lost husband out there somewhere?"

Simon laughed. "Nah. She ain't the cheatin' type."

"So what's your problem, then? If you're so all-fired certain she's too sweet and innocent to have committed any crimes, and she's too purehearted to have a spouse hidden away someplace, what is it you need to know about her, exactly?"

As usual, Casey's straight-shooting approach went right to the heart of the matter. "You make a good point," Simon admitted. Thanks to the Internet and Levi's prying ears, he had far more information than before. Besides, if he quit asking her to talk about bygone days, it would show her how much he trusted her. The only question remaining? How to prove to Julia that she could trust *him*.

Simon unplugged his laptop and snapped the lid shut. "Thanks, cuz. You're the best."

Just then, the kids' voices and footsteps sounded overhead. "Oh great," Casey complained. "Abandon ship now that the pirates have invaded."

"I'd stay, but I've got dinner plans."

"With Julia?"

"None other."

"Gonna ask her to marry you?" It was Casey's turn to elbow Simon's ribs.

"Not tonight."

His cousin's eyebrows shot up and his eyes rounded with disbelief. "So…but…you're gonna? For real?"

"Honestly, I have no idea. Pray on it, will ya?"

"Count on it." He opened the door and, as Simon passed through, Casey added, "When are we gonna meet this amazing, unreal mystery girl?"

"Soon," Simon said with a wink. "If I have anything to say about it, real soon."

* * * * *

He'd expected good things, but this good? Simon licked his lips when she opened the door, stunned into silence by the vision before him. "As I live and breathe," he said, "you're gorgeous."

She blushed, making her look even prettier. As if that were possible. "Thanks."

"You oughta wear that color more often. Very flattering," he said, presenting her with the bouquet he'd picked up on his way over.

"Daisies," she cooed, sticking her nose into the blossoms. "You remembered." *See?* Simon said to himself. *Another thing you already know about her.* "So what do they call that color, anyway?"

She smoothed the sides of her dress, reminding him yet again what a curvy little figure she had.

"It's coral. I think. Or peach." Shrugging, Julia laughed. "Let's err on the side of caution and call it some variation of orange."

"Boy, I'll say one thing about us."

Julia stepped aside as he entered the foyer.

"We could win a small-talk contest."

Crooking a finger as she headed down the hall, she said, "Come with me while I put these in water."

"People are gonna talk," he said as she filled a cut-glass vase with water.

"About…?"

"About why in the world a babe like you is out with the likes of me."

"I'll say one thing for you…." She poked flower stems into the water. "You save me money."

Maybe a guy really could get dazzled by a woman's beauty to the point of being addlebrained. "Uh, come again?"

"Who needs to wear blush with you around?"

Simon walked around behind her and whispered in her ear, "You deserve to hear stuff like that a couple hundred times a day."

"Simon, really now, I—"

"Hey, I don't do it for *you*, you know."

She turned halfway and looked into his eyes. "Really…"

"It's for Him," Simon told her, aiming a thumb at the ceiling. "I figure even God likes hearing 'Good job!' every now and then."

Smiling, Julia clucked her tongue. "Well, I'm finished here." She put the vase in the middle of the kitchen table.

"Heard on the drive over here they're calling for thunderstorms."

"Oh no," she said, leading the way to the door. "Not again."

" 'Fraid so." He took her keys and locked the bolt for her before handing them back. "Guess that means dessert in front of the chiminea?"

A strange expression clouded her face, making Simon wish he had a talent for reading minds the way she had a talent for switching moods. When he was alone later tonight, he'd study those printouts, looking for—

"I didn't know you had a sports car."

"That old thing?" He opened the passenger door. "It's been gathering dust in the garage for years. Thought I'd better take 'er out and give 'er a little air." And then he added, "I didn't forget about your lawn mower, by the way. I figured I could bring it by tomorrow, on my way to church, if that's okay."

Nodding and grinning in response, Julia slid into the leather bucket seat. "Why do you call it 'her'?"

He ran around to his side of the car and started the motor. "Hear that?" he said. "She purrs like a kitten, doesn't she?"

Julia only smiled.

"And she's persnickety. When she's not in the mood to purr, she growls like a tiger. And sometimes she just flat-out decides not to make any noise at all."

"Aha. I think I'm beginning to get the picture." Laughing, she added, "May I ever so politely point out that subtlety is not one of your best-honed conversational skills?"

You may, he thought, grinning. Because he hadn't intended subtlety at all. In fact, he'd hoped it might open the door to a discussion about her *own* mercurial moods.

* * * * *

After arriving at the historic Revere Tavern and Restaurant, Simon suggested they snack on the crab-dip appetizer while waiting for their steaks. When she admitted how much she'd always loved crabmeat, he said, "Baltimore's only a little over an hour from here. They're best in the fall, so maybe one Saturday we'll drive down there. I know a place where they make the best steamed crabs on the East Coast."

How had she let things get so out of control? There he sat, making plans for a future that could not, would not take place. She wouldn't spoil his dinner, since he'd told her on the way over how much he enjoyed eating at the Revere. Instead, when he took her home, she'd let him build that fire in the chiminea, just as he'd suggested. He'd need the warmth to counteract the cold, hard facts about her…and Julia didn't intend to leave out a single detail. That, she decided, would kill two ants with one stomp.

So with her plan firmly in mind, Julia settled back to fully enjoy her last meal with this wonderful, amazing, perfect man.

"Tell me about your family," she said when the waiter brought their appetizer.

"Spoiled only child, I'm afraid, so there's not much to tell."

"Your parents must be very proud of their son the doctor."

Simon only chuckled.

"Do they live nearby?"

"Not anymore."

Now who's being evasive? she thought, smiling to herself. Funny, but he didn't seem to like being on the receiving end of a full-blown inquisition….

"Snowbirds, are they?"

A good-natured chuckle emanated from deep inside him. "No, they haven't migrated to Florida, like so many retirees." He took a sip of his ice water and said, "Mom died of an aneurysm nearly five years ago, and Dad…" He let a deep breath slowly escape his lips. "Dad was diagnosed with lung cancer shortly after we lost Mom. He held on for a little over six months."

Guilt pulsed through her veins, doubling her heartbeat. "Oh, Simon," she said, hiding behind both hands. Then, sandwiching his fingers between hers, she added, "I'm so sorry. I shouldn't have asked. How awful to make you relive such a—"

"Julia," he interrupted, kissing her knuckles, "it's all right. They're with God and His angels, whole and perfect and completely healthy and pain-free. I'm way okay with that. Honest."

Julia wondered if her parents had become believers, as so many of her clients had while in prison. It made her wonder if Simon's folks and hers had met up there in God's kingdom. If Granny had any say in the matter, they had. The idea made her smile a little.

"We have a lot in common," he said, dotting another kiss to the back of her hand.

Funny, but Hannah had said something eerily similar not long ago. She waited for him to tell her what, exactly, he believed they had in common.

"We're orphans, you and I. No parents, no grandparents, no siblings. I've got Casey and his family, and—"

"And Wiley and Windy," she finished for him.

He let go of her hand and said, "Yeah, them, too."

"Which reminds me…I forgot all about our appointment today. I'm so sorry!"

He examined her fingernails and, narrowing his eyes, emulated a German accent. "Where ver you dis ahf-ternoon, Miz Schpenzer?"

"Working in my gardens, just as—"

"Den why iss der no broken feenger-nailz, unt no dirt ground into your skin? I see nuttink!"

Julia laughed. "I discovered the most fantastic invention at the nursery—gardening gloves!"

"Iss dat zo?"

"I watch *Hogan's Heroes* reruns, too, you big nut. And I don't mind admitting, you do a wonderful imitation of Sergeant Schultz."

"Flatterer," he said, poking a cube of sourdough bread into the dip then popping it into his mouth. "It's cool enough to eat now, by the way," he added, scooping a generous dollop of dip onto another cube and holding it near her lips.

She almost giggled when he opened his mouth, the way mommies do when feeding their babies, as she accepted the treat. Her smile faded a little as she wondered if, sometime during the meal, he'd tell her about Georgia. Admittedly, Julia was curious about his first love, the woman who'd shared his heart and his life for—how long had Hannah said?—nearly four years. If *she'd* been his wife, Julia couldn't have denied him anything. Especially not children! How could the woman have said no to something so wonderful?

It surprised her to hear how many loved ones he'd lost. How had he achieved such a complete state of peace?

As she sat considering his history, Simon scooped another generous portion of crab dip onto a crust of bread and held it out to her. Julia had only just leaned forward to take a bite when he said, "You might as well just spit it out, Julia."

"Not on your life," she said around the nibble. "It's too delicious!"

"And you have the nerve to call *me* a nut?" Smirking, Simon shook his head. "I can tell by the look on your face that you're dying to ask me something. So go ahead. Out with it before it drives you even more nuts."

"The longer I know you, the more I believe you're some kind of mind reader."

"If that were true, would I need to ask what you're wondering about?"

"Guess not."

"So ask away."

She couldn't very well say, "So what's your secret? How do you keep from being furious with God when He's allowed so much misery and pain to enter your life?"

Or could she?

Simon's forefinger drew a tiny circle in the air, his silent signal that she was free to open up—the sooner, the better.

"You're right," she began tentatively. "We do have a lot in common. So why are you so… How can you be…so at ease with having lost so many loved ones?"

One shoulder lifted in a half shrug. "It's like I said, they're in a better place, and that's just for starters. I've always been a firm believer that we're all here on Earth to do God's work, for as long as He needs us and not a minute more."

She could only blink in response, amazed at how similar his beliefs were to Hannah's. Was it possible Simon had family ties to the Amish? "You weren't angry or resentful, even at first, when they were taken from you?"

He bobbed his head a time or two. "Oh, I had a few dark moments. More than a few, if I'm completely honest. But I was blessed right from the start with good friends and a supportive pastor who prayed with me. And for me. And before long, anger and bitterness seemed petty and ungrateful. And the instant I let go of all that, I started coping. And healing. I still don't understand it all, and maybe I never will. But I accept things now."

She didn't know whether to admire him or pity him. Didn't he miss having them all in his life? Didn't he want answers to the tough questions, like why God had chosen *them* and why He'd taken each loved one long before their time?

"I miss them, of course," he said, and again Julia wondered if he could read her mind. "I suppose I always will. But with God in my corner, it's easier. So much easier."

She pretended to busy herself by buttering a crescent roll and sipping cool lemony water.

"I have an idea," he said, leaning forward expectantly. "Why don't you come to church with me tomorrow?"

"What makes you think I don't already belong to a church?"

Simon tucked in one corner of his mouth. "Which one? I'll gladly come to yours. I just want to be with you."

"This must be one of those 'gotcha' moments people are always talking about."

"You're wrong. Nobody's judging you, Julia, least of all me. We all make choices about God and church and faith. And we all go to Him at the right place and time. *His* time."

"And you think tomorrow is my place and time, at your church?"

"Who knows. But what can it hurt to try?" His gentle smile warmed the space between them even more than the candle flickering in the center of the table. "If you're not comfortable there, you won't go back. It's a church, not a prison."

Prison? Of all the words he could've chosen, why *that* one? Did he know something about her past, her parents? "Have you seen the Gundens lately?" she asked, hoping he hadn't heard the suspicious edge in her voice.

"I was over there this morning, as a matter of fact. I'd promised to take Levi to the sanctuary, remember?"

Julia nodded. Yes, she remembered.

"Got there only to find out he'd done some mischief and that got him into trouble. In effect, I guess you'd say the kid's grounded."

That touched her deeply. "Oh, poor Levi. I can't even imagine what a sweet boy like him could have done to warrant any punishment!"

"Hey, he's Amish, not an angel." Simon chuckled. "And from what he told me, he earned it."

"What did he do, if you don't mind my asking?"

Simon sat back and, frowning, stared at her for a long, silent moment. Something peculiar glittered in his gorgeous green eyes, something that looked like a cross between pity and confusion and, for a reason she couldn't explain, indecision. It surprised her even more when he avoided her question altogether.

"I told him maybe we'd go to the sanctuary another time."

"Maybe?"

"He didn't seem too convinced that Hannah and William would *ever* let him go."

"But…why not?"

Simon shook his head. "Levi didn't come right out and say it, of course, but he implied that his folks are worried he might get worldly notions, hanging around town with the likes of me."

"Oh, that can't be true. Hannah thinks the world of you, and so does William."

"Oh, do they now?"

What she'd give to be able to know the meaning of those quick-silver emotions flickering across his face! "They've always spoken very highly of you."

"Ditto."

The busboy refilled their water goblets and went on his way. "Ditto?"

"Now don't get any ideas," he said, "but…"

"Ideas?"

Smirking, he added, "More than a few of the Gunden Amish think the two of us would make a good team."

"A good team?"

First looking left, then right, Simon whispered, "Don't tell anybody, but there's a terrible echo in this place."

"A terrible… Oh, I get it. Very funny." But there was nothing comical about the fact that the Gundens had been speculating about whether or not she and Simon would end up together. Speculating with *Simon*. Julia wondered how *he* felt about that and decided to ask him, straight-out.

Two faint frown lines appeared between his eyebrows. "You already know what I think."

"I do?"

"I'm nuts about you, as if you hadn't noticed. When I'm with you, I get all tongue-tied and stupid. And when I'm not with you, I'm so busy *thinking* about you that I get all tongue-tied and stupid. I haven't had a decent night's sleep since we met, because I wake up dreaming of you, missing you. You're on my mind at work, when I'm watching the news, when I'm at the grocery store. I never know when my Julia-crazed brain is gonna ask, 'What would she think of this?' and 'How will she feel about that?' Now really," he said, pursing his lips, "look me in the eye and tell me that all this is a surprise."

Boy, she thought, *when you stick your foot in it, Julia, you don't mess around, do you?* She'd asked Simon what seemed like a simple question and had expected a simple answer. Knowing him as she did, it probably *shouldn't* have been a surprise that he'd go off on a tangent…but it was. As usual, when she couldn't figure out how to deal with an uncomfortable situation, Julia sat quietly.

"Well, good grief, Julia," he said, looking everywhere but at her, "it's not fair to leave a guy hanging this way!" Then he zeroed in on her eyes and, grabbing her hands, added, "Now you listen to me, and you listen good. I know you have some crazy cockeyed notion that something from your past will scare me off and make me wish we'd never met. But you couldn't *be* more wrong, you hear me? I don't give a fig what happened before you and I met. All I care about is the here and now…and the future. I know you well enough to believe you'd never hurt me—at least not deliberately—so it's easy to go forward on nothing but faith."

The waiter approached, carrying an enormous food-laden tray, and Simon waved him away. "Did you *even* hear a word I just said?"

"Of course…of course I did." And thanks to the intensity of his words, so had the diners at every nearby table. Julia's hands acted as blinders to block her view of their inquisitive stares.

"Well…?"

Well, what? she wondered. What did he want from her? By now, her decision to end things tonight was a hazy memory. She tossed her napkin onto the table. Maybe Hannah had been right. Maybe God *did* have a plan for her and Simon. Julia couldn't be sure, but if she let this chance pass her by, she'd never be sure about anything ever again. She'd prayed long and hard about the state of her soul. Each Bible session had drawn her closer and closer to trusting the Lord. Suddenly, Julia's heart started beating faster, and she knew without a doubt that it was time to let go of past doubts and fears and walk in faith.

She leaned in close, so close that their noses nearly touched. "Now *you* listen, you big goof," she hissed. "I'm crazy about you, too. I'm not one to get up on a platform and announce it for all the world to hear, but, yes, I've noticed that you're a bit smitten—"

" 'A bit smitten'?" Simon laughed. "Sorry…continue, O Mistress of Understatement."

"—that you're a bit smitten with me, and God help us both, I've gone and fallen in love with you. Are you happy now?"

"Happy? *Happy?* You bet I am!"

"And don't think it goes unnoticed, mister," she tacked on, "that I said the *L* word, while you only said—"

He was out of his chair and on his feet so fast that his image blurred before her eyes. Before Julia knew what was happening, he'd pulled her up and wrapped her in a big, loving hug. "Man, for a savvy lawyer, you sure can be dense," he said, beaming. "Of *course* I love you. I've loved you almost from the first minute I laid eyes on you, and I'll keep right on loving you till I draw my last breath."

Someone sitting near the windows cut loose with a shrill whistle, and a deep voice by the door bellowed, "Way to go, Simon!" as applause pattered all around them.

"So much for not making announcements from platforms, eh?" she said.

And then he kissed her as he'd never kissed her before. *Dear Lord,* she prayed, *I'll show proper gratitude later, but for now, thanks!*

Chapter Fourteen

....

Julia showed up as scheduled, at six thirty, and just as Simon's secretary snapped the window blinds shut, Julia rapped on the door.

"Sorry," said a high-pitched female voice, "we're closed." Two white metal mini-blind slats parted, forming an eyeball-sized *V*. "Unless there's an emergency." The brown eye gave Julia a quick once-over. "I don't see a pet...."

"I don't have one. Yet," Julia said. "That's why I'm here. To meet with Si...with Doctor Thomas, to choose one."

"Now?"

Julia glanced at her watch, as if the action alone might validate her showing up after-hours. "He said to meet him at six thirty."

The woman muttered something as the blinds snapped back into place. And Julia glanced left, right, behind her, trying to look nonchalant. Where was Simon? Surely he hadn't forgotten that—

Like the answer to an unspoken prayer, the door opened with a *click* and a *whoosh*. "Julia," he said, reaching for her hand, "come on in."

The instant he tugged her across the threshold, he pulled her into a warm hug and kissed her cheek. She might have returned the compliment—and the kiss—if she hadn't noticed an angry blond standing just behind him.

Simon followed her gaze and faced the frowning female. "Debbie," he said, flashing the woman a half smile, "this is Julia. Julia Spencer."

Sliding an arm around Julia's waist, he added, "Julia, this is Debbie, my…ah…my—"

"I'm his secretary, receptionist, bookkeeper, and sometimes assistant," Debbie finished for him. Extending a long-taloned hand, she flashed a small, unfriendly smile.

"Nice to meet you," Julia said, taking the icy red-polished fingertips.

Debbie quickly hid the hand in the pocket of her sweater and aimed a hard grin in Simon's direction. "I didn't see her name in the appointment book."

"That's because this isn't an appointment. It's more like a…" He winked at Julia. "More like an invitation." And to Debbie, he said, "She's thinking about adopting one of our strays."

Chin up and spine stiff, Debbie crossed both arms over her ample bosom. "I see." Raising one dark-penciled brow, she asked, "Can I trust you two alone, or should I stick around and play chaperone?" Debbie cut an icy glare in Julia's direction. "Wouldn't want people *talking*. A girl's reputation is important in a small town."

After a millisecond of uncomfortable silence, Julia realized she'd been standing with her eyes wide and lips parted, like a kid caught with her hand in the cookie jar. *Doesn't take a genius to figure out the woman considers Simon her property,* she thought. A quick look at his stern glare made his disapproval quite clear. "What do you recommend?" she asked Debbie. "Cat or dog?"

Debbie rolled heavily mascaraed eyes and sighed. "I'm not the person to ask," she snapped. "Never had a pet, never intend to get one."

"Why not?" Julia blurted. Then, in response to Debbie's glare, she quickly added, "I figured since you work for a vet, you must love animals— that you'd have a tough time not wanting to take *all* the strays home."

Debbie narrowed her eyes. "You figured wrong. I've got a kid at home and no husband to help raise him. I don't have time for pets or"—she shot an angry glimpse at Simon—"dating."

"Are the charts filed?" Simon asked.

Julia heard the ire in his voice and said a silent prayer for Debbie. If his posture and tone were any indicators, the woman was in for an earful in the morning.

"I didn't quite finish, but I'll get to them," Debbie said. "We had that emergency today, don't forget, and that threw me off schedule."

Simon grabbed her coat from the wall rack and walked behind her, his not-so-subtle hint that she should leave. Now.

Bristling as she stuffed her arms into it, Debbie said, "Such a gentleman. Thanks, Doc. See you at nine?"

He was halfway to the door before he answered. "You bet. Actually, why don't you come in a half hour early so you can catch up on that filing. I'll pay you double-time."

He didn't wait for her to respond. Instead, he opened the door and held it until she stepped outside. "Tomorrow isn't your carpool day, so it won't be a problem, right?" And with that, he closed the door—and locked it.

"Sorry about that," he told Julia. "She's a…" He shook his head. "Suffice it to say that she's a long, long story."

"Personally," Julia said with a grin, "I've never been a fan of horror stories, but I'll listen to that one, if talking about it will keep you from having nightmares…."

"Nut," he said, pulling her into his arms. "Man, you look gorgeous," he whispered. "I was up half the night thinking about you."

She hadn't slept much either. In all her years, Julia had never felt this way about a man. She'd *thought* she'd been in love a time or two, but after her frightening experience in foster care, she'd always talked herself out of relationships before they had a chance to develop. For the first time in her life, she wasn't afraid to admit how she felt, wasn't afraid to show her true feelings, wasn't afraid of being judged inferior or tainted or—

"You really *don't* have a romantic bone in your body, do you?" he asked, laughing.

"Ah…I…" Julia frowned. "What?"

"I just admitted I was up all night thinking about you. You're supposed to reciprocate, you little nut."

"Oh." Julia giggled. "Okay." And because she knew he expected her to say "Ditto" or "Me, too," or echo his words to the letter, Julia stood on tiptoe, wrapped her arms around his neck, and kissed him square on the lips, fully expecting him to return it with gusto.

He caught her totally off guard when, instead, he started to laugh. It began quietly, emanating from deep inside him, then bubbled up and overflowed until he'd tipped his head back to fully vent his merriment.

"And you say *I* don't have a romantic bone in my body?" The sound was contagious, and it took a healthy dose of self-control not to join in. "You must really trust me," she said, tilting her head slightly. She gave him a moment to process her words, acknowledging that she trusted him more than anyone since Granny or Gramps.

"I read someplace that guys rarely expose their throats this way. Dunno why, exactly," she continued, lightly dragging her fingernails across his Adam's apple. "Must have something to do with a deep-seated fear of—"

"Julia," he said, boring into her eyes, "did anyone ever tell you that you talk too much?"

"Only you."

"Then shut up and kiss me again."

"But what about the adoption? Shouldn't I—"

His gentle lips silenced her, and as she absorbed the warmth of his arms and the tenderness of his kiss, Julia thanked God for sending her this wonderful man, this wonderful love. She hadn't been old enough to understand how blessed she'd been when Granny and Gramps had been part of her life. But Julia was old enough now to praise Him for these gifts.

Simon's stomach grumbled just then, sending her into a fit of giggles. "Didn't you eat at all today?" she asked, still standing in the protective circle of his arms.

"Didn't have time. My 'secretary, receptionist, bookkeeper' made so many mistakes, I spent half the day picking up the pieces."

"Then what say we save the pet adoption for tomorrow," she suggested, patting his stomach, "and get something into that belly of yours before every critter in here has a panic attack."

"Panic attack?"

"How would you react if you were a defenseless animal, alone in a cage, in a sterile clinic environment…and you heard growling like that?"

"I won't keel over for at least a half hour. That's plenty of time for you to choose a housemate."

What would he think if he knew she'd like nothing better than to marry him and make *him* her housemate?

"All in good time," he said, taking her hand.

Julia's heart thudded. Had her emotions been that visible?

"You can't do it all in one night, of course," he continued, leading her into the back room. "But you can at least get a sense for whether you'd like a dog or a cat."

"Or both," she said, quoting what he'd told her not so long ago.

The instant he flipped on the light in the next room, the barking and meowing began. Julia bit her lower lip, grieving already for the dozens of loving animals pacing near their cage doors that she couldn't take home with her.

A small gray-striped tabby sat watching Julia, its big green eyes glowing like marbles. It tilted its head then poked a forepaw through the bars.

"What're you doing?" she asked it, leaning closer. "Waving hello, or trying to shake my hand?"

She stuck out a finger and stroked the soft fur. "How old is this kitten?" she asked Simon.

"That isn't a kitten," he said. "She's nearly three years old. Someone left her on my doorstep, literally, with a box full of other kittens."

"Where are the others?"

"Gone. Years ago." Simon opened the cage and scooped the tabby into his arms. "But nobody adopted this one."

"But she's so cute!" Julia said, scratching between the cat's ears.

"Until you walked in, she never came near the cage door before."

Julia's hand froze, and when it did, the loudly purring feline rubbed a cheek against her palm.

"She always hovered near the back of the cage," Simon continued, "doing that flat-eyed 'Don't mess with me' thing cats are notorious for." He shrugged and handed the tabby to Julia. "Guess she was waiting for Miss Right to walk by, too."

Too? she repeated mentally.

"Oh, don't look so puzzled. You already know I'm nuts about you. And so is Mouser, here."

The cat snuggled into the crook of Julia's neck. "Mouser?"

"At the first sign of a rodent, I let her roam free for a night or two." He snapped his fingers. "And that's the end of the problem."

Looking into the cat's eyes, Julia said, "Maybe he should've named you Killer, then!"

The tabby replied with a happy meow and went back to purring.

"I want her," Julia said. "Can I take her tonight?"

"No, you'll need some supplies first. Litter box and litter, food, bowls, a bed, some—"

"She won't need a bed. Mouser will be sleeping with me." She hugged the cat. "Won't you, cutie pie?"

"Julia, I hate to break it to you, but cats have minds of their own. This little critter here might just have other ideas."

"All right. I'll get her a bed. But you'll see…she'll prefer cuddling up with me to sleeping alone."

"Tomorrow after work," he said, taking Mouser from her arms, "I'll take you to the pet store for bowls and a bed and stuff. I'll set you up with some of the food she's used to so her adjustment will be easier. She's had all her shots, and she's neutered. Plus, she's been microchipped so that if she ever wanders off or gets cat-napped, any vet in the nation can read the numbers and contact her owner—*you*."

"I hate to leave her," Julia said, fighting tears as Simon closed the cat's cage.

"She'll be just fine for one more night. This has been the only home she's known for years."

Julia's gaze swept up and down the aisle at the dozen or so other cats and dogs that watched them from inside their own cages. "How long have the rest of them been here?"

Simon pointed at a cocker spaniel. "She's been here about six months. The German shepherd? Just over a week…"

As he went down the list, naming breeds and the length of time spent in his clinic, Julia's eyes filled with tears. "How do you do it?" she asked, sniffling. "How do you go home every night, knowing they're here all alone?"

"It isn't easy," he confessed. "But the truth consoles me. If they weren't *here*, they'd be out *there*, abused, neglected…or worse. I make time for all of them every day. And I've got a few schoolkids who volunteer to stop by and play with 'em whenever they can."

Simon headed for the door and laid his hand over the light switch. "Living here isn't the best life they could have, but it sure beats the alternative."

She pulled a tissue from her coat pocket and dabbed at her eyes. "Something tells me you will have a very special place in heaven, Simon Thomas."

He turned off the light and closed the door behind him. "Maybe. But if that's true, then everybody who has adopted a pet and given it a loving home will be right there beside me."

The plight of these homeless creatures made Julia think of the wolves at the sanctuary, each stolen from the wilderness to satisfy humans' desire to play zookeeper despite regulations that make it illegal to raise wild animals. Whether or not their intentions were pure at the start, they discovered all too soon that the beautiful beasts needed fresh meat—and lots of it—and quickly grew from adorable cubs into enormous animals too powerful to handle. "I need to get to the sanctuary. With my crazy court schedule and Hannah's miscarriage, I haven't been there in *weeks*!"

"Let's go now."

"Now? But, Simon, it's seven o'clock, and you haven't had supper!"

He shrugged into his coat. "We'll grab something on the way."

"The staff will have left for the day, and it's nearly a half hour's drive each way...."

"Ninety-nine percent of the staff are volunteers, but Matt's there twenty-four hours a day, seven days a week. Besides," he said, "the wolves do their best howling in the dark."

So far, Julia's visits to the wolf sanctuary had been during the day, and the rare wolf howl had been an electrifying, exhilarating experience. But to stand amid the sanctuary's wooded acres under a coal black sky? A shiver snaked up Julia's spine at the prospect. "Can we stop at my place first so I can grab my boots? We can slap together a couple of sandwiches while we're there...."

Simon leaned back and gave her a quick once-over. "Yeah, I guess high heels aren't exactly 'hiking the grounds' footwear, are they?" He pulled her into a hug. "But I'd sure like to be the guy you call on to warm you when your feet get cold."

"You accomplish that," she said, kissing his chin, "just by being there."

* * * * *

He'd seen her with the wolves before, so Simon shouldn't have been surprised at her reaction.

The faint light of a crescent moon illuminating her gorgeous face, she looked for all the world like a child visiting a toy store for the first time. He didn't think she could look more beautiful than when she gasped quietly behind her fingers in response to the first haunting notes—when her big eyes filled with tears and her lower lip quivered as she reached for his hand.

"Oh, Simon," she whispered, "it's…it's like a haunting melody. I could listen to it forever!"

He'd had a pretty good life with Georgia, but she hadn't shared his love of animals and definitely didn't "get" his fascination with the wolves. Julia, God bless her, she got it. Better still, she got *him*. Unable to speak, he hugged her from behind, content to stand with his eyes closed as he buried his face in her thick auburn waves.

She leaned her head against his chest and hugged his forearms to her waist. It felt good, holding her this way. Felt *right*. His earlier doubts about God's intentions for the two of them vanished.

Somehow she'd managed to deal with Debbie without insulting her. He'd been putting up with the woman's nonsense for weeks now, giving her a paycheck for work she didn't do. But tonight, when she'd mistreated Julia? Well, that had been the last straw. Casey's neighbor or not, she'd crossed the line, and tomorrow he'd spell things out nice and clear. He'd give her two weeks to shape up or—

"Why so quiet?" Julia asked.

"Just…" He knew only too well that with that big heart of hers, she'd come to Debbie's defense if he told her the truth. "Just counting my blessings." It wasn't a fib, exactly, because he did consider her a blessing. A big one. Simon kissed the top of her head. "Warm enough?"

"It's an inside-out thing, so yes, I'm more than warm enough."

He turned her slightly, needing to see her face, needing to look into her eyes. "An inside-out thing?"

She turned slightly and laid a hand on his cheek. "You've touched me, Simon. All my life, I've been afraid of one thing or another, of being rejected, of being judged." Nodding toward the tree line where Casper and Fawn paced, frustrated by their lone wolf status, she sighed again. "I was just like them…always on the outside looking in. Always wanting acceptance. Never thinking I deserved it."

He held her tighter, hoping with everything in him that he *had* made those differences in her life, because she'd sure made a big difference in his!

Julia wriggled free of his embrace and stood beside him. She slipped an arm around his waist and leaned her head on his shoulder. "There are things I need to tell you, Simon, things you need to know if we're to…if we're to—"

"All I need to know is that you love me."

She patted his side. "Then let me rephrase things. There are things *I* need you to know about me. It's because I love you that I believe you deserve to know the truth—all of it." She inhaled a long, shuddering breath. "Because if you can still claim to love me after you know everything?" She nodded. "Then I won't just hope it's true, I'll *know* it is."

Wolf songs echoed all around them as storm clouds gathered overhead. Soon, the bright glint of starlight and moonlight went as dark as the blanket of night that held them aloft.

"Ever hear of the Internet, Julia?"

Her quiet laughter tickled his ears. "Of course I have. What's that got to do with—"

"Have you ever had occasion to dig into a client's background?"

He felt her stiffen, heard the breath catch in her throat. "Many times," she said tentatively.

"Well," he said, tightening his hold on her, "it just so happens I own a computer with access to cyberspace."

The night grew deathly still—so quiet that Simon heard her breathe, heard her blink, heard her swallow.

"Is that your way of saying you had me checked out?"

Gripping her upper arms, he forced her to meet his gaze. "No, I didn't 'have you checked out.' " Kissing her forehead, he added, "I did it myself. Considered paying a company and decided against it."

"So you know? About my parents? About the kind of people I'm descended from?"

"They made mistakes. Stupid mistakes. Big mistakes, and lots of them," he said. "The biggest was giving you up." He kissed her again. "But before they got all tripped up on drugs and booze, before they started committing crimes to provide for their habits, they were good kids."

Julia blanched. "And what about the molestation? Did you read all about the big investigation that happened because of me?"

"Investigation?"

"Into the foster care system. The county turned their office upside down, spent months hammering other foster families after they found out what my foster father had been doing to me." Shaking her head, Julia stared at her shoes. "If it hadn't been for an observant teacher…"

Her voice trailed off as she bit her lower lip. Simon prayed that God would provide him with the wisdom to know whether it was good for her to get this off her chest or harmful to bring it all back into the present.

"They put me in the hospital, so they could prove their case against him. And kept me there until they could find a family with room for 'a troubled young girl.' "

Her voice didn't hold the bitterness Simon might have expected. Instead, she seemed relieved that the truth was out—even the most agonizing truth about her past. She continued. "And did your investigation tell you the authorities had to let him go?"

"No," he said quietly.

"One of those 'my word against his' scenarios. I can hardly blame them, now that I understand the law. I mean, what were they to do without a shred of evidence to back up what I said after my teacher filed the report? He was a virtual pillar of society. A family man. A deacon in the church. Naturally they believed him over a kid who'd been bounced around by the system for years."

Julia exhaled a shaky breath. "He died years ago, in a drunk driving accident. Fortunately, no one else was hurt."

"If he hadn't, I'd be tempted to kill him myself." Simon's quiet voice shook with emotion.

She looked away, toward the stealthy shadows of Fawn and Casper. But Simon needed her to look at him, so she could see with her own eyes that every word he was about to say was the truth. He cupped her chin and brought her face back into line with his own. "You aren't like those lone wolves, Julia, and you aren't like your parents. You grew up practically on your own, and look how you turned out! I'd bet anything that you blame yourself for what that creep did to you, like your parentage gave him an excuse to violate you. And I'm here to tell you you're wrong, one hundred percent." He bracketed her face with both hands and stared into her eyes.

"Do you think for one minute if your 'defective DNA theories' were true, you could have become an upstanding, successful young woman all by yourself?"

She felt so small, so vulnerable, standing there in his arms, that he wanted to find the people who'd had the audacity to call themselves her parents and box some sense and reason into their self-centered heads. If someone had told them about the damage their actions would cause their innocent, good-hearted child, would they still have led such selfish lives? *Probably*, Simon thought, but none of that mattered now. They'd paid for their sins.

Julia had asked nothing of life but to belong, to be accepted and loved, and to love in return. And he wanted nothing more than to provide her with proof that those things had always been hers for the asking. How sad that, believing she'd been contaminated by her parents' sins, Julia had never felt worthy to ask.

Simon said all that and more, adding, "You inherited only their best qualities and none of the worst."

She wanted to look away again; he could feel her trying to distance herself, trying to avoid his eyes.

"I know the whole story, Julia, and none of it matters a whit to me. In fact, I love you *more* because of what you've endured, what you've survived! I can't tell you how much I admire and respect you, because you're stronger than—"

Simon never finished his litany of compliments, for Julia silenced him with a well-timed, tender kiss that outlasted the long lone howl that pierced the night.

Chapter Fifteen

....

From early autumn to Thanksgiving, an overcrowded court docket made finding time to spend with Simon a challenge. She found herself wishing for extra hours to share with the love of her life, and her wish had been granted.

She'd met Casey and his family at church—her church now, thanks to Simon—and they'd invited her to share Thanksgiving dinner at their house.

"You sure you want to volunteer to bring dessert?" Simon tossed a loaf of bread into her grocery cart. "You like rye, right?"

"Love it," she said. "Of course I want to bring something. It's the least I can do."

"Did Casey tell you there are never fewer than twenty-five people around their table on Turkey Day?"

"Twenty-five!"

"Sometimes more."

She gaped at the lone can of pumpkin filling in the bottom of her cart. "Guess I'll need a few more of those, won't I?"

He popped a noisy kiss to her cheek. "Takes a lot to rattle you, doesn't it?"

After they paid for the groceries, he drove her home, and Julia thanked him for taking her to the store.

"Happy to do it," he said, helping her off-load bags from the bed of his pickup. "I'd offer to help with the baking, too, but I have a couple of appointments this afternoon."

Julia made him a sandwich to eat on his way to the clinic and sent him on his happy way, laughing when half of the sandwich was gone even before he fired up the truck. She spent the rest of the day baking cookies and pies and cheesecakes and spent the evening wondering aloud during their late-night phone call how she'd get all of it to Casey's house. "Leave it to me," he said before hanging up. And sure enough, it was Simon to the rescue on Thanksgiving morning, with cardboard boxes and a freshly scrubbed pickup truck bed.

Dinner was delightful, as were Simon's relatives—and the two dozen friends who'd happily crammed into the narrow dining room. A light snow was falling when they drove away from Casey's, making Julia glad they'd taken his four-wheel-drive pickup instead of her sensible sedan. "The roads will be a mess by morning," she said, slouching in the passenger seat. "Sometimes I'm tempted to move to Lancaster just to avoid that highway drive to and from the courthouse every day."

"Yeah," he said, patting her hand, "but then you wouldn't have that big beautiful house to come home to."

"And I'd be farther from you."

"Well," he huffed, "that goes without saying."

She'd always loved her house. Work-related stresses and the cares of the day wafted from her mind the minute she set foot in the quaint foyer. And now, with a purring, chirruping Mouser to greet her? Traffic to and from Lancaster was a small price to pay for peace and joy like that!

She'd managed to foist most of the leftover desserts on Casey's dinner guests, left some for Casey and his family, and still ended up bringing home a pie, half a cheesecake, and a huge bucket of cookies.

"My freezer isn't big enough for all this stuff!" she wailed, staring at all the food spread across her kitchen table

"Should have thought of that before you decided to make like the Pillsbury doughboy."

Grinning, Julia clucked her tongue. "Thanks for your support." Then, "I have an idea…. You can take some to the clinic and give cookies away to kids and parents who bring in pets for checkups."

"And you can do the same at your office. Now, how 'bout if we have a slice of pie right now?"

She glanced at the clock. "It's nearly nine!"

"So?"

"Déjà vu?" she said, grinning.

"No, no sanctuary tonight. Even Matt takes a day off every now and then." He hugged her. "I just don't feel like saying good night yet."

"I miss you already, and you're not even gone?"

"Something like that."

They shared a cup of herbal tea and a slice of pie as Mouser purred in Julia's lap.

"So, is she sleeping in the bed you bought her?"

"Nope. What a waste of money!"

"Hey," he said, glancing at his watch, "do you realize it's ten forty-five?"

"I know."

"What's wrong with us?"

Julia shrugged. "Pie addlebrained, I think."

Chuckling, Simon got to his feet and put their dishes into the sink. "That's as good an explanation as any. Better than saying we're lovesick."

Hand in hand, they walked to her front door. Julia buttoned his jacket then pulled the collar up.

"Sleep well."

She opened the door. "Goodness, look at how much snow fell since we got back! There must be a foot and a half on the ground!"

He hunched into the wind. "Can't remember the last time it did this on Thanksgiving."

"Be careful."

"Lock up tight once I'm gone." He gave her one last kiss. "Don't want the wind blowing snow under your door."

"Call me once you're home, so I know you got there safely."

He snapped off a smart salute and grabbed the doorknob. "Get inside before you catch your death. I love you," he said, closing it before she could respond.

"I love you, too," she hollered through it.

Julia did the dishes and decided to have one last cup of tea before heading up to bed. Hopefully sleep wouldn't elude her too long. She hugged herself as the wind rattled windowpanes and sent crisp leaves skittering across the porch. The lights flickered then dimmed, and in a blink, the power went out completely.

Snow-thunder boomed as Julia scampered around, lighting candles and oil lanterns. Thankfully she'd had a cord of wood delivered just last week, and the day before, a chimney sweep had cleaned years of creosote from the stovepipe. As soon as she got into her PJs and robe, she'd build a toasty fire, make up the sofa bed, and wind Granny's ancient alarm clock. Only one thing could improve the nearly perfect early-winter night…

…but Simon was halfway home by now.

* * * * *

Leave it to Julia, he thought, pulling into her driveway, *to make a house look warm and cozy even on a storm-riddled, no-electricity night.* Smiling, he locked up the truck and long-stepped through the drifting snow to her front porch.

She'd built a fire in her woodstove, and whiffs of the peat-scented smoke permeated the frigid air, reminding him of all those nights they'd sat talking near her chiminea—though the weather had been balmy back then.

Habit made him press the doorbell's button. "Idiot," he laughed to himself when it didn't ring. He knocked on the leaded glass sidelight beside the heavy oak door. "Julia," he called. "Julia, honey… it's me, Simon."

His ear craned near the window, he heard Mouser inside, alternately meowing and chirruping. "Hey, kitty…go get your mommy. Tell her there's a nice man out here freezing his fingers off on her porch."

The unrelenting wind wailed and bawled, threatening to blow Simon off balance. Shivering, he knocked again, harder this time. "Julia…open up! It's like a blizzard out here!"

He saw her shadow on the other side of the glass and heard her sleepy, timid voice. "Simon?" she said as the door opened. "What on earth…?"

"Tree's down. Huge one. Must be a hundred years old, if the size of that trunk is any indicator. It's completely blocking the road, and I can't get around it. Nobody can. Must be a dozen cars down there trying to figure out which way they'll go."

"Well, goodness gracious sakes' alive," she said, grabbing his sleeve, "come in here, will you, before I'm forced to chisel you from the floorboards!"

She slammed the door behind him and immediately began tugging off his wet gloves, scarf, and baseball cap. "Get out of that coat," she said, frowning as she hung his things on the coat rack. "Shoes and socks, too. I've got a nice hot fire going in the family room. Stand there and warm up while I get you one of Gramps's sweaters."

"But…I haven't brought back the last stuff you loaned me."

"Oh, what a feeble protest," she teased, giving him a playful shove toward the hallway. "Now what's your preference…cocoa or herbal tea?"

"You built a fire, lit the lanterns, *and* made cocoa?"

Smiling, Julia shrugged. "I almost made tea, but then I got to remembering that night you made cocoa…."

"Man, oh, man," he said, hugging her, "God broke the mold when he made you."

"Unhand me, sir, or I'll be forced to call a constable!"

Laughing, Simon stood back. "Unhand… Call a…call a *what*?"

"Seems the appropriate choice, since we're living like it's 1800. And since it seems you're stuck here for the night, I need to change into something…into something proper."

Ah, now that his brain had thawed some, she was beginning to make sense. Some puritanical sense of right and wrong had raised its self-righteous head, making her think her attire might look provocative. He resisted the urge to chuckle, because he thought her modesty and old-fashioned notions were adorable. "Julia," he said, arms spread to emphasize his point, "you're covered up more right this minute than you were last spring when we walked along the river. Why, I saw your bare arms that night. And your naked knees, let's not forget!"

She hugged the shawl collar of her fuzzy robe tighter around her neck. "It was warm outside then," she said, more than a little defensively. "And besides, that's entirely beside the point."

Julia was halfway up the stairs when she leaned over the railing to say, "Soon as I change into sneakers and sweats, I'll fix you that cocoa. And if you're a very good boy, I'll put a dollop of whipped cream on top."

Grinning, Simon stared after her, wondering what—in her old-fashioned-girl opinion—he'd have to do to qualify for "good boy" status. With a shrug, he decided to follow orders and headed for the family room.

Her woodstove boasted a rectangular window in its door, and when he caught sight of the fire's amber radiance, it became easier still to follow Julia's instructions.

She'd tossed a fading, frayed afghan onto the couch cushions, and the Good Book lay open on the end table. Mild curiosity made him wonder which of the poetic verses in Isaiah she'd been reading.

He heard her padding down the wooden stairs and pictured her tiny white-socked feet. What made her think she'd be less alluring in sweats than in her thick pink robe? The woman was femininity personified—not even a suit of armor would have hidden that fact—but Simon would humor her.

Carrying two gigantic mugs into the room, she placed one on the table beside the recliner and one at the end of the couch near the Bible. "This is your bed for the night," she said, pointing as she opened the ancient wooden trunk beside the big leather chair. "It opens almost flat, so you can stretch out and catch a few winks." Julia pulled out a thick cream-colored blanket and hung it over the arm of his recliner. "We're stuck here in the family room, I'm afraid, since the woodstove is our only source of heat until the power comes back on."

Simon wondered where the fuse box was in this aging farmhouse. If he knew, he might unscrew every one of them to ensure that the lights and heat would stay off even if the power came back on. He grinned to himself at the thought. "That's fine," he said, sipping his cocoa.

"Will Wiley and Windy be okay, home alone?" She cuddled on the far end of the couch and hugged her knees.

"They'll be fine," he said, releasing the recliner's footrest. "I filled their food and water bowls before I left this afternoon, and Wiley can get outside through the doggy door."

"Windy won't use it?"

"Nope. Stereotypical scared-cat, that one." He chuckled then scanned the room. "Where's Mouser, speaking of cats?"

Julia lifted the corner of the afghan. "Voila!"

"I guess that's one good thing about her being declawed. She can't tear up that old thing any worse than it already is."

"Hey, what're you calling an 'old thing'? My gran made this for me," Julia said, sliding it onto her lap, "when I was a wee girl of four." Her smile faded when she added, "I couldn't take it with me when…"

Her voice trailed off, and he sipped some cocoa, hoping she'd continue, uninterrupted.

"When I got home, it was nice to find it, all folded up and smelling like lavender, on my bed."

"Bet it was something to behold when it was new."

A dreamy, wistful expression lit her face as she stared into the fire. "Oh, it was. Scraps from every old sheet and towel, every dress and shirt she could get her hands on, every square hand-stitched onto a thick flannel blanket."

"Bet it's warm, too."

Nodding, she fingered the threadbare satin trim then got to her feet with the afghan draped over one arm. "See for yourself." She covered him with it. "I won't take no for an answer," she said, taking the blanket she'd set out for him.

"But Julia…"

"But Simon…"

He knew what that quirked brow and half smile meant and held up his hands in mock surrender. "Your house, your rules." And just for fun, he tacked on, "But if you change your mind, it's—"

"I won't." Then, "I promised myself earlier that this would be the very last night I'd use it. It's too tattered and worn to be washed, even by professionals. So…I'll have to muster up the backbone to do what I should've done years ago."

"Seems a rotten shame."

She sipped her cocoa. "I have a transistor radio in the kitchen drawer. Want me to get it? I could probably find a station that plays some good 'snowed in' music."

"Nah." He didn't mind that she'd changed the subject. The lull in conversation gave him time to mull over the idea that had begun to brew in his brain. "I'd much rather listen to the music of your voice."

"I sure hope they get that tree out of the road by morning. I have to be in court at nine…."

"I wouldn't worry about it. If that mess out there keeps up, they'll have to cancel it, anyway."

They spent the rest of the night that way…Julia curled up on the sofa and Simon stretched out in her grandfather's well-worn recliner…talking and laughing, scheming and dreaming about their future together.

One day soon, Simon would stop by the jewelry store in Paradise and see what sort of rings they kept on display. And while he was in that part of town, he'd drop off her grandmother's afghan at the framers' shop. The trick would be getting the thing out of her house without her noticing….

Julia would fuss and croon over her engagement ring, but he knew in his heart that no diamond would compare to having that treasured possession of hers forever protected and framed under glass.

Chapter Sixteen

....

Paradise still shimmered with the last remnants of Christmas decorations. Whistling as he walked down the street, Simon drove his hands deeper into his coat pockets and withdrew them occasionally to return the friendly waves of the shopkeepers he passed along the way. Shoulders hunched against the cold wind, he wondered how long it would be before the garlands wrapped around every lamppost blew loose and slithered down Main Street like shimmering snakes.

White plastic snowflakes and silvery stars suspended from street signs and overhead power lines clanked merrily with nature's blustery breaths, and the two-inch blanket of snow that had fallen on New Year's Eve still lingered in heaps and piles alongside the roads and sidewalks and glittered in the noonday sun.

What a gorgeous little town, Simon thought, smiling. What a gorgeous day. What a gorgeous *life* he had since Julia agreed to share it with him! He hadn't felt this good, hadn't been this happy since long before Georgia's diagnosis. He sensed that she would have approved wholeheartedly of his relationship with Julia, and the knowledge filled him with calm and peace about the future.

"Doctor Thomas! Doctor Thomas!"

He'd have recognized the voice anywhere and turned to see Levi halfway up the block, bundled in a muffler and mittens, poking his head out the side of William's dark gray carriage. "Hey, kiddo!"

he called back. "Better watch out…you'll get a windburn on your cheeks, hanging around that way!"

The boy glanced at his father, whose patient grin told Simon he was about to get an earful of youthful Amish wit and wisdom, delivered straight from Levi's lips. "That's what all the Townies say!"

Laughing, Simon shook his head as William guided the horse parallel to the curb in one of several parking spots reserved for Amish buggies. Even before his father's boots hit the pavement, the boy hollered, "I will wait here for you, Papa."

"But, Levi, it is cold."

"Under this coat, Mama put two sweaters and two pairs of pants on me this morning." He wiggled his own booted foot to add, "And three pairs of socks. I can barely move my toes!"

"As you say, then. But stay in the buggy. I will be back soon," William muttered before disappearing into the hardware store.

Simon continued walking toward his clinic. He'd pay for those extra moments at the bakery, sipping coffee and munching hot-from-the-oven blueberry muffins. No doubt there'd be a short line of patients outside the—

In the reflection of a shop window, Simon noticed three teenage boys lurking near the intersection, two blocks back. Something about the way they stood, peering up and down the street, caught his attention. Everything about them seemed eerily out of place on this beautiful, snow-sparkling morning, and a sense of unease and dread settled over him. Simon thought he recognized two of the three as owners of pets who came to him for treatment for the animals. He thought the third boy looked like Michael Josephs, whose reputation for vandalism, assault, and breaking and entering had long been a

topic of gossip throughout Paradise. His age, Simon knew, was the
only thing preventing WGAL-TV news from reporting his crimes.

They were up to no good, that much was clear, and knowing it
set Simon's teeth on edge and raised the hair on the back of his neck.
No doubt they aimed to pull some mean-spirited prank on William's
horse and buggy. Simon had seen enough of that to know how costly
their graffiti might be and how terrifying it could be for the horse.

Simon turned, intent on marching right up to those rascals and
giving them a piece of his mind. Burning Amish barns and shooting
livestock and frightening horses, overturning carriages, and hurling
stones and cruel words at the gentle farmers was bad enough. But
Levi was in the back of *this* buggy. If these delinquents had decided
to pick on an Amishman, they'd picked the wrong day.

One of the two kids he'd recognized noticed Simon looking
their way and pointed at him. A series of nods and gestures quickly
followed, telling Simon they understood that he aimed to have a
cross word or two with them. The one who looked like Michael lifted
his chin in defiance, as if daring Simon to interfere with whatever
mischief he and his minigang had planned. "Nobody can do anything
about it," he yelled, "because Clapes are stupid and too chicken to
press charges!"

Simon hated it when ruffians like these referred to the Amish as
"clapes." Bad enough they'd chosen the hard-sounding nickname.
Worse still, when their acts of aggression were so frequent, even the
cops referred to the abuse as "claping."

The boys on either side of the portly one shook their heads and,
hands in the air as if in surrender, backed slowly away. They hadn't
gone three feet before the leader stuck his hand under his down-filled

jacket and locked onto Simon's gaze…a bold, vicious glare that chilled him more than winter's biting winds.

In the back of his mind, Simon was aware of the big clock in the square, ticking off the seconds:

Tick: sunlight, glinting from a glass bottle…

Tick: the white rag in its mouth, riffling in the wind…

Tick: a cigarette lighter, sliding from the boy's pocket…

Tick: its aluminum lid snapping back…

Simon ran toward the boy, his boots thudding over the ice-and-snow-patched sidewalk as…

Tick: the wick ignited as the boy held the bottle high above his head…

Tick: the golden liquid sloshing inside the bottle glinted in the sunlight…

"Gasoline…" Simon said under his breath. And understanding what it meant, a coarse "Nooo!" growled from him as the flaming bottle flew, end over end, closer, closer to William's buggy.

Something gleamed silver inside it. Bolts? Nails? Had this crazy kid actually built a crude bomb? Running full-out, Simon bellowed, "Nooo!"

In one eyeblink, the fiery bottle landed with a quiet *think* on the buggy's front seat. Simon, arms outstretched in the hope he could right it before the flaming rag-wick reached the gasoline, raced for the vehicle. In the next, the bottle rocket fell onto its side, instantly igniting the fuel and spewing fiery liquid, nails, and screws in a hundred different directions. The cutting wind whistled through the buggy's windowless doors, fanning the flames, and in the next instant, the floorboards, walls, even the ceiling were afire.

The startled horse reared up, trumpeting with fear, then thundered down the street, dragging the blazing buggy behind it. As it passed by him, Simon felt the wave of heat left in its wake; at the same moment, he heard Levi's plaintive voice shrieking in panic and pain.

Shocked shoppers, tourists, and store owners stopped in their tracks. But Simon barely noticed. "Somebody call 911!" he roared. *"911!"*

When the horse tried to round the corner, it snapped the harness and breastplate. Freed from the fiery buggy, it quickly disappeared from view. For a precarious moment, the buggy teetered on two wheels before it continued down Main Street, its now-loose reins flapping like black ribbons…until it crashed headlong into a parked car.

"Find William Gunden!" Simon shouted to no one in particular. "The boy's father…he's in the hardware store!" Already blue-orange flames licked low-hanging tree limbs above the buggy as Simon closed in. Shrugging out of his coat, he plowed through the billowing tornado of thick black smoke and draped it over Levi's scorched clothes. Gently lifting the boy into his arms, he grimaced when he had to tug a bit to separate Levi's trousers from the melting vinyl seat.

Blond-lashed blue eyes fluttered open, crinkling slightly at the corners as Levi recognized Simon. "Doctor Thomas," Levi rasped around a feeble smile.

"Shh," Simon told him. "Help is on the way." He slumped to the curb, cradling the child in his arms. Things looked bad, real bad, and Simon considered the possibility that even if an ambulance arrived in the next instant, it might be too late. Poor Levi looked like a human pincushion, thanks to dozens of carpenters' nails that had been added to the gas-filled bottle. Shards of glass protruded from his chest, thighs, and throat. Thankfully, his face had been spared from the daggerlike projectiles and sizzling heat, and Simon could only presume God protected it to spare Hannah and William from having to carry that grisly image with them for the rest of their days.

"Hurts," the boy croaked, "hurts everywhere…very much…."

"Levi," Simon interrupted, lightly pressing a finger to the child's lips, "please don't talk, son." Fear and agony sparkled in the boy's eyes, and Simon resisted the urge to gently lay a palm over them. "Shh," he said again, rocking forward and back, forward and back. His heart thumped as the enormity of the situation engulfed him. In one beat, he felt sadness and regret that he hadn't reached the buggy sooner—in the next, unbridled, blinding rage toward the boy who had committed this hateful act. "Shh," he repeated, "save your energy for—"

His voice trailed off as he wondered what, exactly, he expected Levi to wait *for*. Simon had never been a fatalist, had always believed in holding onto that last web-thin thread of hope. But things looked bleak. He'd seen the mutilated bodies of deer, of cats and dogs that clung to life after run-ins with speeding cars and trucks, but Simon couldn't remember an instance when a living being looked closer to death without actually being dead. How ironic that the same fluid that powered those vehicles was also responsible for this unspeakable crime.

Tenderly clutching the now-shivering little body tight to his own, Simon closed his eyes and prayed for words that would comfort Levi. But none came. A great sob ached in his throat, yet he couldn't give in to it. Not when the suffering child huddled against him needed reassurance and strength, needed to believe help *would* arrive soon to ease his excruciating pain.

A small crowd had gathered, but Simon barely heard their shocked gasps and moans. He heard just one voice: "I…I am afraid," Levi sputtered. "Is…is Mama coming…will she soon…be here?"

"Don't you worry, little Levi, you'll see your mama soon enough." Simon felt no guilt for the bold-faced lie. Instead, his guilt came from knowing that Hannah wouldn't be with her boy again on this earth because *he* hadn't reacted fast enough when he spotted those boys clustered on the street corner. Hadn't run fast enough to catch the bottle of fire. Hadn't reached the buggy in time to pull Levi to safety.

Where was William? And the paramedics! Had anyone responded earlier, when he'd hollered for someone to fetch the boy's father, to call 911? *Get word to William, Lord*, was his silent scream, *so Levi will have at least one parent with him when—*

He couldn't finish the thought.

Simon felt dampness on his lap and, without looking, knew that Levi's blood had soaked into his trousers. The snow between his boots, pushed toward the curb by a Paradise plow, had gone scarlet, and much as he wanted to put pressure on Levi's wounds, there were simply too many, and he couldn't stop the steady flow.

"Will you…pray?"

Oh, Levi, Simon thought, *Levi, please don't ask that of me*. "Help me, Lord," he whispered, his face tilted to the heavens. "Help me comfort him."

The instant the words exited his lips, Simon knew what Levi needed to hear.

Soon, the heartrending tones of his lone baritone floated on the frigid winter wind. He didn't remember having sung the song before, yet somehow he knew the lyrics as well as if he'd penned them

241

himself. God, Simon believed, had put the words of Isaiah 40:31 onto his heart:

" *'...and He will raise you up on eagles' wings...'* "

Three verses sighed soft into the icy air before a woman stepped closer. Sitting beside Simon, her voice blended with his: " *'...bear you on the breath of dawn....'* " Within seconds, a virtual choir, made up of Paradise citizens and visitors alike, formed a circle around Levi and the grieving man who held him close, their shoulder-to-shoulder bodies blocking the cold wind while they sang in sad harmony: " *'...and hold you in the palm...of his hands.'* "

When the hymn ended, Levi's faltering voice crackled. "So... beautiful," he sputtered, "...like...like the voices of angels...."

The Amish didn't worship with melody and lyric, organ and fife. Maybe that explained why these sweet strains plucked a restful chord in Levi. The Lord had sent calm in a most unusual way to this small, frail boy, and the proof was written on his now-peaceful features.

Simon hung his head, unable to gaze upon this innocent face a moment longer. *Thank You, Father,* he prayed, *oh, thank You for this miracle.* Dare he hope it was a sign? That the Almighty intended to save Levi despite how bad things looked? That Hannah and William would have years and years to watch their youngest son fumble through adolescence and grow into manhood?

The rude, piercing wails of emergency vehicles interrupted his hopeful prayer, growing louder as they drew closer, while Simon pictured the smirking teen who'd caused this misery. It took every bit of willpower he could muster to unclench his fists and jaw. There would be time enough later to ensure justice. For now, it was more important to put Levi safely into the waiting ambulance, where EMTs could—

"D—Doctor Thomas?"

Simon laid a palm on the boy's cold, pale cheek and leaned in close. "Shh," he repeated. "Can you hear the sirens? They're here to take you to the hospital. They'll fix you right up, good as new. Okay?"

One weak nod was all the answer Simon would get.

Levi grasped Simon's hand and, with a power that contradicted his condition, held on tight. "Are we…are…we really are friends?"

"You bet we are, big guy. I'm so very proud to call you my friend."

Eyes closed, a satisfied smile tugged at the corners of the boy's pale blue lips. Then, "I…I love you, you know. Almost as much as I love Papa."

Grief groaned deep inside Simon, for instead of "I love you," he heard "Good-bye…I'm dying." He knew what the Amish said about death—that when God thought a person had lived out his usefulness, He called him home. Surely that couldn't be the case for Levi. Not yet. He was barely more than a baby!

"I—I love you, too, Levi." And he had, from the day the boy entered this world, to this very moment. And no matter what happened today, he always would. Simon knuckled at the tears pooling in his eyes. *Save him, Lord. Sweet Jesus, save him, please.*

The boy's grip tightened still more as he glanced around, searching the faces that hovered above and mouthing *Mama? Papa? Seth? Rebekah?* And realizing they were not among those gathered, he gave a sad little nod, as if resigned to the fact that he'd meet his Maker today alone.

"Tell them…tell them I am sorry," Levi ground out. "And tell them—"

"Levi," Simon said, giving his shoulders a tender shake, "you have *nothing* to be sorry about!" He gentled his tone to add, "You have a job to do, kiddo…and that's to concentrate. Hang on, little buddy. Stay with me, you hear, 'cause you're gonna be fine, just—"

"No," came his hushed reply. "It is time."

"Aw, c'mon, now," Simon said, faking a goofy grin. "How can you say a thing like that? Why, you're nothin' but a wet-behind-the-ears little pip-squeak, for the love of Pete!" He gave him a hug then kissed his chalky cheek. "You be quiet now, you hear me? Be quiet and let the paramedics and doctors do their thing. Got it?"

"Psalm…cha–chapter eight, v–verse two…"

Simon knew the verse well but had no intention of reciting it. At least not now. "Levi, I'm not kidding," Simon said, shaking a paternal finger under the boy's nose. "You're supposed to mind your elders, so you quiet down and rest, so—"

He felt the boy stiffen, saw him grimace and try to lift his head. Simon's efforts to blink back hot tears failed in that moment. "Levi," he croaked past an aching sob, "I'm not kidding! Be still. Be quiet. Lie back and—"

" 'Out of the mouth of babes and sucklings,' " Levi recited in a pure, clear voice, " 'hast thou ordained strength because of thine enemies, that thou mightest still the enemy and the avenger.' " He grew quiet for a mere moment as one corner of his mouth lifted in a sad, slow smile. "I will miss your silly jokes, Doctor Thomas," he said. "I will miss *you*."

And then his tiny body went completely slack.

"Oh my," wept the woman who'd sat beside Simon.

"How awful," said another.

"Heartbreaking…"

"Tragic!"

"Who did this awful thing?" someone demanded.

"Those punk kids," said another voice. "I saw them, running, when the buggy caught fire. And the fat one was laughing…."

The next voice Simon would have recognized anywhere:

"What is this?" William asked, shouldering his way through the crowd. "What—"

His words stopped as surely as if a hangman's noose had tightened around his throat. A myriad of expressions darted across his rugged, bearded face, from bewilderment and disbelief to concern…and unabashed grief.

And in those same silent seconds, Levi's soul left him. His gaze, still locked on Simon's face, proved the truth of his final words. On his lips, the elfin grin that Simon had come to know and love, forever frozen in time.

Knowing Levi was beyond pain now, Simon drew him into a fierce hug and buried his face in the bloody, hand-knitted scarf wound round his neck. What began as a muted murmur grew in volume and intensity until every man and woman stepped back. "Nooo," he moaned. "Not Levi. Why Levi? *Why*?" Sobs wracked Simon's body as tears splashed upon Levi's angelic face. His mournful "Nooo!" echoed from every window and wall on both sides of Main Street.

A light snow had begun to fall as William took hold of Simon's forearm. "Get up, Simon Thomas," he said. "Get to your feet now, and give me my boy."

Simon heard the agony in William's stern command. The man had shared home and hearth, workdays and meals, laughter and chastisements with this child, every day for nearly six years. If the loss had impacted Simon this deeply, how much more lamentable must it be for the boy's *father*?

An ambulance and squad car jerked to a halt not ten feet from where the buggy still puffed smudgy spirals of smoke into the cloudless blue sky. Even if the day had been a gray and stormy day, the sight would have looked alarmingly out of place.

He thanked God for the men and women who answered official questions in his stead, for it took all the strength he could muster to grind out a pathetic, "I'm sorry, William, so, so sorry," as the man took his boy's limp body from Simon's arms. "I wasn't fast enough...."

"Will you drive us to the undertaker's, Simon?"

The simple question snapped him to attention. Horse long gone and his carriage destroyed, William had no transportation. Leave it to an Amishman to put his grief into perspective, to consider what must be done. "Of course," Simon agreed. "Anything…" He could see on the man's haggard face how desperately he wanted to be home with Hannah, with his other children, but this first stop was a miserable necessity.

Feet planted in the blooded snow, William raised his bearded chin. "I will wait here," he said, staring into his boy's face, "while you fetch your truck."

A moment later, when Simon parked at the curb, several uniformed officers stepped up, intent on taking the boy to the hospital, getting witness statements, arranging for an autopsy. But William was adamant. "No!" he grated, "no hospitals. No autopsy. We can easily see what killed him." He put his back to them. "My family and I, we will handle this in our way. *God's* way," he stated.

"I'll come to the station later," Simon told the nearest officer. "For now, let him go. And let me help him."

Every policeman present had lived in Paradise long enough to know that the Amish had rules for things like this. Nodding, each stepped back, making room for William to carry the lifeless body of his youngest son to Simon's pickup.

It wasn't a surprise, really, when the man climbed into the truck bed. He sat with his back to the wheel well, holding Levi close and dipping his head, his face hidden in the shade of his wide black hat brim. It would have been warmer in the front passenger seat, but Simon understood the man's need for privacy in these last minutes with his son.

It was a short drive to Brown Funeral Home. Simon could have parked out front, where the red-and-blue strobes of emergency vehicles, reflected in every shop window, were clearly visible. Instead, he drove around back and, girding himself for yet another look at Levi's battered little body, hurried from the cab. "I'll go inside," he said as William scooted from the truck bed, "and get old man Jakes to roll a gurney outside."

William's black hat dipped further as he nodded his agreement.

Minutes ago, Simon had loped up the street, counting his blessings and listing the ways the little town seemed like a little slice of heaven.

How quickly things can change, he thought, stepping into the dim hush of the funeral parlor, because right now, Paradise seemed like anything but.

Chapter Seventeen
....

Hannah's work-hardened hands trembled as she tucked the quilt under Levi's chin. "He was a good boy," she said, giving it a loving pat, "never asked for much." A shaky sigh passed her lips. "Just a quilt…"

Her quiet confession reminded Julia of that day in the café, when Levi had teasingly asked why strangers had his mother's beautiful creations on their beds but he did not.

"Just a quilt…"

Julia rested a hand on her friend's forearm and gave a slight squeeze. Throughout the day, Hannah managed to hold her composure through dozens of compassionate embraces and soothing words offered by family, friends, and neighbors. But this gentle touch unlatched the gates of Hannah's carefully guarded heart, and the usually stoic woman fell sobbing into Julia's arms. As her wristwatch counted the seconds, Julia prayed the Lord would help her find the right words to comfort this grieving mother. "You are such a good mother," she whispered, patting Hannah's back. "Levi thought so."

Hannah took one step back and blotted her tears on a corner of her apron. "You…you think he did?"

Julia nodded. "I *know* he did." She recalled the way Levi's face would light up as his mama entered a room or how he put his whole body into every hug he gave to or accepted from her.

"They will take him to the graveyard soon," Hannah said. She gripped Julia's hands tightly. "Will you come?"

"Of course I will." She'd attended Amish viewings before, parking her car amid dozens of horse-drawn buggies outside simple farmhouses. Her comments at each service had been heartfelt, but she'd always slipped away before the funeral. Today, Julia had arrived early to help the neighbor ladies wash dishes, refill bowls of food, and arrange cakes and pies on the very table where she'd shared so many meals with the Gundens.

To get even one invitation to dine with an Amish family was an honor in itself. But by asking Julia back dozens of times—and including her in the family prayers—they'd made it clear she'd become a friend. She treasured the title, so yes, she'd stay.

All day, people came and went, paying their respects and praying over the body of the little boy whose traditional white Amish burial clothes were hidden beneath a crazy quilt of flannel and cotton that more than made up in intricate stitchery and designs what it lacked in bright color.

"I will miss him," Hannah said, tracing one of the feathers she'd sewn into the fabric.

"We'll all miss him. But he took a big step ahead of us, and we're blessed that we don't have to mourn his passing, as people do who have no hope of the afterlife."

For the first time during that long, sad day, Hannah's smile reached her eyes. Clasping both hands at her waist, she said, "Well, listen to you, Julia Spencer. Praise His holy name, for He helped you figure it out, finally." She flung an arm around Julia's shoulders for a sisterly hug. "Am I to expect you'll become one of us, then, and live Plain?"

Difficult as it was to fix her gaze on Levi's gentle, ever-sleeping face, it was easier than telling Hannah that nothing of the kind would ever happen. She didn't have the courage to live as these good people lived, sacrificing modern conveniences, saying no to bright colors and fashionable clothing, enduring the curious stares of tourists. And laying to rest an innocent little boy who died a horrible death because an Englisher had been led by judgmental hatred to kill. Worse still—being expected to openly forgive the boy who had taken Levi from them, because to do anything else was, in their minds, as serious a sin as the killing itself.

No, Julia didn't possess strength of character like that, and never would. But she'd never say so to Hannah. Today, of all days, the woman deserved to be surrounded—and supported—by friends and loved ones who shared her deep grief…and respected her beliefs.

Hannah finger-combed Levi's blond bangs into place then patted his cheek. "At least he is not part of this sinful world anymore."

Julia swallowed the sob that ached in her throat, remembering how those now-forever-closed blue eyes had sparkled with boyish enthusiasm. Oh, what she'd give to hug him one last time or hear one of the silly rhymes he made up to make her laugh.

"It is time," William said, one hand pressing his wide-brimmed black hat to his chest. He'd already donned his winter jacket and held Hannah's with his free hand.

Nodding, Hannah relieved him of her coat. "Would you look at that," she said, pointing.

Julia glanced toward the door, where Simon sat on a long wooden bench between Seth and Rebekah, an arm slung over each of their shoulders. Tears glistened in the children's red rimmed eyes, and in Simon's, too, as he spoke softly, first to one and then the other. "He may not be Plain," Hannah added, securing her black bonnet under her chin, "but he is good to the bone."

He looked up just then, and when his green-eyed gaze locked on Julia, it nearly took her breath away. Oh, how she loved this wonderful, bighearted man who was like a magnet for lost animals and brokenhearted children. He popped a kiss to each child's cheek and then joined her.

"They're leaving for the cemetery now." Watching his jaw muscles bulge and relax as he fought tears reminded her how he'd looked when she opened her door on the night of the accident and found him on the porch, still wearing a bloodied shirt and pants. It had taken him nearly an hour, between bouts of sobbing, to tell her what had happened as she quietly stroked the back of his hand, knowing that words would have been of little value to this man who'd seen Levi take his first breath…and watched him draw his last.

Now, as they stood in foot-deep snow, she patted his hand as he and the rest of the sorrowers squinted into the face-prickling wind, holding hats and bonnets with mittened hands. Those gathered huddled together for warmth, sobbing and crying as the bishop recited hymns in High German. More than an hour later, she watched as Simon mouthed silent prayers and closed his eyes as four strapping Amishmen lowered the small coffin into the gaping hole in the earth. Then more prayers—louder this time, to drown out the grim clatter of dirt being shoveled onto the lid—and, finally, as the men positioned a blank marker at the head of Levi's grave, it was over.

The rattle of buggy wheels and the steady beat of horses' hooves mingled with the fading murmur of departing voices, for although winter's brutal grip had seized Paradise, everyone present had left an assortment of chores behind in order to share the Gundens' loss. The adults had cows to milk and pigs to slop, eggs to gather and meals to prepare, and for the children, lessons to learn in their one-room schoolhouse. Even the Gundens had formwork waiting for them at home, and so the graveyard slowly emptied…

…except for Simon and Julia, who stood side by side near the mound of fresh-dug earth.

"His whole life," Simon said, "summed up by a number on a map of the graveyard in the bishop's office, marking the spot where—"

"Shh," she said, patting his hand. "It's their way. It's always been their way."

And though he nodded in agreement, Simon had made his point: It grieved him deeply that Levi's tombstone would stand stark and bare, just like every other in the small cemetery, devoid of his name or birthday or the date of his death, echoing the Amish belief that no particular man, woman, or child is special in God's eyes—that He loves them all exactly the same.

"It's always been easy before," he said, "respecting their ways, but…" After a long moment of brittle silence, he added, "But this… *this* was…my little *Levi.*" He launched into a short list of Levi's pranks and jokes, and how Levi had yearned to grow up and become a hardworking man like his father.

"Your hands are like ice," she said when he paused. "Let's go to the car, out of the wind."

"Okay," he said, following her across the snowy field. "Did you know other Amish kids his age don't even speak English?"

Simon sounded so proud of the fact that Julia couldn't help but smile a little. "I might have heard something like that."

"They speak Pennsylvania Dutch," he continued, "and don't even begin to learn English until they go to school at six." Simon chuckled.

"But Levi? He's been talkin' a blue streak every bit as well as you and me since he was in diapers." Pausing to fish his keys from his pocket, he sighed. "And smart? Man, he was smart! Picked stuff up just by watching and listening. He told me once, 'I learn a little here, a little there.' "

Once they were settled in his pickup, Simon leaned his forehead against the steering wheel. "Julia," he ground out, "I still can't believe what happened. If I'd spotted those good-for-nothing hoodlums sooner...or if—"

"Simon," she interrupted, "you'll drive yourself crazy with thoughts like that."

But he shook his head. "If I'd have been faster, maybe—"

"What if it had been me that day in town, instead of you?" she asked. "What if I was sitting here, beating myself up because I didn't notice something happening three blocks away, or because I didn't run fast enough? What would you tell *me* right now?"

The longer he stared at her, the deeper the frown line between his brows grew. Unshed tears pooled in his eyes and shimmered on his long, dark lashes. He blinked then reached across the console for her hand. "I'd tell you to knock it off."

"Why?"

"Because I know you, that's why, and there's no way anyone could convince me you didn't try everything humanly possible to..."

His voice trailed off as she squeezed the hand wrapped around her own. "I know you, too, Simon Thomas. There's no way anybody could convince me *you* didn't try everything humanly possible to save Levi." Another squeeze, and then, "So knock it off."

He ran both hands through his hair then leaned back against the headrest, spent.

She got out of the car, slamming the door as he said, "Where are you going?"

Julia jerked open the driver's side door and aimed a thumb over one shoulder. "Out."

"What—?"

"You've been promising to let me drive this ugly old rig since our first date. Time to pay up, buster."

Amazingly, he did as she asked, and as he hiked around to the passenger side of the pickup, Simon said, "Just don't give 'er too much gas too soon. She tends to—"

Julia didn't know why he didn't finish his thought. But instead of asking why, she turned the key and fired up the engine. The original plan had been for him to drive her back to the Gundens' to fetch her car then follow her to her place, where she'd made beef stew for their supper. But her nondescript sedan would be just fine parked outside her friends' barn for the night. Tomorrow she'd hire a cab to take her back there and pick it up. Right now, Julia only wanted to get Simon to her house, in front of a roaring fire, where he could continue reminiscing about Levi's life…

…or weep at his passing, instead.

* * * * *

The weeks passed slowly after the funeral, and though Simon tried hard to behave like his usual jovial self, it didn't take much to remind him of Levi. A child's voice, a toy commercial, even the apple pie Julia made for dessert woke memories of the boy he'd so loved.

He hadn't talked much about it since the night of the funeral, except to whisper, "He died in my arms" or "Lord, why wasn't I faster?" when he thought no one was listening. Often she caught him staring into space, as if he thought Levi might materialize if only he stared hard enough. As Julia saw it, her function was to stand beside him, listening if he needed to talk, remaining quiet when he preferred not to, and pray that soon his melancholy and deep-seated anger would lift.

Then one evening when she answered the front doorbell, he stood on the porch and held out his arms. "Sorry, pretty lady, to put you through all these weeks of me acting like a basket case."

Julia didn't know which felt better—seeing that old familiar grin on his face or feeling his arms around her again. "I just put a potpie in the oven. Hungry?"

He ran his fingers through her hair. "Starved," he said, "for affection." Holding her at arm's length, Simon met her eyes. "Why'd you let me go on and on, feeling sorry for myself all this time?"

"You loved him, Simon, as much as if he'd been your own. Losing him has been hard, and you needed time. Time to hurt and cry and get angry that he left you."

"Left me? Levi didn't leave," he growled. "He was *taken*."

The source of his hostility was Michael Josephs, who'd thrown the pipe bomb. The mere thought of him was enough to alter Simon's entire being, from eyes that glittered with loathing to a face contorted with rage, low-hunched shoulders and hands balled into white-knuckled fists.

She hadn't told Simon the latest about the boy....

When Julia learned that Michael's parents—embarrassed by this latest in a series of scandals—had turned their backs on him, she'd pitied the boy. With no one to post bail, he'd been thrown into jail with a coarse assortment of hardened felons, where he'd stay while awaiting trial. Ironic, she'd thought, that he might be safer there than on the streets…if Simon had his way.

Sooner or later, she'd have to tell Simon that she'd been assigned Michael's case. Would he understand that it was nothing personal? That filing pleadings and preparing for jury selection were routine parts of her job and that Michael had as much right to a fair trial and legal representation as every other citizen of this country? Julia sighed to herself, because if she didn't believe it, how could she expect *Simon* to?

Worrying about how he'd react is what had prompted her to pay her boss a visit weeks ago. "I've known the Gundens for years," she'd explained, quickly adding that she also had a personal relationship with the prosecution's key witness.

"I don't have time for this nonsense," he'd bellowed, slamming his office door. "You're like everybody else in this office, putting in ten- and twelve-hour days because we're seriously understaffed. So grow up, Julia, and dump the Pollyanna attitude. Nobody on our side is the least bit interested in your *relationships*. And you can bet the *other* side ain't gonna complain if it seems you're guilty of partiality." Then he opened the door, her signal to get back to work. "You're outta your mind if you think you're gettin' out of—"

"What's going on in that pretty head of yours?"

The sudden sound of Simon's voice startled her so badly that Julia slopped hot tea onto her hand. Her heart pounding, she grabbed a napkin and dabbed at the spill.

"Come on," he coaxed, "out with it."

Forcing an "I don't get it" expression, she grinned nervously. "Can't a girl's mind stray a little without people thinking there's *stuff* on it?"

"Some girls can, but Julia Spencer?" Simon lowered the recliner's footrest and leaned forward to gently tap her temple. "There's *always* something going on in that head of yours."

She swallowed. Hard. "Must've been nonsense, then, because I…I don't know what you're talking about."

Left brow raised and right eye narrowed, Simon shook his head. "I dunno. From the look on your face, I'd have said you were thinking scary thoughts. Real scary."

Well, it was scary, knowing her job was on the line if she refused the case. And worse—wondering how Simon would react to the news.

Maybe she should just blurt it out, get it over with.

But one look at his weary face told her to wait, let him catch up on lost sleep, give him more time to adjust to life without Levi. If the boy's death still occupied such a huge part of her mind this many weeks after the funeral, how much more must he be in Simon's *heart*?

There were hundreds of things to do before the trial began. Later, as the date drew closer, she'd tell him. And in the meantime? She'd pray as she'd never prayed that the media wouldn't jump all over this story as they had the Amish schoolgirls' shooting years ago.

"I'm in the mood for popcorn," she said, standing suddenly. "How 'bout I make a batch while you stoke the fire?"

Simon got to his feet and pulled her to him. "Something tells me *some*body is trying to evade something important."

Heart pounding, she kissed his chin. "And sometimes," she echoed, "*some* people are too quick to judge."

"Okay, have it your way," he countered, tucking a tendril of her hair behind her ear.

"Ahh, so I can make double-buttered popcorn, then."

When he chuckled, a bit of the joyful spark she'd grown to love returned to his beautiful eyes, and Julia sent a silent prayer of thanks to the Almighty…then quickly tacked on, *I sure could use a healthy dose of good timing, Lord.*

But even as she thought *Amen*, Julia knew that what she needed most…was courage.

Chapter Eighteen

....

"Michael Josephs for you, counselor." The guard held the door as a portly teen entered the interview room.

"Thanks, Dave," Julia said, as the officer secured the boy's shackles to thick metal clips bolted to the concrete floor. "Remind me...do you prefer to be called Michael or Mike?" she asked as he flopped onto the chair across from hers.

He shrugged. "My parents call me *Michael*, but since they've disowned me, I guess it's time for something new." Smirking, he said, "How 'bout *Mike*?"

She ignored his sarcasm. "And you can still call me Julia," she reminded him. "I'm sure you know why I'm here." She slid a thick accordion file from her briefcase and pushed PLAY on the tape recorder beside it. "I need to record our talks in case I need to refer to anything while preparing for your trial."

"Hey," he said, balancing both elbows on the table, "do what ya gotta do."

As she'd reread the contents of his file and some of the charges brought against him in the past, Julia had cringed....

At six, he'd stolen firecrackers from a neighbor's back porch and used them to launch his mother's stew pot high into the air...and when it landed on the hood of a parked car, the explosion had left its driver scarred for life.

Michael was seven when he set fire to kerosene-soaked rags he'd hidden in his lunch box and flushed them down the elementary-school toilets…destroying the plumbing and flooding the boys' bathroom.

Shortly after his eighth birthday, he made a bow from balsa wood and strung it with heavy-gauge fishing line then fashioned arrows from quarter-inch-thick wooden dowels sharpened to a dagger-like point…and used them to kill robins and rabbits in his backyard.

By ten, he'd formed the "Here Comes Trouble Club" in his neighborhood and taught boys to fashion slingshots, used to pepper passersby with pea gravel if they dared to walk or bicycle near the clubhouse. Their antics blinded a two-year-old in a baby stroller.

Enraged when disgruntled former club members stole his basketball net, Michael glued thumbtacks to its rim, costing one prankster two fingers and a thumb.

In junior high school, Michael graduated to breaking and entering, burglary, assault and battery, and muggings. And most recently, a young female art teacher at the high school had accused Michael of cornering her after class. If not for a janitor who had come upon them, there was no telling what might have happened.

Michael's dad, a prominent businessman who'd made regular and generous contributions to politicians' campaign funds, managed to call in favors to keep the details of every incident out of the public record. High-priced lawyers and disreputable judges ensured light— or nonexistent—penalties.

But this time, Michael had deliberately planned and executed the killing of a five-year-old Amish child, in broad daylight and in plain sight of a half dozen witnesses. Humiliated, Gus Josephs and his socialite wife washed their hands of the boy…ensuring that this time, he'd face the full extent of the law.

"This is quite a file you have here," Julia said, flipping through the pages.

"My biggest crime was stupidity."

Julia removed her reading glasses and looked up from the folder. "Stupidity?"

"I got caught."

What a waste, she thought, staring into gray blue eyes that sparkled with intelligence. If Michael's parents had sought help after his first offense, perhaps they'd have discovered a way to prevent the rest. Instead, payoffs and pretense designed to protect their own reputations guaranteed their son's emotional demise.

She grabbed a blue-lined yellow tablet. "So tell me about the day of the accident."

"Ahh," he said, leaning closer, "you've been misinformed."

"How so?" she asked, clicking her pen into "write" mode.

Michael ran a hand through straight dark hair. "Lucky me," he said, mostly to himself, "I get a hot, *stupid* lawyer to defend me." Then, "It wasn't an accident."

If not for the smug expression on his pudgy face, Julia might have thought she'd misunderstood. "Okay, tough guy," she said, narrowing her eyes, "how about we start with *why*."

"The Clapes are dirty, for starters. And slow. And always in everybody's way."

"First, in my presence, you'll call them 'Amish.' Got it?"

Blinking, he nodded.

"So why *that* boy, *that* day?"

"Because," Michael said around a bored yawn, "he was there."

"So you *knew* he was in the buggy?"

"Sure. What would be the point of blowing up an empty one?"

It took hard work to keep her emotions at bay. Harder still admitting that she'd wrangled his freedom after the shoplifting charges. If he'd been in jail, serving time for that… Swallowing, Julia decided to leave such thoughts for later.

"So how'd you feel afterward? When you realized the little Amish boy had died, I mean?"

Michael shrugged. "I dunno…how was I supposed to feel?"

"How about bad? Guilty? Sorry? Anything to indicate you wish you hadn't done it?"

A halfhearted grin, then, "Not really."

"Do you know that Levi Gunden had a mom and a dad, a brother and a sister?"

Rolling his eyes, he said, "I do now."

"Do you feel bad about the grief you've caused them?"

"Why should I? Those…those *Amish*…they reproduce like rabbits. Give them a couple months and they'll have another to take that one's place."

Julia couldn't help but remember the agony Hannah had gone through with her recent miscarriage. No one but God knew if she was capable of having more children…. So the question was, did Michael have a capacity for empathy at all, or was he truly devoid of human compassion? She met his cold, gray eyes and knew that deep down he felt nothing. Nodding, Julia closed the file and returned it to her briefcase.

"We're done? Already?"

"Oh, don't worry. I'll be back." After he'd undergone a physical and a complete psych workup. He'd confessed to cold-blooded, calculated murder and would be tried as an adult. But even with the testimony of professionals to show the jury proof of Michael's mental problems, Julia had her work cut out for her if she hoped to spare him the death penalty. She owed him that much, didn't she? Because if she'd recommended mandatory in-patient psychiatric care to the judge who'd heard Michael's shoplifting case, he would've been in a juvenile facility on the day of the accident.

And Levi would still be alive….

Thoughts like that are counterproductive, she told herself. She'd never make it up to the Gundens, a tough fact to cope with, especially knowing that Hannah and William would be the last people to censure her for doing her job and doing it well. But that didn't stop the pangs of guilt from echoing deep in her soul. "Don't talk to anybody, *anybody,*" she told Michael, "unless I'm in this room with you. Got it?"

"Whatever."

She wondered if he even had it in him to pretend, at least, to feel remorse for what he'd done….

* * * * *

Simon couldn't understand why the public defender's office didn't hire a few recent law-school grads. That way every attorney in the office would enjoy a lighter caseload, including—especially—Julia.

Last time she'd cancelled dinner, Julia explained how the entire staff had been told they must put in extra hours. During the past few weeks alone, she'd backed out of a dozen lunches and quiet evenings together, claiming the need for time to write pleadings to prepare documents for trial. But when she backed out on the party at Casey's, he couldn't help but worry about her health.

He'd grown tired of eating fast food. Alone. Burgers and fried chicken had been staples in his diet before Julia, and it hadn't taken long to grow accustomed to hot, home-cooked meals, shared with the love of his life. Knowing her, she'd been skipping meals altogether rather than make do with the greasy beef patties between stale rolls he'd been consuming.

Well, if Mohammad wouldn't go to the mountain…

When his last patient left at three, he sent Debbie home with a "Good job these past few weeks!" pat on the back and headed for the grocery store. His culinary capabilities were limited, at best, but he'd learned a few things, standing beside her in the kitchen these many months.

Standing at her stove, Simon added garlic powder, Italian seasoning, a sprinkling of sugar, and a dash of ground cloves to a jar of store-bought spaghetti sauce, and put it on to simmer while he set the table. As he tossed the salad and buttered the garlic bread, he decided to announce at dinner that she would put her feet up for a change while *he* did the dishes. With his plan firm in his mind, Simon grinned. How could she object to a quick, quiet dinner even if she brought home a briefcase full of homework?

With nothing left to do but boil the water for the pasta and run the garlic toast under the broiler, Simon decided to get the ol' woodstove going while watching the evening news. The mid-March weather had grown increasingly warmer, and this could very well be their last fire of the season. Maybe once he'd filled her belly with tasty spaghetti, Julia would agree to share her favorite dessert here in her cozy family room. Vanilla ice cream in sudsy root beer took no time to make.... And maybe after *that*, she'd consent to cuddle on the sofa for just a few minutes so he could tell her how much he'd missed her as she'd burned the midnight oil.

It hadn't been easy, getting through those weeks following Levi's funeral, but Julia stood beside him all the way and made coping more bearable. She'd been so sweet and supportive, quietly enduring his rants and tirades about Michael Josephs. "I've heard the rumors about that nutcase," he'd fumed the last time they were together. "I know about the crazy crimes he's committed in the past," he'd said just last week. "I've gotta believe in the justice system. Maybe his rich daddy won't be able to bail him out this time. There's no rehabilitating a lunatic like that; I hope they fry the demented beast so he'll never harm anyone again."

She'd been strangely quiet and fidgety, and he'd chalked it up to the fact that she'd loved Levi and missed him, too. He decided to put more effort into avoiding talk like that. A lot more, because she deserved to be protected from the unpleasant things in life.

Kicking up the footrest of her grandfather's recliner, Simon laid the evening paper across his lap as the TV meteorologist predicted a cold and windy night. *Perfect woodstove weather,* he thought, yawning. Minutes later, as Simon snored beneath a blanket of headlines that read Teen's Lawyer Demands Psych Evaluation, a blond anchorwoman announced breaking news in the Michael Josephs murder trial as reporters surrounded his pretty young public defendant, Julia Spencer.

* * * * *

The aroma of spaghetti sauce filled the air as Julia dropped her briefcase on the foyer table and hung her coat on the hall tree. Down the hall, she spied a fire dancing in the belly of the woodstove as, in the family room, Simon snoozed contentedly in her grandfather's big chair. *What a wonderful welcome,* she thought, smiling at the sight of him buried under pages of newspaper as the colorful light of the TV flickered blue and red and white over his handsome features.

But her smile faded as her own image filled the screen. "No comment," she heard herself say as she plowed through the gaggle of reporters surrounding her. Grabbing the remote from the end table beside him, she hit the Off button and breathed a sigh of relief.

Until she realized that similar pictures had dominated the front page of every newspaper in the area. But how would she retrieve it when his hands rested, one atop the other, hiding the horrible headline?

She'd been meaning to tell him about getting the Michael Josephs case, waiting for just the right time. Unfortunately, the right time hadn't presented itself. And now Julia stood face-to-face with the folly of her wavering bravery.

It wouldn't be fair for him to find out watching TV or reading the evening news. She owed it to him to 'fess up. Somehow, before this night ended, she'd have to tell him…and hope for the best.

Simon had always been one of the most levelheaded, fair-minded men she'd ever known. That couldn't be said where anything relating to Michael Josephs was concerned, however. What he felt for the boy who'd killed Levi had long since passed loathing and hostility and moved straight into hot-blooded hatred. No telling how he'd react once he found out it had become her job to get

Michael the lightest possible sentence. She eased up to the chair and stooped, ready to grab the paper as she woke him with a gentle kiss.

Simon's long-lashed eyes fluttered open the instant her lips made contact with his. "Hey, pretty lady." Chuckling, he added, "If somebody ever figured how to make an alarm clock do that, nobody would hate Monday mornings."

She almost felt guilty. Almost. But since she planned to tell him the whole truth tonight, absolutely and for sure, Julia didn't feel too bad about her trickery. "What are you doing here?" she asked, taking hold of the paper.

"Thought you could use a break and a decent meal and some companionship. You've been working your little fingers off."

"You're a sweetie." As he yawned and stretched, she dashed to the woodstove to chuck the newspaper inside.

"Hey, I haven't read that yet."

Julia jabbed the poker through the glowing coals a few times as the paper caught and flared then added a log to the fire. "Oops… sorry." She walked back to the chair. "What smells so scrumptious?"

"Spaghetti." He dropped the footrest and got to his feet.

"I repeat, you're a sweetie." Hugging him, she added, "I think it only fair to warn you…I brought work home. Lots of—"

"Yeah, I figured. But you have to eat." He kissed the tip of her nose. "How else are you gonna keep putting in sixty- and seventy-hour workweeks without keeling over?"

"Hungry?"

"Starving. Everything is ready. Well, nearly ready. You have time to change out of your stiff-upper-lip business suit and into something more comfortable while I finish up."

Melting into his arms, Julia sighed. "Is this what being married to you will be like? I'll come home after a hard day in court and you'll have a delicious meal waiting for me?"

Pressing a palm to her forehead, Simon said, "Mmm…you don't *feel* feverish."

Oh, how she loved this handsome, pun-loving man! Julia grinned and waited for the explanation she knew would follow.

"It says in plain English in the small print on every marriage license that it's the *wife's* job, not the husband's, to have healthy, mood-improving food on the table at the end of a hard day." He punctuated the joke with a merry wink. "But maybe as a savvy attorney, you can add a codicil to the agreement."

She grinned and decided to take him up on his offer to get into something less confining while he put the finishing touches on the meal. "I'll set the table once I've changed," she said, heading for the stairs.

"Already done," he called after her.

"Then I'll toss the salad."

"Also done."

She was halfway up the stairs and hung over the railing to say, "Fill the glasses with ice and water?"

"Sorry, nothing for you to do but sit down and eat…and tell me about all the down-on-their-luck people you helped today."

No way she'd ruin the mood he'd set by telling him who her most recent hard-luck case was. There'd be plenty of time to destroy his good mood after they'd eaten.

Fifteen minutes later, when she walked into the kitchen, Julia fought happy tears as she scanned the room. He stood at the sink, a kitchen towel tucked into his belt, draining pasta into a colander.

A vase of daisies—no fewer than three dozen yellow-eyed white blooms—were stuffed into a glass vase in the center of the table. Beside them, in a basket lined with paper towels, were slices of golden garlic toast. "Simon," she said, fingering the delicate petals, "wherever did you find them this time of year?"

"Oh, it ain't tough for people in the know." He winked. "You like 'em?"

"I love them." He was stirring noodles into the sauce when she hugged him from behind. "I love *you*. This is such a nice surprise."

"Hey, it isn't all for you, you know," he said, turning to wrap his arms around her. "I've missed the daylights outta you, so this is for me, too."

Julia looked away, unable to meet his trusting eyes. "I'll try to do a better job of clocking out at a normal time from now on," she said, meaning it.

"I wish I knew who to credit for one of my favorite adages."

"Which?"

" 'Do or do not,' " he quoted, fiddling with the radio dials, " 'there *is* no "try." ' "

He settled on an oldies-but-goodies station, and in no time they were chatting quietly as they ate, stopping now and then to sing along with a line from a favorite tune. If he'd mentioned Levi or the accident or Michael Josephs, she might have found the courage to tell him everything, even amid the amiable atmosphere. But either he'd decided to avoid all unpleasant topics, or he suspected something….

"If you can afford a couple minutes more away from your briefcase," he said, stacking the dishes, "I've got dessert, too."

She glanced at the clock. Nearly eight. She had research to do and needed to get started on interrogatories, but what difference could a half hour make, especially considering how often she'd disappointed him lately. "Seems you've thought of everything," Julia said, opening the dishwasher.

"Oh no, ya don't," he said, playfully muscling her aside. "My job isn't over till the last spoon is washed. Have a seat, m'dear."

"Spoon? We didn't need spoons for dinner. Does that mean what I think it means?"

"Root beer floats."

Minutes later, side by side on the sofa, they scooped creamy vanilla ice cream from tall soda-filled glasses as Julia asked him about his day. Mouser purred between them, occasionally lifting her gray-striped head for a pat as the fire emanated cozy warmth and provided the only light in the room.

"You know, I could stay forever," he said once they'd emptied their glasses, "but it's after nine, and I know you have things to do. If I want you to get any rest at all tonight—and I do—I'd better head on home."

Julia remembered a time not so long ago when she didn't think she deserved love at all, let alone the love of a man like this. But Simon, with his big and giving heart, patiently taught her how wrong she'd been. She didn't want to tell him about Michael Josephs after an evening like this, when he'd gone to so much trouble and been so thoughtful.

But how could she *not,* was the haunting question that echoed in her soul.

"Simon," she said, "I have something to tell you, and you aren't going to like it."

He scooted closer to the edge of the cushion and turned slightly to study her face. "Maybe I don't want to hear—whatever it is—if that look on your face is any indication of how *much* I won't like it."

Taking his hands in hers, Julia said, "You know how much I love you, right?"

"Sure I do." And as if to prove it, he kissed her.

"And you know how much I appreciate all the gifts you've—"

"Aw," he said, "just trinkets. No big deal."

"They were a big deal, a very big deal to me, and I love them all!" If he kept looking at her that way, could she tell him? Or would she chicken out? "But it's not the presents I'm talking about. It's the other gifts, like the caring way you taught me to believe I'm normal and lovable and worthy of a happy future, complete with children."

"All true, Julia. Every word of it and then some." He frowned and ran a hand through his hair. "I don't mind telling you, you're scaring me a little, babe."

Lord, she prayed, *help me do this, please. And help Simon understand….*

After taking a deep breath, she said, "I'm representing Michael Josephs at trial."

Simon shook his head and grimaced. A long, horrible moment of silence passed before he said, "You're…you're *what*?"

"The office is understaffed and overworked. The case landed on my desk, and I have to—"

"You have to turn it down. *That's* what you have to," he snarled.

"I can't, Simon. My boss all but said that if I didn't take it, I'm out of a job."

"So? You're smart and talented. You'll find work elsewhere. No way can you convince me that you want to represent that…that… *animal.* You loved Levi, too!"

He was on his feet now, pacing, one palm clapped to the back of his neck, the other waving in the air. "Your grandparents left you this house and plenty of money in the bank. You don't need that rotten job. So *let* them fire you! Where's your sense of right and wrong? Where's your decency, Julia? Where's—"

"Simon, Michael is sick. Very sick—and has been for most of his life. I can't go into detail because of client-attorney privilege, but there are things…horrible things…that go way back to when he was a little boy himself. Things that his parents didn't bother to—"

"I can't believe what I'm hearing. That monster *murdered* Levi. Burned nearly every inch of his little body. You weren't there, Julia. You didn't see what I saw, didn't hear what I heard. But I've told you. I've *told* you."

His voice was cold. Colder than she'd ever heard it. Colder than she knew he could sound. "I know it seems crazy, me representing Michael, especially considering how I felt about Levi, but Michael has rights under the Constitution, and I'm sworn to uphold them."

He'd been stomping back and forth on the other side of the coffee table, big feet pounding the floor hard enough to make the spoons in the soda glasses clatter with every step. But he stopped when she referred to the Constitution, planted his feet shoulder-width apart and shook his head. "Do you actually believe the nonsense you're spouting?"

"Yes," she said timidly, "of course I do. Michael has no one. His parents have turned their backs on him, and his so-called friends have, too. There's no one in his corner, Simon, no one but me."

He drove a hand through his hair and grabbed a fistful of sandy-colored curls. Then he aimed a stiff forefinger at her. "*Your* childhood," he spat, "was way tougher than—than that spoiled-rotten freak of nature—and you didn't spend it maiming innocent animals and blinding babies. You didn't have anybody in *your* corner, so why do you want to be in his?"

She exhaled a shaky sigh. "Because…because it's the right thing to do. God hates what that boy has done all his life, but He loves the *boy*. I can't turn my back on him."

"Can't?" An uncomfortable beat in time passed before he added, "Or won't?"

So far, his reaction was pretty much what she'd been afraid of, and why she'd put off telling him about her involvement in the first place. "Look," she began, "I understand why you're angry, and hurt, and confused. I understand why you think you hate—"

"I don't think it, Julia. I have good reason to despise that sorry excuse for a human being."

She took a deep breath and launched back into her explanation. "Okay, so I get why you hate Michael. He killed Levi, after all!" Julia clasped her hands, prayer fashion, and asked God to guide her next words. "What I don't get," she said, "is why you can't see past your fury. Where's all the compassion, all the acceptance, all the Christian forgiveness you showered on me?"

"Apples and oranges!" he barked.

Simon stared her down, as if willing her to stop talking. For the moment, she humored him.

"So which is it, Julia? Can't or won't?"

"Is there a difference?"

He blew a frustrated blast of air through clenched teeth. "So I take it to mean you're gonna do this awful thing…a slap in the faces of Hannah and William. I thought they were your friends."

She'd been over that ground dozens of times since accepting the case, praying that God would lead her to do the right thing. It hadn't been coincidence, Julia knew, that at the conclusion of every heartfelt prayer, she was left with the reminder that the Amish considered it a sin to harbor feelings of hate, judgment, or vengeance. The Gundens would understand, but in Simon's present mood, she couldn't very well point that out. "I'm sorry," she said, meaning it, "but it's part of what I do for a living. Sometimes the people I represent aren't the most upstanding, law-abiding citizens. Sometimes they're—"

"Baby killers and arsonists and creeps who torture their fellow human beings with thumbtacks, stones, and firecrackers? Oh, don't look so surprised. I've lived in this town a long time. Long enough to have heard horror stories about that wacko. And it just so happens I know some of the *people* he hurt, too."

He marched around the coffee table until he stood a foot in front of her. Gripping her upper arms, Simon gave her a gentle shake. "You can't save him, Julia. He's beyond saving. I've always known you're naive, but surely even you realize that he's hopeless."

"He's going to prison for what he did. I can't save him from that. I don't *want* to save him from that." She could tell him that she felt largely responsible for what Michael had done, because if she hadn't gotten him off on the shoplifting charges, he'd have been forced into therapy, where a talented analyst would have been working with him on the day he chose to kill Levi. And maybe that therapist would have reached him. *Not likely,* she thought, *but why give up all hope even before treatment began?* "There's no escaping the fact that he's sick." She tapped her temple. "Sick, Simon, and after all these years, I doubt there's a cure. But I couldn't live with myself if I didn't at least *try* to get him some help, so that when he gets out, he'll—"

"When he gets out?" he roared. He gave her another little shake. "You're actually planning to work toward getting that homicidal maniac *out*? So he can kill somebody else's little boy? Are *you* out of your mind, Julia?"

A sob aching in her throat, she fought the tears that burned behind her eyelids. " 'There but by the grace of God,' " she whispered. " 'There but by the grace of God.' "

The expressions skittering across his exquisite face went from anguish to frustration to utter defeat. Julia reached up to touch his cheek, just a small gesture of love and comfort…but he shoved her hand away. He held her gaze long enough for her to read the misery glittering in his eyes. Then he crossed the room in four long strides and took his coat from the hall tree. "Gotta go," he ground out, slipping his arms into it. "I…you…" And shaking his head, he walked out.

If he'd slammed the door, Julia would have had reason to hope that his mood would shift, that in the morning he'd see things differently. But the door closed softly, quietly, as if deliberately shutting her out of the rest of his life.

Julia reached for her Bible, flicked on the lamp beside Gramps's chair, and prayed for all she was worth that God would help her put one foot in front of the other tomorrow…and every day until Simon came back to her again.

Chapter Nineteen

· ·

The last time Julia visited Paradise, it had been a lovely early spring day, nearly two months after Simon stormed out of her house. She hadn't seen or heard from him in all that time—unless she counted the dreams that tormented her as she tried to work and as she tried to sleep. She'd barely noticed the aroma of budding honeysuckles that sweetened the warm air or the colorful strokes painted by tulips and daffodils blooming along the walkways.

But she'd noticed Simon, a half block away, in animated conversation with a uniformed police officer. Fear kept her rooted to the spot, unable to go to him, incapable, even, of waving. Because what if he turned from her, as he had upon leaving her house that awful night? Or worse, what if he met her gaze…and she found no trace of love glimmering there?

She understood that he needed time, lots of time, to wrap his mind around what she must do as part of her job. Julia believed that fervent prayer would soften his heart…if only she could resist the temptation to rush him.

The blue sky went suddenly dark and thunder rolled as lightning sliced the horizon. Ominous clouds swirled overhead as an angry wind whistled through the streets of Paradise. Julia didn't pray that the rain would hold off until she'd run her errands, like every other person now running for cover. Instead, she simply asked God to spare her a run-in with Simon.

Stepping into line at the bakery, she dug through her oversized purse for the ten-dollar bill she'd stuffed inside it that morning. It was her turn to provide donuts for the Friday coffee klatch at the office, and she hadn't had time the night before—thanks to last-minute pleadings and jury selection notes—to bake them herself. *I hope you appreciate all I've sacrificed for you, Michael*, she thought, knowing even as the words formed in her mind what an impossible scenario *that* was. She'd given up sleep, food, and time with her friends to work on his defense. Most important of all, she'd given up *Simon*.

Two more days, she thought, *just two more days before the trial begins.* It wasn't likely to last a week, not with all the evidence the prosecution had against Michael, so—

"Hello, Julia."

The voice startled her so badly, she nearly dropped her purse. "Hannah," she said, turning. "Hannah…how are you?" The woman had aged many years in the months since Levi's death. She appeared thinner and toil-worn. "Come," Julia said, taking her elbow, "sit with me a minute."

Nodding, Hannah followed to a small table in the corner. "I saw you through the window. You looked so sad, standing here alone, that I just had to come in."

"I've been meaning to stop by," Julia admitted. But the case had eaten every spare moment…and most of her courage. Telling herself the Gundens were understanding, forgiving people was entirely different from looking into their grief-stricken faces, knowing that for all intents and purposes, she'd taken the side of the boy responsible for their painful loss.

"You have been busy, I am sure," Hannah said, laying a hand atop Julia's. "But even with all you have to do, I knew that William and I, and Rebekah and Seth, were in your prayers, always." She gave the hand a little squeeze. "And you in ours."

Surely they'd heard that Julia had been assigned Michael's case. Despite their lack of telephones, radios, and televisions, very little escaped the knowledge of the Amish. And yet they prayed for her. Julia dipped her head low, unable to look into Hannah's big, friendly eyes..

"It is hard for most to understand, I know," Hannah said, "but we do not hate those who hate us. Judgment is God's and God's alone. Besides," she added, leaning closer, "that Josephs boy needs someone like you to stand up for him. I pray your influence will change his heart before it's too late for him."

Julia felt the sting of tears behind her eyelids and looked away, unable to face Hannah's unabashed kindness and goodness. She remembered wondering once, when Simon had made a comment about forgiveness and understanding, if he might have a little Amish in him. Julia couldn't have been more wrong about that, but that didn't stop her from wishing he was a little more like his friends the Gundens, especially now!

"How is William doing?" Julia asked.

A long, shaky sigh exited Hannah's lips. "Better every day," she said. "Hard work is a big help."

"And Seth and Rebekah?"

"They are well," she said, nodding. "They miss Levi, of course, but like us, they know he is in a better place."

Julia knew that the image of Hannah's children, red-eyed and sniffling at Levi's grave, would never leave her memory.

It was Hannah's turn to ask a question. "And Simon," she said. "How is he?"

Julia couldn't bear to add to Hannah's troubles by telling her the truth. "He's been very busy," she said, choosing her words carefully.

"He is overly proud, that man of yours."

Julia closed her eyes for a moment and prayed he would someday be "hers" again.

"He thinks his wrath is loyalty, well-placed because he is our friend. What he has yet to realize is that we do not need him to defend us. God is our defender, all we will ever need."

So Hannah knew that Simon had broken things off with her after all. Julia shouldn't have been surprised. Under different circumstances, she might have smiled at that fact. Instead, she said, "It's just that Simon loved Levi so much…."

"Oh, that was never a secret," Hannah said. "The night he helped me bring the boy into the world, I would not have needed a lamp in the room. His face lit up like the sunrise when Levi dropped into his waiting arms." Sighing, she continued. "I remember how his eyes filled with tears, and when at last he could speak, he said, 'I am holding in my hands living proof that there is a God.' " With a nod, Hannah added, "Do not worry, Julia. He will soon come to his senses, and when he does, Simon will see that his angry ways are not God's way. And he will see another important thing, too."

Julia met Hannah's blue eyes, waiting for the wisdom of the Amish that so often held the promise of hope and comfort in times of trouble.

"He will see that you are his intended, and he will come to you, seeking forgiveness."

"Forgiveness? *I'm* the one who should ask forgiveness!"

"For doing what God leads you to do?" Hannah shook her head. "I know you English think that we Amish are without temper, or anger, or spite. You believe we are incapable of hate." Eyes narrowed and lips thinned, she said, "I am here to tell you this is not true! We are Amish, yes, but we are human. We feel all those things and more! The difference is that we lay our hatred in God's capable hands and ask Him to release us of it." She held a finger aloft to conclude. "Those emotions imprison our hearts and souls and keep us far, far from the loving mercy of our God. There is no worse fate than to be separated from Him." She gave another nod. "I believe Simon will wake one day and see that this is true."

"From your lips to God's ear," Julia said, hugging her cherished friend.

* * * * *

The trial began on Monday, presenting Julia with a major problem to contend with right from the start. Not the ill-fitting clothes Michael's mother had grudgingly delivered, making her son look like a ripe pear in a navy suit. Not the jury's reaction to opening statements. Not the judge, for experience had taught her that he was a fair and reasonable man. And not even Michael's defense, for Julia had prepared well, practiced her speeches, and knew the case inside and out. Barring any last-minute surprises by the prosecution, she'd hold her own in the courtroom.

No, Julia's problem had a name: Simon, who made a point of sitting front and center.

She knew that the Commonwealth of Pennsylvania would call him to the stand at the end, to ensure that the last thing the jury would hear were his faltering, impassioned words, describing the cold-blooded crime Michael had committed that awful January day… and how it had cost little Levi Gunden his life.

Much as she'd hated to, Julia prepared well to interrogate him. She didn't look forward to questioning the opposition's main witness, for it meant standing two feet from arms that had once held her tenderly, from eyes that had glowed with affection for her, and from hands that had performed a thousand gentle acts of love.

Instead, when she took her place in front of the witness box, she'd face his rage and reproach—and the heartache of wondering if he still loved her, if he'd ever forgive her. No amount of planning and practicing could prepare her heart for that.

The days passed grindingly, slowly, as the DA introduced blood samples, finger- and shoe prints, and hair samples found at the scene, each directly linking Michael to the crime. Gasps of shock and horror echoed through the courtroom as photos, taken by a local reporter just moments after the fact, showed fiery reminders of Michael's heinous act, seared into the Paradise pavement.

Things shifted a bit in Michael's favor when Julia entered doctor and psychiatrist findings into evidence, and she watched as the jury read each page, as they listened with undivided attention to the experts' testimony. Perhaps like her, they held out hope that the professionals could help explain the ruthless barbarity of Michael's actions…and that he wasn't doomed to repeat them if they decided against the death penalty.

Ordinarily in a case like this, the sadistic acts he'd performed as a boy would not be entered into evidence, but in order to prove the teen's long history of disturbing behavior—that went unpunished *and* untreated—Julia presented the court with pages of detailed documentation that made his mental unbalance shatteringly clear. Through it all, he sat beside her, drawing ferocious monsters on a sketch pad, looking up only now and then to glower at the prosecutor, a member of the jury, the judge. No matter. She'd use it all in her summation…and pray he'd finally receive the help he so desperately needed.

Then came the day she'd dreaded—when Simon was called to the stand. Once he'd been sworn in and situated himself, she approached the polished oak box surrounding him and said, "Doctor Thomas, would you please state for the record your full name and residential address?"

As Simon rattled off the necessary information, Julia prayed. Prayed the Lord would guide her actions as well as her words, for she had no intention of skewering Simon in order to spare Michael.

"And would you tell the court if, on January second, you were alone in Paradise?"

"I was," he stated. But his eyes said, *You already know the truth....*

"Do you recall why you were in town that day?"

"I work in Paradise," came his gravelly reply.

"In your veterinary clinic?"

"Correct."

"But that's located at the other end of town, is it not?"

"It is. I'd stopped at the bakery for breakfast. Donut and coffee. Same as I do most mornings on my way to the work." And his glittering glare said, *But you know that, too....*

"Did you have occasion to converse with anyone as you walked down Main Street?"

"Other witnesses to the murder, you mean? You bet I did."

"Your honor," Julia said, "please instruct the witness that his personal opinion has no place in this trial."

The judge leaned closer to the witness box. "Keep your responses to 'yes' and 'no,' Doctor Thomas," he said.

Glowering, Simon nodded.

Julia continued. "When the police questioned you after the accid—"

"Accident! What that punk did was deliberate, calcula—"

"Your honor…?" Julia interrupted.

"I don't want to have this conversation again, Doctor Thomas," he warned. "I'll thank you to stick to yes or no answers."

"Yes, your honor." But Simon had fixed his hard gaze on Julia, not the judge, as he spoke.

"Will you tell the court, please, Doctor Thomas, who you saw on the street that day?"

Simon named the shopkeepers he'd spoken with and the townsfolk who'd waved hello. "And then I saw *him*." He stabbed the air with his forefinger, indicating Michael, who nonchalantly continued sketching monsters at the defense table. "He was standing with those other two, Paul and Walt, until he pulled that…that bottle from under his coat and they hightailed it."

"Let the record show," Julia said, "that the witness has indicated the defendant, Michael Josephs." And then she faced the jury, mostly because she didn't want to look into his face as he answered her next questions. "Now, Doctor Thomas, will you tell the court what you saw after Michael removed the bottle from under his coat?"

Simon inhaled a deep breath, let it out with a *whoosh*, and told the jury exactly what had happened. His voice cracked several times, and tears came to his eyes as he recounted the tragedy. Julia squeezed the railing surrounding the jury box so tightly that her fingers ached. *Just a few more questions,* she told herself. *Just a few more minutes....*

"Would you say, Doctor Thomas, that Michael seemed in his 'right mind' as he perpetrated this evil deed?"

"What?" Simon all but shouted. "Did he…did he *what*?"

She needed to get him to repeat what he'd told her that night in her living room…that Michael looked wild-eyed and insane, cold and far removed from his horrible act. But could she continue punishing Simon to get the testimony she needed, particularly since she knew better than anyone how much that day had changed him, changed his life?

"What I'm getting at, Doctor Thomas," she said as gently as possible, "is whether or not it seemed to you that Michael appeared to be rational."

"Objection," called the prosecutor. "Leading the witness…"

"Overruled," blurted the judge. "I want to hear where the defense is going with this. But I caution you, Ms. Spencer, to take care…."

Nodding, Julia continued. "Would you say Michael had targeted the Gunden buggy?"

"Absolutely."

"And it was clear to you that Michael knew Levi was *in* the buggy?"

Frowning, Simon blinked and licked his lips. "I…I don't see how he couldn't have known." He stared at the enormous double doors at the back of the courtroom as if they'd become a wide-screen TV where he could view the grisly scene as if on film. "Everybody on the street that day saw Levi, waving, saying hello to passersby, chattering like a chipmu—" Simon's words caught in his throat, and he pinched the bridge of his nose in an attempt to regain his composure.

Oh, how Julia yearned to go to him, to comfort him! But she had a job to do, like it or not.

And she definitely did *not*. "How far would you say Michael was from the buggy?"

Simon cleared his throat. "Half a block, maybe less, by the time he tossed the bottle."

"How many yards would you guess that to be?"

"Sorry. I didn't have a tape measure with me."

"Would you be so kind as to hazard a guess?"

On the heels of a ragged sigh, he said, "Twenty, twenty-five yards."

"So," Julia interjected, "a distance similar to where you're sitting and that blue van in the parking lot, out the window over there?"

Simon followed where she'd pointed and said, "I guess."

"Objection," the prosecutor interrupted. "Calls for speculation."

"Sustained," said the judge.

"I know what you're trying to do, *Miss Spencer*," Simon steamed, "but the best I can do is provide an educated guess." He leaned closer to add, "I *am* under oath, after all."

As the judge tried to quiet the quiet chuckles that floated through the courtroom, Julia realized she'd have to try another tack if she hoped to get Simon to admit that Michael had been too far away to know for certain if Levi had been in the buggy. Clasping both hands behind her back, she faced the jury again. "Did Michael move closer to the buggy *after* he lit the wick on the bottle?"

"He ran full-out," Simon blared. "Held that flaming thing above his head, bellowing like a bull moose, all the way from the corner to where William had parked his buggy."

Then Simon slapped both hands on the rail surrounding the

witness box, his eyes boring hot holes into Julia's face as he quoted Ecclesiastes 5:8: " 'If thou seest...violent perverting of judgment and justice...marvel not...for he...is higher than the highest.' "

"Your honor!" shouted the prosecutor. "Objection! A Bible verse? In open *court*?"

But before the judge could comment, the squeal of a chair, dragging across the marble floor, echoed through the wood-paneled room. On his feet now, Michael banged both fists onto the defense table. "You've got my confession, you bunch of idiots, so why are you wasting everybody's time and money?" he demanded. "I wrote it in my statement: I saw the stupid little Clape in the buggy. I threw the bottle. That's that."

"Sit down, Mr. Josephs," came the judge's booming voice, "or I'll have you removed from this courtroom!"

Shrugging, the teen upturned both palms. "Do it."

"Miss Spencer, if you can't restrain your client...."

Julia was at Michael's side in an instant. "Michael," she whispered, "sit down and be quiet."

"Why? So you can save me from the death penalty? What do I care if they kill me?"

"Your honor," Julia said, "the defense requests a recess."

"Gladly," said the judge. "Doctor Thomas, you are excused." He looked over his half-glasses at the jury panel. "Ladies and gentlemen, you will disregard Mr. Josephs's comments and will refrain from discussing the case in any way or with any person." He scribbled notes on the file before him before adding, "Court will reconvene on Monday at nine a.m." With one last glance over the magnifying lenses, he added, "And Miss Spencer, I trust you'll have your client in hand by then?"

I hope so, she thought. But "Yes, your honor" is what she said.

After one bang of the gavel, the judge said, "Court is dismissed."

As the guards led Michael from the room, he continued ranting about his guilt, about having earned the death penalty, about having nothing to live for. Julia tried not to notice the curious stares of people in the gallery, and then a shadow fell across her paperwork.

"Ironic, isn't it, that I never had a chance to watch you at work… before this case."

Simon. Julia didn't want to look up, didn't want to see abhorrence and revulsion on his handsome face…directed at her. "I'm sorry," she whispered, slowly meeting his eyes.

"For what? For doing your job?"

Julia's head snapped up in surprise. If he truly felt that way, why had he been avoiding her all these weeks? But whatever ill will she'd tried to muster to help her get through those long, lonely days had never fully ripened. And now, standing so near the very arms that had made her feel loved and protected caused an ache inside her like none she'd ever known. She looked deep into his eyes and confessed the truth: "I've missed you, Simon."

She watched his Adam's apple rise and fall above the tidy Windsor knot of his blue silk tie. Heard him sigh. Felt the brittle air that had gathered between them like an impenetrable wall warm slightly. Was it too much to hope that—

"You're very good at what you do, Julia."

It wasn't a compliment. That much was evident in his crisp tone. Before, when he'd said her name, it sighed into her ears like a song… three delightful notes that told her he enjoyed the poetic music of saying "*Jyoo*-lee-ah." In all her life, no one had ever pronounced it that way, and she'd treasure the memory of it, always. But just now, two harsh syllables, making it clear that his feelings had changed—dramatically.

"Plans for the weekend?"

It was all she could do to croak out, "Not really."

"How's Mouser?"

"Fine," she said, snapping her briefcase shut. Had he walked over to the defense table for the sole purpose of torturing her? Of reminding her what she'd had…and deliberately given up on behalf of a murderer? If so, he'd accomplished what he'd set out to do.

"See you Monday morning, I guess…"

Had she imagined it, or did he sound almost like his old loving self? Julia didn't dare look up to find out. "Right," she said, amazed that her voice worked at all. "Monday."

As he helped her shrug into her blazer, Julia longed to feel his powerful hands resting on her shoulders, the way they used to when he performed this gentlemanly task. For the briefest moment, her prayer was answered as he quickly patted her shoulders, as his hands skimmed down her upper arms, stopping just above her elbows. She chanced a peek at his handsome face and nearly burst into tears at the hint of a smile playing at the corners of his mouth. She'd freeze the moment in her memory and pray even harder that his heart would soften as the days passed.

She didn't trust herself to speak, and so Julia hurried toward the big double doors at the back of the courtroom.

"I've missed you, too," Simon called.

But Julia never heard him, for she'd ducked into the ladies' room to hide her tears.

Chapter Twenty

....

It would have been easy to wallow in self-pity indefinitely. She'd probably lost the love of her life, after all, and didn't intend to search for a replacement, ever.

It would've been easy to pretend she'd grown angry with him, too, but Julia really did understand how he felt, and why. Levi had been the closest thing to a son he'd ever had, and she'd consciously gone against his wishes by representing the young man responsible for his brutal loss. And it would've been easy to focus on the ache in her heart.

Julia chose, instead, to remember the many wonderful things about him, about their relationship. She'd come into his life an emotional wreck, believing she'd inherited her parents' less-than-stellar traits, and Simon had shown her how wrong she'd been. Once, she'd believed herself defective, so defective that she didn't deserve to have children of her own, ever, and he'd taught her that the opposite was true.

She'd given up the promise of a loving, happy future for her so-called career. In court, he'd quoted Ecclesiastes, and even as the prosecutor objected to the blatant melding of religion and law, Julia understood only too well what Simon had been trying to tell her. And his words, echoing in her dreams night after night, helped her decide that this would be her last trial. Because if she continued representing people like Michael, how could she look at her own reflection in the mirror?

Simon had been right to point out that she didn't need the job—her grandparents had left her a sound house on three acres, a sizable bank account, and a portfolio of stocks and bonds. What more did she require than a modest weekly salary to provide food and utilities?

For years, Julia had dreamed of hanging a shingle to advertise her one-woman law office, where she'd represent folks who might not have the means nor the access to legal representation. Thanks to Simon, she'd developed the confidence to make that dream come true.

Her only regret?

That she couldn't share it with him.

* * * * *

"What're you doing here in the middle of a work day?" Simon asked.

"Curiosity." He snorted. "Just wanted to see what a real live crazy man looks like."

Though Casey hadn't said so, Simon had a feeling that the visit was directly related to his breakup with Julia.

Shaking his head, Casey frowned. "Still as stubborn as ever, I see."

"I'm not…I didn't…I—I—"

"Oh, quit your stammering," Casey interrupted. "Reminds me of that time when we were kids and we got caught smoking in my folks' attic."

"That was your idea, not mine."

Casey shrugged. "You're the one who brought the matches…"

Simon's memory took him back to a day nearly twenty years ago, when Casey had sneaked a pack of cigarettes from their grandfather's den. They'd spent the better part of a summer morning trying to figure out where and how to light up, just one of many adventures he and Casey had shared as boys.

"Yeah," Casey said, grinning, "but it was your coughing and wheezing that brought the grown-ups down on us," he pointed out. "I'm amazed to this day that somebody didn't call the fire department."

"I repeat: You brought the matches…"

…which had ignited not only the tips of their cigarettes, but a stack of yellowing newspapers, as well. When Casey's grandfather lumbered up the steps, hollering and waving his arms like a furious windmill, Simon had stuttered a slew of excuses and thrown open the round multipane window.

"And it still amazes *me* that Grandpa actually understood your incoherent babbling." He gave Simon's shoulder a playful poke. "You never could handle that kind of heat."

Simon could only shake his head. "At least the episode taught us both to avoid tobacco products after that."

Casey jabbed a finger into Simon's chest. "This time you're in up to your ears in it, Sie." Shaking his head, he added, "And frankly? I don't think the shovel's been manufactured that can dig you outta this one."

"Who says I need to dig out?" His defensive tone reminded him yet again of days long gone, when he'd thought that nothing more than a defiant statement could redirect blame that ought to rest squarely on his own shoulders.

"Oh, gimme a break, why don't you. You're sneakers over baseball cap in love with Julia. And why wouldn't you be? I can't name a single other woman who'd tolerate your 'holier than thou' nonsense." Casey paused and screwed a fingertip into Simon's chest. "Except maybe

Debbie. And if you don't shape up, that's *just* the kind of woman you'll end up with."

Simon didn't like the mental image Casey's words conjured.

"Gotta go," Casey said.

"You just got here."

"You need time alone, to sort stuff out. Julia may not have danced to the tune you assigned her, but she didn't do anything wrong, either. Except maybe disagree with Mr. High and Mighty."

"Hey, what's up, Case? First I'm holier than thou, and now I'm high and mighty?"

"If the insult fits…" He snickered. "Just a little more for you to mull over once I hit the road." He opened the door. "How'd you get so lucky *twice?* I always liked Georgia. And then you had Julia. That girl's *made* for you, Sie, and if you'd rather stick to your guns than admit that, well then, I guess you'll do all right, spending the rest of your life without her."

He'd been anything *but* all right since the night Julia told him she'd represent Michael Josephs in court. Since then, the days had dragged endlessly, and the nights were longer still. If more than a half second ticked by without something to occupy his brain, there she was, dominating his thoughts.

Casey chuckled. "If that sad-eyed, hound-dog expression is any indicator, you're already regretting the stupid things you said."

"She *told* you what—"

"Nope."

"Then how—"

Simon's cousin groaned. "*You're* the one who told me, you big lummox, just now, with that…I can't decide if that look on your face is caused by guilt or regret!"

If Casey had asked, Simon would have said, "Both."

"I've known you all my life and survived enough squabbles with you to know that you sometimes fight dirty."

Good grief, Simon thought as the third insult registered. What sort of man had he become if people viewed him this way? Maybe Casey was right. Maybe he *did* need some time alone to sort things through, to fine-tune his attitude. Maybe—

"If you come to your senses," Casey said from the porch, "Joanna and I will throw you and Julia an engagement party." He paused on the top step and, finger in the air, frowned. "But…if you don't wise up and admit what a boob you can sometimes be, is it okay if we stay friends with Julia? 'Cause we're nuts about her, and it'd be a shame if—"

Shaking his head, Simon grinned then waved him away, "Give my love to Jo and the kids."

"Will do." He winked as a crooked smile split his face. "Love you, too, cuz."

Simon closed the door and stared at the empty, now-silent foyer, remembering the first time Julia had stood where Casey had just been, oohing and ahhing about the house and about his pets. A sob ached in his throat as he exhaled a long, deep breath. Pacing the length of the hall, he pummeled the palm of one hand with the fist of the other. Why hadn't he blubbered this way when Georgia passed away? Maybe it was knowing that, while cancer had *taken* her from him, he'd *driven* Julia away.

Casey had been right when he'd said Simon needed time to think about…everything.

He headed for his study and grabbed the Bible, flopped into an easy chair, and opened the Good Book on his lap. "Show me, Lord," he whispered. "Show me how I've gone wrong—and how to make it right."

* * * * *

It had been a month since they'd carted Michael Josephs, rambling and raging like a madman, from the courtroom. Her legal finesse had spared him the death penalty, and Julia could only pray that while he served his sentence—life with a chance at parole in twenty-five years—God would touch his heart and spare his soul. Meanwhile, she could rest easy, knowing the innocents like Levi would be safe.

She remembered all too well the sentencing hearing, when two burly guards led Michael into the courtroom, shackled at the wrists and ankles and garbed in a garish orange jumpsuit. As she watched him scan the gallery, Julia caught a glimpse of childlike longing in his eyes—and a tiny spark of hope for parental support that might flare into full-fledged love. But his face went blank when he realized that neither his mother nor his father had come to offer words of comfort, or hug him good-bye or promise to visit. That instant of innocence was replaced by the moody, mistrustful, malignant expression so evident during his trial—an expression that remained on his face even as the judge spelled out his fate.

How easy it would be to blame his parents' disinterest for the way Michael had turned out. But she'd been in this business long enough to know that sometimes people went bad—even those who got the benefit of every bit of help available—for no definable reason. The "why" of such things could drive sane people mad, could harden even the gentlest of souls. Julia had no intention of traveling down that road. She'd borrow a page from the Amish, instead, and trust her newly remembered faith in God to provide her every need.

Faith. Something she'd never fully understood. Until Simon…

She'd trust that the Lord would provide clients and anything else she'd need. The public defender's office had been seriously understaffed, even as she struggled alongside coworkers to balance the county's caseload. Her resignation would make it tougher for everyone who remained, but she'd prayed on it, long and hard, alone and with the assistance of her pastor and fellow parishioners, and believed that when she'd put the long white envelope on her boss's cluttered desk, it had been the right thing to do.

Freedom from doubt—yet another gift to thank Simon for.

She would start her new life with conviction and self-assurance partly because he'd gently coaxed her from her lonely pit of despair. If she'd stayed there? Julia shuddered to think what might have become of her.

Eyes closed, she hugged herself as the image of Simon floated in her mind. She smiled, picturing his dark-lashed green eyes; the smile that seemed to start in his heart and reflect the warmth and kindness of his soul; the masculine laughter that began deep in his chest and echoed out, making anyone within earshot feel a little happier just by hearing it. Maybe now he'd have a chance to find the woman who'd bring him the joy and happiness he so richly deserved.

It wouldn't be easy in a town this size to see him living that life with someone else. God had helped her survive other pain and disappointment. He'd get her through this, too. But oh, how she'd miss—

In a moment of blinding clarity, she realized that Simon *had* been there for her, right from the start. When her life seemed bleak and hopeless, he'd compassionately encouraged, tenderly taught, and lovingly lifted her from a life of recrimination, self-doubt, and despair.

Just moments ago, she'd acknowledged that the vile acts of people like Michael could drive a sane person out of his mind and could turn a gentle, caring man into a bitter and angry loner. Levi's death had done that to Simon....

Had the things he'd said to her hurt? More than she cared to admit! But knowing Simon had said them because he was suffering? Julia's heart swelled with love for the big, wonderful man who'd made such a difference in her life. She wanted to go to him, right now, throw her arms around him, and kiss him until her lips were chapped!

Time, patience, and prayer, Julia knew, were the keys to healing. He'd invested all three in her, without giving up on her, and she wouldn't give up on him!

Buoyed by optimism, Julia felt happier than she had since before their quarrel. Grabbing her purse and keys, she raced out the door and headed for the one place where she could think...and plan.

Chapter Twenty-One

He didn't understand his new habit of driving aimlessly around town, but Simon questioned very few things these days. Like the little velvet box he continued to carry in his pocket. He needn't *see* the glittering diamond inside to be reminded that when he had purchased it months ago, he'd intended it to be a symbol of love and the promise of a long, happy future with Julia.

He'd become a growling, grumbling, grumpy old man. Would Levi have wanted to be friends with a guy like that? Would Julia have wanted to *marry* a guy like that?

Okay, so he'd been disappointed—no, borderline furious—when he'd heard she intended to represent the kid who killed Levi. It hurt like crazy, thinking she didn't get it, didn't get *him*. But had he really expected her to give the Commonwealth reason to fire her, just to appease him?

Casey had hit the old nail on the head when he'd said it was about time Simon took a long hard look at himself, analyzed his own behavior, and listened to the tone of his own self-absorbed rants. And when Simon took that good advice, it shamed him to admit what he'd become. No…what he *might* have become, if not for his hardheaded cousin's words to the not-so-wise.

Grinning to himself, Simon wondered how many minutes it would have taken Casey to agree with his self-assessment.

He'd fed and watered the cat and dog an hour ago, before beginning this latest driving tour of Paradise. "Long as you're home by dark, they'll be fine," he muttered, putting the pickup in REVERSE and then heading for the place where he'd always done his best thinking.

* * * * *

He had a lot to make up for. And if God was on his side, he thought as the lone wolves howled, Julia would forgive him for every stinging word. The sun had begun to set, and their music would soon echo throughout the sanctuary, an eerie blend of jubilation and heartsickness. Simon believed the majestic beasts had the capacity to feel gratitude for the daily care they received here. But he also theorized they knew where they'd come from—even those born here at the sanctuary—and mourned the vast wilderness and unfettered freedom that could have been theirs, if uninformed humans hadn't intruded.

Fawn approached slowly, and right behind her came the leader of Wolf Pack B. "Well, I'll be," he said, squatting and extending a hand, "got yourself a boyfriend, have you, girl?"

She looked over her shoulder at the big male then brought her head up and sent Simon her best wolf smile.

"I'm happy for you, Fawn. Real happy."

But her good fortune wasn't shared by Casper, who paced nervously along the tree line, watching the huge alpha that stood between him and the friend who for so long had shared his lone-wolf status. "Sorry, pal," Simon whispered. And he meant it, too, because now the poor animal would truly *be* a lone wolf.

Just then he spied movement to Casper's left. Another wolf—one Simon hadn't seen before—moving steadily closer, head down and tail tucked. Simon froze, not wanting his human instincts to interfere with the wolves' natural inclinations. "Watch yourself, buddy," was his quiet warning to Casper, " 'cause there's trouble at two o'clock…."

Matt had told Simon that a newcomer would soon arrive at the sanctuary. He must have only just been delivered, or the caretaker would have called to arrange a thorough exam and vaccinations.

He'd seen members of the packs head for Fawn and Casper for doing little more than trying to enjoy a biscuit or standing too near the others. And while it pained him to watch as they relegated the pair to a distant corner of the sanctuary, it was the wolves' way, and he was duty-bound to accept it.

For a time, the loners held their own. But all too soon they were forced to succumb to peer pressure and the strength of wolves twice their size, thanks to a ready supply of food that the smaller pair could eat only when granted permission. He'd doctored injuries inflicted on Fawn and Casper by claw and fang, and miraculously, they'd survived. This newcomer, leaner and lighter than Casper, would have a fight on his hands if he planned to go after the white wolf.

Then an amazing thing happened. Casper turned and nudged the brown and gray wolf. "Ahh," Simon said to himself, "so you guys are friends already, are you?"

"You shouldn't be surprised. Even outsiders are accepted, sometimes…"

He'd know that voice anywhere. Oh, how he'd missed hearing it all these months! But Simon didn't get to his feet, for fear the movement would spook the wolves. Especially Fawn and her new beau, who'd never been as accepting of the volunteer vet as most of his cohorts.

Julia eased nearer and settled down beside him, and when she laid a hand on his knee, he thought his heart would burst with gratitude and joy as Fawn and her partner pranced away. He didn't deserve this act of kindness. Didn't deserve her forgiveness, and he would've said so if she hadn't chosen that moment to softly sigh.

"I'm happy for her," Julia said, her gaze following the female wolf, "and for Casper, too." She stared into the thicket where the loners paced. "Does the new one have a name?"

"Haven't met him yet." He chanced a peek at her profile. Was it possible she'd grown even lovelier during their months apart? "If Matt hasn't already chosen something, I'll bet he'd let you pick a name."

He watched her grin and wished she stood square in front of him instead of crouched at his side, because Simon longed to look into her eyes and see for himself if hope for the two of them glimmered there.

"So how're Windy and Wiley?"

"Fine." Were they back to making small talk, thanks to his cantankerousness? "And Mouser?"

"I've taught her a few tricks. She's a smarty, that one."

He chuckled despite himself. "You can't teach a cat tricks. They're stubborn, with minds of their own." But he had to consider he'd said it to the woman who'd taught him that even cold-blooded killers deserved a little grace now and then.

She shrugged, but only a little. "Guess you'll just have to come see for yourself."

"Guess so." *Does that mean,* he thought as gratitude swelled inside him, *there's hope for us after all?*

"Are you here to inject the newbie with various drugs? Or give him a mild sedative so you can check for parasites and injuries and signs of abuse?"

"Neither, actually. Matt said last week there'd be an addition to the

population, but I didn't realize he'd been delivered until I got here."
Simon wondered if the continued small talk was a good thing…or a
sign of doom.

"Do you have the stuff you need in the office? To do it now, I mean?"

Simon nodded, wondering where Julia was heading with her line
of questioning.

"I could help…if you need an extra pair of hands, I mean."

"Probably better if I come back tomorrow."

"Ahh…easier to see what you're doing in the bright light of day?"

"Everything looks better in the bright light of day."

She shifted slowly to face him, and when she blinked up at him
with those big golden eyes, Simon believed he knew how Levi must
feel, looking into the eyes of angels every day up there in heaven.

"I never stopped loving you, you know. Not for an instant."

The heat of thankfulness pulsed through his veins, making his
eyes burn with unshed tears and his throat ache with a sob. He'd
planned a long apology, where he'd confess what a fool he'd been just
before begging her forgiveness. But "I'm an idiot," was all he could
think to say.

"I know." She allowed a moment to tick silently by then giggled
quietly. "And so am I." Winking, Julia added, "We make a pretty good
team, eh?"

The wolves seemed to grow tired of waiting for treats from the
babbling humans, and they trotted back toward their Matt-made dens
of wood and cast-off carpeting. Simon slowly got to his feet and ever-
so-gently brought Julia to hers. She melted against him like butter on
a hot biscuit. Peripheral vision told him the wolves didn't know what
to make of this two-legged sign of affection. He might have called

Julia's attention to it, too, if she hadn't risen up on her tiptoes to press her lips to his.

A pretty good team, he thought as her fingers combed through his hair. *A pretty good team.*

* * * * *

"You go on ahead and unlock the door. I'll be right behind you." And once she'd made her way up the flagstone walk, Simon tossed aside the tarp that had been hiding her gift. Holding the brown-wrapped package behind his back as he made his way down the hall, he stepped up behind her at the stove and kissed her cheek. "You spoil me," he whispered as she poured lemonade into two icy glasses. He put the package onto the corner of the table. "Go on, open it."

She stood for a moment just looking at him, one hand on her hip while the fingers of the other tapped her chin. Simon wondered if he'd ever get used to being on the receiving end of that "I love you and always will" expression.

Julia slid the bow aside then peeled the shimmering pink wrapper from the package. "Simon," she said on a sigh, "is this what I think it is?"

He chuckled.

"It looks like…like a keepsake box." She hugged it as he told her how he'd gone back to Zooks' and looked through everything available but hadn't found anything to suit him. A half dozen failures in as many other stores told him there was but one way to give her the box she truly deserved. And so Simon made this one himself, starting with oak scraps left over from when he'd repaired his staircase. Using every tool and trick he'd picked up during his years working construction to pay his way through vet school, Simon crafted a mini hope chest of sorts, sanding and polishing until the oak was so smooth it wouldn't snag even an old silk tie. Stained and sealed to match her grandfather's trunk, he'd lined it with pillowy white satin. The finishing touches were brass hinges and a push-button latch.

"Well," he said, "open it."

She held his gaze for a long, silent moment then slowly did as he asked.

"A…card?"

"Remember what else you said that day in the gift shop?"

Julia's brow furrowed, and he could almost see the gears meshing in that never-stopping mind of hers as she thought back and tried to recall every word she'd uttered. Her hands trembled slightly as she unstuck the flap and slid the card from its envelope. "A blank-inside card," she said softly, "so you could tell her exactly what she means to you."

Simon held his breath, waiting for her to read what he'd written.

"Sorry, Simon," she said, her voice thick and trembly, "but I can't see to read it." She held out the card and sniffed, pointing at her teary eyes.

Grinning, Simon wrapped her in a loving embrace. It surprised him when, as he began reciting what he'd written, tears stung in his own eyes:

"*Beulah Land, Eden, Avalon. Many places claim to be heaven, but there's only one Paradise…and it will become my heaven if you agree to be my wife. I love you as I've never loved anyone, and I always will.*"

Then he kissed her.

Epilogue

. . . .

"Seems a waste," William said, "to spend so much hard-earned money on wild animals...especially animals that eat livestock!"

"Somebody's gotta make up to 'em," Simon said, "for the stupidity of humans."

William shrugged then went back to stacking hay bales in the loft.

"People try to make pets out of them," Simon continued, "and when they get too big and start eating them out of house and home, they abandon the wolves...or let them starve."

"Cruelty of any kind is sinful, I think." He nodded. "But you did not come here today to give me a lesson in caring for wolves, wild or otherwise. You are here to invite me to your wedding at the sanctuary, ya?"

Simon was about to ask how the man knew the purpose of his mission even before he'd versed it when William said, "Our women, they have been talking." Leaning an elbow on a tower of hay, he added, "*You* are a doctor. Is there a cure for this talk-talk-talking disorder?"

"None that I know of."

"You should put on your thinking cap, then." Pausing a beat, William added, "The man who concocts a tonic like that will be the richest on earth, I think!" And he punctuated his joke with a hearty laugh.

William's laughter was a good thing to hear. Simon had barely seen the man so much as crack a smile since before Levi was killed. "We couldn't have a wedding without asking if you and the family will join us."

William clapped a hand to Simon's back. "You are a good man, Simon Thomas." He winked. "And smart."

"For choosing Julia, you mean…."

The farmer returned to his work. "The Gunden family will be honored to watch as you and Julia are married."

"And we'll be proud to have you there."

Three weeks later, on the Saturday before Easter, Simon stood in the sanctuary gift shop, decorated by Matt and other volunteers to resemble a chapel, fidgeting as he waited for his bride-to-be to walk down the hall.

The Gundens sat on folding chairs beside Casey's family, and an odd assortment of Paradise shopkeepers and residents filled the remaining seats.

Thirty-five guests in all to share their glorious day.

Although their more liberal brethren sometimes decorated wedding ceremonies with flowers, the Old Order Amish did not. And since the Gundens were strict Old Order, Julia, out of respect for her dear friends, opted not to adorn the makeshift chapel with floral arrangements. The only blossoms visible would bloom in Julia's bouquet.

In place of the haunting strains of the "Wedding March" chorusing from a church organ, Rebekah had offered to provide a traditional Amish song. She stood guard outside the storeroom door where the bride hid, donning the finishing touches for her eager groom.

A trickle of sweat inched down Simon's spine, and he ran a finger around the stiff white collar of his pleated tuxedo shirt. Why hadn't he opted for a pre-tied bow instead of the do-it-yourself kind? In his nervousness, he'd pulled the knot a mite too tight.

"Stand still," Casey whispered from the corner of his mouth as he elbowed Simon's ribs. "You're making *me* nervous."

"Where is she?" he asked, tugging at his cuffs.

Casey peeked at his watch. "Relax. She has five minutes yet before she's supposed to make her grand entrance. And weddings never start on time."

"How do you know so much when you've only had one?"

"Joanna is addicted to that wedding show on cable…." He chuckled. "See what you have to look forward to? Decorating shows and talk shows and…"

Simon was about to tell his cousin that maybe he should've chosen a best man with fewer insights into women, marriage, and television when the door opened at the rear of the gift shop.

Rebekah's pure, sweet voice rose in a blissful accappella melody that was more chant than song…and then Julia appeared in the doorway.

He leaned forward then side to side to get a better look. But since she was silhouetted by the window behind her, Simon couldn't make out the details of her gown, couldn't see her eyes or her smile or—

"Relax," Casey said again. "You'll be lookin' at that face for the rest of your life."

"A guy can hope."

She took a few steps into the light, allowing Simon his first glimpse of his bride-to-be. "She's…she's breathtaking," he whispered. "I've never seen anything lovelier."

Julia had bragged, just last week, what a great deal she'd gotten on her dress. "No ruffles or bows, no sequins or lace. Just a plain little A-line off the rack, and I love it." If that's what she called "plain," Simon didn't think he could stand to see her idea of "fancy."

The gown of dazzling white clung to her petite figure, accenting every womanly curve. In place of a flowing gauzy veil, she wore a tiny circlet of daisies on her head like a flowery halo. He could see the gleam of her engagement ring, but it paled in comparison to the radiance of her smile and the lovelight beaming from her eyes. She carried a handful of daisies, and even from where he stood, he noticed the slight tremor that shook every petal in the basketball-sized bouquet. And on her tiny feet were shiny white shoes with the toes cut out, exposing pink-painted nails that glinted in the overhead light.

"Breathtaking," he said again. "Has it been five minutes yet?"

"Almost," Casey answered, "but, dude…don't wish your life away, okay?"

Their pastor stepped up to the provisional pulpit and faced the small gathering. "Ready, Simon?" he asked over his shoulder.

"Absolutely."

"Should I start?"

"Definitely."

"Think your bride is in agreement?"

Her gaze held his and, smiling, she sent him a little wave.

"Positive."

"Then let's get this show on the road!" the reverend said, opening his Bible.

Rebekah's song ended at the precise moment a wolf howled, its long, lone note rising in pitch and volume as a second joined in, blending its voice with celestial harmony. Soon, a chorus of calls hung on the humid air.

"That's weird," Simon heard Matt say, "they don't usually *all* go at it during the daytime this way."

Simon silently agreed, and when he glanced to the end of the hall to share Julia's reaction to the unrestrained symphony, he saw that she'd faced the window, one delicate hand pressed to her lips as the other hugged the bridal bouquet to her bosom. Had she wiped away a tear, or did he imagine it? *Lord,* he thought, *how did I merit a woman like this, who's as sensitive as she is beautiful?*

The pastor and all those gathered stood in awe as the wild and wonderful ballad continued. And then, as suddenly as it had begun, the serenade stopped, leaving everyone blinking and bewildered, almost as if they wondered in unison, "It isn't really over, is it?"

Then the ceremony began, and like the wolves' melody, it ended, leaving each man, woman, and child amazed at how quickly and competently the pastor had united Simon and Julia in the bonds of holy matrimony.

As they walked arm in arm into the sizzling sunshine, Simon realized that with the recitation of a few ordinary words and the proclamation of a simple man of the cloth, he had become Julia's husband and she his wife. He watched her, smiling, as friends and neighbors hugged her, as she thanked them for their well-wishes and laughed at their jokes. And though he appreciated the people who'd drawn together in support of their decision to join two lives into one, Simon wished the shop—the entire sanctuary!—would empty, so he could commit every moment to memory.

"Don't worry," Casey said, clapping his shoulder, "this isn't something you'll ever forget."

Simon chuckled. "How'd you know what I was thinking?"

"It's written all over your face, cousin, all *over* your face."

That ain't nothin', he thought, *compared to what's written on my* heart.

* * * * *

Simon surprised Julia by booking the honeymoon suite at the Inn at Speedwell Forge, the lovely, historic bed-and-breakfast located adjacent to the sanctuary grounds. She spent most of the night happily snuggled in his arms, listening to the mournful song of the wolves. Though she hadn't slept more than a few hours, she felt rested and refreshed when they went downstairs on their first morning as man and wife.

The innkeepers had set out a wonderful buffet, and the newlyweds piled their plates high. Seated at a table overlooking the sanctuary, Simon took her hand. "Happy?"

"Very." And heart thudding with boundless love, she said, "Any regrets?"

Brow furrowed, he considered the question for a long moment. "Just one…"

Simon leaned over their table settings, with his elbows resting on the table edge, and said, "…that I'll never have the pleasure of asking you to marry me again."

POST CARD
CARTE POSTALE
Love Finds You

Want a peek into local American life—past and present? The *Love Finds You*™ series published by Summerside Press features real towns and combines travel, romance, and faith in one irresistible package!

The novels in the series—uniquely titled after American towns with unusual but intriguing names—inspire romance and fun. Each fictional story draws on the compelling history or the unique character of a real place. Stories center on romances kindled in small towns, old loves lost and found again on the high plains, and new loves discovered at exciting vacation getaways. Summerside Press plans to publish at least one novel set in each of the 50 states. Be sure to catch them all!

NOW AVAILABLE IN STORES

Love Finds You in Miracle, Kentucky by Andrea Boeshaar
ISBN: 978-1-934770-37-5

Love Finds You in Snowball, Arkansas by Sandra D. Bricker
ISBN: 978-1-934770-45-0

Love Finds You in Romeo, Colorado by Gwen Ford Faulkenberry
ISBN: 978-1-934770-46-7

Love Finds You in Valentine, Nebraska by Irene Brand
ISBN: 978-1-934770-38-2

Love Finds You in Humble, Texas by Anita Higman
ISBN: 978-1-934770-61-0

Love Finds You in Last Chance, California by Miralee Ferrell
ISBN: 978-1-934770-39-9

Love Finds You in Maiden, North Carolina by Tamela Hancock Murray
ISBN: 978-1-934770-65-8

COMING IN JUNE

Love Finds You in Treasure Island, Florida by Debby Mayne
ISBN: 978-1-934770-80-1

Love Finds You in Liberty, Indiana by Melanie Dobson
ISBN: 978-1-934770-74-0

summerside
PRESS